NAREK MALIAN

POINT ZERO

POINT ZERO

by Narek Malian

NAREK MALIAN

POINT ZERO

Translated from the Armenian by Haykuhi Babajanyan

GLAGOSLAV PUBLICATIONS

Contents

1. Mass (Clermont, AD 1095)

On a cold November evening in 1095, Pope Urban II summoned all believers to attend Mass at Notre Dame de Clermont. The noble knight stepped out of one of the many coaches driving up to the cathedral and, adjusting his mantle, walked toward the entrance. A man in shabby clothes got out of his stagecoach, emptied the contents of an ointment into his palm and started massaging the leg of one of the horses. It was the groom, Mark. On the day of Urban's sermon, he arrived at Notre Dame with his master, a noble knight. One of the knight's horses had slipped a few weeks ago, and it was necessary to apply some healing balm to its leg, which needed massaging at hourly intervals. The veterinary surgeon had said that the injury was not particularly severe, but that the horse's leg needed care for some time. For this purpose, the knight had employed Mark, who was to follow his horse everywhere and take care of its leg in a timely and conscientious manner, which he did. Mark would stop the horse from time to time, rub the healing balm into the areas the doctor had indicated and massage its right hind leg. The horse obviously enjoyed the massages; it had no problem letting Mark get close and would snort with satisfaction while being massaged.

The master of the horse had decided to attend the Mass that the pope was to deliver that day. There were rumors going around the country that Urban had a special message to deliver. Therefore, all those who had the opportunity to get there took it and arrived at Clermont Cathedral. Having finished massaging the horse's leg, Mark stood in the churchyard feeling bored and cold. Yawning from idleness, he looked around and tried to guess which region each approaching coach had come from. Most coaches, lavishly decorated with old-fashioned ornamental sculptures, would stop in front of the cathedral. The ones with gilt statues, thick dark red curtains and decorative arbors were pieces of art – absolute masterpieces. There were a few such coaches in the yard, and their dazzling beauty added a particular significance to the event that was taking place in the church. It would take a master craftsmen years to make such a coach, and those who had them did not gather in one place for just anything. Mark imagined how immense the desire to go everywhere would be if one owned such a coach – at the very least for showing off their gilt. The majority of the chariots that had gathered in the churchyard were not particularly expensive, yet ordinary people couldn't afford them.

Finally, the nobility arrived. Mark could see that the most luxurious carriages had gathered in the churchyard within a one hundred-mile radius, and he realized that quite an important event would be taking place inside the cathedral. After a short while, there was hardly any room left in the churchyard, even for standing.

Mark suddenly remembered that he had to drop by the baker's shop on his way home. He did not fancy that prospect much, as he also remembered that during a recent visit the baker had hinted that it was time to pay off the debts that had accumulated for him and the grocer. Mark could sell something to pay off his debts, but he didn't have many belongings. The pawnbroker had already pawned his meager household items, and now Mark couldn't imagine how he was going to preserve the last vestiges of his financial stability by massaging a horse's legs.

The large crowd was so tightly packed inside the church that it seemed like it wasn't a crowd of separate people at all, but rather one large body with thousands of arms and legs. It was practically impossible to get into the cathedral. Mark poked his head through the church door. The scent of the crowd's collective breath, flavored with sweat and various other unpleasant smells, immediately hit his nose. Although, the people in the crowd came from all walks of life, they all immediately fell silent as Pope Urban II appeared at the cathedral's altar. He sat on his throne solemnly and, with a slight movement of his head, ordered the Mass to start. The cardinals and priests began the ceremony of blessing; the sounds of the organ resonated from above.

"In nomine Patris et Filii et Spiritus sancti," the Bishop of Bologna said in prayer.

Though cramped and crushed together, the attendees crossed themselves as far as they could. This caused a great deal of movement to begin in the crowd, which did not turn into a brawl, only due to the sacredness of the event and the God-fearing worshippers who had gathered in the cathedral.

Usually these kinds of people are fond of brawls, especially during events with massive amounts of people. The desire to enjoy themselves is what makes them gather during rural fairs or public executions held in city squares, and of course the best way to enjoy such events is to deplete the wine barrels and break each other's jaws without reason and end up covered in blood. Then later, after getting home, they eagerly discuss the brawl, which had surely broken out over a trifling cause, and exaggerate the strength of each other's blows. Those same people behave differently inside a church or during religious rituals. Most people are too afraid to display such behavior in the house of God. To show they are devout believers, they readily forgive each other for things like being elbowed by the man standing close to them or smelling the foul odor of another man's breath emanate as he prays from the row behind. Whereas the same reasons could easily turn into bloodshed at any common inn, it simply does not happen in church. Church is the house of God. Here, people behave like guests, utilizing every bit of etiquette that they know.

Mark tried to break through the crowd to get into the cathedral, but not because he was very religious. Rather, it had become completely dark and quite cold outside and he could not stand out there any longer. He was even ready to venture underground to the hottest parts of hell just to find a little warmth. The organ's smooth, soothing sounds were the only pleasant thing inside the church; everything else that was happening only expressed pain and agony, much like what God's only begotten son had endured when founding Christianity.

Some of the bishops had surrounded the pope in a semi-circle and were staring at the sacred altar where the main rituals of the Mass were taking place. The celebrant archimandrite was directing his prayers to God, begging for peace after each quatrain. The sounds of the organ and the celebrant complimented each other perfectly. Naturally, Mark could not understand anything that was going on because he didn't know Latin, but also because he was standing at the very end of the crowd from where hardly anything could be seen. He was the very last man standing at the back of the church.

The Mass was concluding, and the celebrant made his call for peace with an already hoarse voice. With the last sounds of the organ, Urban II stood up and walked to the altar quietly. This caused a flurry of excitement among the crowd, which began to shout, "Dieu le veut!" The pope motioned with his hand for them to be quiet and walked forward to give his sermon, but the crowd refused to calm down. They continued to interrupt the pope's speech, shouting "Dieu le veut!"

Mark had heard the pope's messengers announce beforehand that Urban II was to make an extremely important statement in his sermon. The people gathered inside the church couldn't even guess what the pope would say. Some of them pretended to know everything and were telling those standing nearby that the pope was going to declare another anathema and pronounce another series of curses directly from the altar onto any antipopes. Some speculated that the papal treasury was on the verge of being empty, and Urban II had thought of some plan to fill it. Others were confidently claiming that the tension between the pope and antipope had reached a point where Urban had decided to attack Rome with his army.

The fragrant smoke of the incense had spread throughout the whole cathedral. The bishops' clothing, woven with gold threads, shone under the candlelight, creating an illusion of grandeur. The Mass attendees exhibited a buzz of restless excitement, like bees in a hive. Urban was no less excited, yet he was hesitating whether to begin his sermon or to wait a bit longer until passions subsided. "Dieu le veut!" was reverberating throughout the church. Pope Urban turned toward the voices and blessed them.

"Dear and pious faithful, as you already know, I have an important message for you, for my faithful flock," Pope Urban II began. "The knife with its edge turned obliquely upwards has reached the bone, making forbearance impossible. Therefore, today I must make a very important appeal."

"Dieu le veut! Dieu le veut!" the crowd continued to shout in encouragement.

"Yes, dear faithful. God wills it. As you are well aware, not a leaf falls from a tree without it being God's will. Today I want to share with you my concerns. For quite a while, we've been receiving disturbing information about acts of lawlessness committed by non-believers against Christian pilgrims visiting the Holy Sepulcher of Christ in the Holy Land. Saracens are plundering the caravans of our pilgrim brothers, raping and killing women and selling children into slavery. The road to the Holy Land has become a sea of blood. Christians have been deprived of the chance to fulfill their religious duty. I used to think that these sorts of crimes were carried out as simple robberies, but when I heard that they have been happening continually and are committed with such atrocity, I realized that this is nothing other than them trying to settle the score with believers. This is an encroachment on faith, and not on just a certain person or his property."

Shouts of discontent were heard from the crowd.

"I share your indignation. Since I am the pastor of the Christian Church, each Christian's pain and sorrow is felt a hundredfold by me," Urban continued. "It's already a firmly established fact that our Christian brethren are in danger. Saracens have conquered the holy city of Jerusalem, the tomb of our God, and are trampling the Holy Land under their feet. They are walking on the Holy Land like they are the owners and are doing everything possible to suppress our brothers and sisters in Christ. Blood and tears are irrigating the fields and deserts. Believers are leaving their ancestral home in despair and fleeing the Holy Land with their families. The Holy Land has now become the land of God's perdition and torments. Every day I receive numerous letters in which my faithful flock is begging me for help so that they can somehow manage to survive. Brethren, we can't bear this anymore. Each day of forbearance will cost a believer's life."

Urban raised his head and, looking at the church ceiling covered in colorful patterns, shouted, "Now is the time for us to protect our brothers and sisters! The hour of reckoning has come. It is time to establish God's justice in the Holy Land and throughout the whole world. To arms, my dear faithful flock!"

"Dieu le veut!" the crowd shouted in response.

The voices from the crowd spread like a wave. People were outraged and angry. They agreed with Urban II that they could no longer tolerate such treatment toward Christians. The crowd finally settled down when Urban gave the sign of peace.

"Every night the souls of martyred Christians visit me in my dreams and demand fair retribution," Urban continued. "And as a pastor of the Christian flock, I recall them in my prayers every day, but the situation, unfortunately, is such that we must do more than pray. Christian meekness is applicable only to Christians. There is only one language in which you can talk to non-believers, and that is the language of weapons and intolerance against them. Not a single non-believer is good. All Saracens are under the eternal curse of God, and their earthly punishment is in our hands."

Urban paused to take a breath and then continued.

"From this moment on, all believers going on pilgrimage will take with them a weapon, in addition to the pope's blessing, to withstand the ordeals along the way. The ultimate aim of pilgrims visiting the Holy Land will not be to pray at the tomb of God, but to finally liberate the Holy Land from non-believers. The Holy Land needs to be cleared of Muslims. That is the will of God, and we must all do our utmost to perform that sacred task."

The crowd chanted "Dieu le veut!" once more. People were slightly embarrassed; they didn't really understand how the liberation would take place, who would actually go to the Holy Land, or how they would get there. The emotional atmosphere was so intense, however, that those questions were pushed aside. Each person assumed that the other might be aware of the Holy Land liberation plan and dared not ask any questions, not wanting to reveal their ignorance.

"I myself am ready to enlist for this heavenly goal. May there be no victims and let it be I who will have to go through any difficulties and hardship, for blessed is the man who will endure them to reach the Kingdom of Heaven." Urban's voice trembled with excitement. "Standing here at the altar, I also want to announce that all those who will choose to become soldiers of faith will immediately be exempt from taxes and duties. I will personally hand them small crosses cut from papal vestment, which will keep them safe along their way, and those soldiers of faith will have their steady place in the Kingdom of Heaven as martyrs in case of death, even if they die during the journey from disease or other causes. May the blessed cross, received from my hand, preserve them from all kinds of troubles and comfort them in times of hardship or distress. From this moment on, you all, my dear pilgrims, will be called Crusaders.

The crowd erupted with joy with joy. They were happy to finally be given the chance to restore justice. They did not have a particularly deep understanding of what was required of them, but they were sure that God willed it so.

2. Emperor Alexius' Letter to Urban II (Clermont, AD 1095)

Upon finishing his sermon, Urban imperceptibly turned from the altar to where Odo, Urban's faithful adviser and closest friend, was sitting. Odo was to blame for all this, but was now unnoticed by the faithful crowd. He was quietly following the Mass, and more specifically the pope.

It was typical of Odo to avoid public life. He and Urban were complete opposites. Odo was a secular man, so secular that it was surprising how he remained among the confidants of the most powerful religious leader. Moreover, he held a position as sort of an advisor, a position that required a great deal of trustworthiness. Odo repeatedly tested Urban's patience. He was in the habit of bothering the pope with his extreme frankness. There were instances where Urban would not receive Odo for months. *We shouldn't pamper him*, Urban thought. After a while though, papal mercifulness would win over and Odo would recommence his regular visits to the palace. Urban tried not to show that he attached importance to Odo's advice and comments, though Odo himself was not particularly interested in whether his advice was followed. He was overconfident that his every action would strengthen the papal supremacy, sometimes going beyond the boundaries of what was acceptable.

Urban never talked to Odo about religious, theological or doctrinal topics. He didn't even know whether Odo was a believer or not, and at that point in their relationship it didn't really matter, since Odo had done much more for the church than many of the cardinals or bishops, with their pseudo-sanctimonious prayers and exclusively demonstrative faith. Odo, unlike those mentioned above, was a man of action. Minimal philosophy, maximum work: this seemed to be Odo's motto. Besides, no one seemed to be as deeply aware of people's inner worlds and motives as Odo was. Each report by the secret police passed through his hands first. He and Urban would decide together whether to forgive a sinner or punish him, and they would even discuss the severity of the punishment. No decisions were made without hearing Odo's opinion first.

Everyone in the palace knew this, and they were all unanimous in their hatred of Odo. Of course, they never expressed their hatred in any way, but there was no lack of rumors about Odo throughout the corridors. The courtiers, hearing Odo's name, would explicitly express their dissatisfaction with their facial expressions and would bow to Urban as if wanting to say, "The will is yours, high priest, but if we were you, we would not tolerate that cynical, arrogant Odo even for one minute."

Unlike the courtiers, the higher aristocrats, namely kings and emperors, would simply pretend not to understand who was being discussed. They would snobbishly deny knowing Odo. This approach slightly amused Urban. The pope had known Odo for so long that he couldn't even remember when they had met. He knew that Odo was stubborn and that he couldn't see anything beyond himself. Odo was the only living being on earth who was free and unconstrained in contradicting Urban and could even argue better than him. Since the papal infallibility was the cornerstone of the Catholic Church and taking into account the infinite power Urban had in the secular life as well, Odo's position required a lot of courage. To some extent, this infallibility could be viewed as a violation of one of the fundamental dogmas of the Catholic Church. Every moment, Odo was in danger of losing his own head. Of course, it was possible that one day Urban could finally become so angry that he could retaliate, but this didn't affect Odo's courage at all. He continued his assertions, which usually went beyond the general opinion. Some courtiers had tried to replicate Odo's daring approaches to win Urban's favor, but they were removed from the palace at the first sign of insubordinate behavior. Odo was brave but not reckless. He was an advisor able to give profound reasons for having formed this or that opinion. In this case, that's what happened.

A few months before Urban's sermon at the Notre Dame Mass, a letter of request had been received from Byzantine Emperor Alexius. In his letter, the emperor described the wonders of Constantinople. He explained that twenty new fountains had been installed, more than half of the city had been paved, three new cathedrals had been constructed, the renovation of the Hagia Sophia had been completed, four new prefectures, two new hospitals, twelve new schools, and one new theater had been built and bathhouses had been completely repaired. The emperor then cordially invited the high priest to visit Constantinople to see the world's most beautiful and comfortable city at any time and for any period convenient to him. Alexius spared no words in describing the remarkable city. Apparently, the letter had not been written by him, but by a poet specially employed for that purpose. At the end of the letter was a request. Alexius asked Urban to allocate one hundred – one hundred fifty soldiers from the papal army to the security patrol services in his beautiful Christian capital. Alexius explained that the newly built and reconstructed parts of the city could be destroyed unless they were properly protected, especially since expensive materials had been used for the renovations. The emperor wrote that, because of this, the city attracted thieves and looters, and living there had become dangerous. At the end of his letter, Alexius again expressed his gratitude to God, asking for many years of good health for the high priest and once again restating his open invitation.

"I wonder how much it will cost the papal treasury to maintain one hundred soldiers for a year in Constantinople?" Odo asked after reading the letter aloud to the pope.

"I do not think it will be very expensive," Urban said.

Urban liked the idea of visiting Constantinople. He even started to consider acquiring a summer residence there. Indeed, Constantinople was the most beautiful city in the modern world. One could not imagine a city that could compare to it, with its exquisiteness and allure. The pope particularly liked that the world's most beautiful city belonged to Christians and not to Saracens.

"Compounded yearly, it would make up a rather large sum. According to rough estimates, about two thousand pieces of gold, not including the transportation and other expenses like medical, postage, uniforms, etc.," Odo counted out.

Urban frowned. It was quite a large amount of money. The papal treasury was not at its best. The war against the antipope had used up their money, and the saddest part was that it wasn't just the war, but the various attempts to attract noblemen to stick to the true pope's side that had been putting a dent in the treasury. Urban also liked to demonstrate his papal extravagance by holding lavish receptions. During those receptions, the whole strength of the papal power was displayed. World-renowned musicians were invited who would simultaneously play in different corners of the palace for days on end. Snacks were served from overseas, prepared by chefs whose language no one could understand. Theatrical groups performed plays depicting important historical events of the ancient world. A special Mass was served using utensils that had been handcrafted by the most famous goldsmiths and lapidaries. Urban tried in any way to show off the immensity of the papal power and wealth, but each luxurious event would seriously reduce the content of the treasury.

But there was another danger. Noblemen who appeared to be of the same mind with the pontiff missed no opportunity to enter into secret negotiations with the antipope, wishing to serve two masters at the same time. To ascertain such conspiracies, Urban used the secret police to keep surveillance on all suspicious persons around him. It didn't even occur to the majority of noblemen that their every move was being studied in detail, whether it was a love affair, friendly meeting, political conspiracy, or secret trade deal. Urban was kept thoroughly informed about everything, and these services continued to exhaust the treasury's funds. In certain cases, the secret police cost more than the extravagant events. Good information is a precious commodity. Sometimes more than a dozen people had to be bribed in order to extract valuable information – information that helped prevent numerous unfavorable events. Almost everything had been prevented by the efforts of the secret police, from assassination attempts to secret political agreements. The basis of the papal infallibility was that he was well aware of the real life he wasn't witnessing. The courtiers spoke in the corridors about how the pope was not infallible, but rather well informed. Important state decisions were impossible to make without reliable, well-grounded information that Urban was abundantly given.

"And which expenses are you going to cut?" Odo asked, seeing Urban's hesitations over Alexius' letter. "You aren't going to raise taxes or increase the amount of non-existing tax, are you?"

"It's not possible to impose new taxes. The people's condition is quite hopeless and will remain so until the day of resurrection. The same applies to raising existing taxes, but we need to help Alexius."

"Really?" Odo gave a smile. "And how do you suggest doing that?"

"I don't know. We should think it over. Alexius emphasized in his letter that he recognizes and accepts my spiritual authority, which means he will defect to the antipope unless we lend him a helping hand."

The papal treasury had already been squeezed dry by the long-lasting and complicated geopolitical situation. Besides, the controversy over the right to consecrate bishops and noblemen was being fought against Henry IV. It had always been the right of the pope, but Henry was trying to usurp it. Having that right was also quite profitable, and since there was a need for money, ending the meaningless fight in Urban's favor would be beneficial. Most of the military operations were regulated by Odo. Urban would intervene only when it was absolutely necessary, when decision-making demanded personal responsibility. He would regulate the movement of both active and reserve forces, the directions of attack and defense on grounds of expediency, as well as the amount of the soldiers' remuneration.

This certainly did not imply that Urban had no interest or role in political or military affairs. Quite the contrary, everything was kept under Urban's direct control. Each day began and ended with Urban's reports, and there were also interim reports, such as information brought by messengers, which were read upon arrival. All correspondence was handled by Odo, but only under Urban's immediate awareness. Odo was too secular for ecclesiastical affairs, while Urban was too spiritual to assess the military and political actions. This union was ideal for both of them, since one made up for the other's weaknesses and leaned on the other's strengths. After all, it was Pope Urban to whom all the numerous military successes achieved during his papacy were attributed to. In the modern world, he had a reputation of being a good strategist and commander. Very little time had passed since his anointment, but all the European potentates were already sure that the papal ferula was in good hands. Not only did Urban II not concede his predecessor's positions, but he strengthened his powers, and now, just a few years after his anointment, not a single nobleman in the whole of Europe would question his authority. Against this background, the existence of the antipope became a sort of fictional tale. The antipope had surrendered almost all his estates and withdrawn to his residence in Rome, where he tried not to make many appearances.

As for Henry, the military operations initiated by Odo had put him in a tough spot. It seemed like now he was just following policy to not give up the influence of his words in order to preserve his current position. Urban's envoys were already working on the negotiation process to bring down Henry's boyish ambitions and to reach a mutually beneficial declaration of peace.

"I don't think Alexius will be that stupid that he would defect to the antipope, especially now that we have already been so successful in the fight against the antipope. A few more military operations and his power will remain a memory," Odo said proudly.

"The antipope still exists, and it means that we must be more sympathetic to our friends. Nothing makes a man more compassionate toward his friends than the enemy," Urban said. "Odo, how can we fulfill Emperor Alexius' request?"

"Well, we could save a lot of money if we abstain from celebrating Assumption Day."

"And how much could we save?" Urban asked.

"I can't say right now. I need to count, but I think it will be enough to cover the annual cost of paying for one hundred fifty soldiers. Or maybe we could abstain from holding Mass that day."

"Have you gone mad?" Urban shouted. "What do you mean? How could we abstain from the Mass? We can abstain from everything, but never a religious ritual. You have become so obsessed with political intrigues that you probably forgot my authority is spiritual. Spiritual! Please always remember this when giving me advice."

Odo smiled. "Wonderful!" he said quietly.

"What's wonderful?"

"With your permission, I will think it over and tell you how to solve this seemingly unsolvable problem."

"Have you thought of anything already?" Urban asked hopefully.

"Maybe," Odo smiled.

"Well then tell me."

"Maybe the solution is much more obvious than we thought. But I need to make sure before reporting to you. Give me some time."

"Okay. You can go," Urban said.

This was the kind of man Odo was; he could always find a way out of any situation. Emerging from the pope's room, he instructed a courier to invite the head of heralds to the pope's residence. He warned the courier beforehand that the invitation was secret. The courier bowed to signal he understood the importance of confidentiality. Odo then sent another courier to Italy to invite one of the local philosophers to the pope's residence. He was determined to thoroughly research his plan before carrying it out, and he intended to consult with leading specialists who had great influence on people's consciences. He wanted to consider the whole depth of the pope's mind.

3. Young Sayid's First Steps (Damascus, AD 1115)

Sayid did not remember his parents. He didn't know much about who they were or where they came from. Having lived in various Arab countries since he was born, he stood out from the crowd with his unique appearance. Sayid was a blue-eyed fellow with white skin and blonde hair. Being a tall, broad-shouldered nineteen-year-old who was unusually burly for his age, he differed greatly from his small dark-skinned, brown-eyed friends. He had grown up on the street and made money begging or running errands. The notion of having parents was incomprehensible for Sayid. He had become accustomed to solving his problems by himself.

Sayid lived in Damascus, where markets differed from other similar eastern markets because of their abundance of arms dealers. Sometimes sword sellers would even cut people's heads in the middle of the narrow, winding streets, trying to convince passersby that the sword had the power to turn them into a famous commander. Loudly praising the strength and deadly strikes of their bladed weapons, they would show off their colorful daggers. It was believed that no one could escape the strike of a Damascus dagger. Anyone wounded would die within a few days.

So, this was Sayid – street roamer and errand runner. It was his regular, but not chosen occupation. Sayid himself realized that it could not last long and that it was time to look for real work. And then there was old Ahmed, who lived on the same street. This old man would voluntarily help those in need. Ahmed would say that when the gates of heaven opened up before a believer, Allah would assess the path they'd traversed based on such deeds. It was therefore necessary to take care of others and to always be useful to those around, even if just to give a piece of advice on life.

But Sayid wouldn't listen to old Ahmed's words unconditionally and apply them to his life. At his age, everybody turned a deaf ear to the words of his old neighbors. Without anyone in the world, Sayid had simply gotten used to Ahmed because he was the only man in his life that he could poke friendly fun at or go to for a piece of advice. Every morning old Ahmed would come out of his house at sunrise and pray, looking toward the rising sun, and then he would take his seat on the outdoor porch and smoke the hookah that sat on his table. He'd drink his tea and blow a few rings of smoke. After sunrise, the street would grow lively with artisans hurrying to work who would say hi to old Ahmed. He always had a look of accumulated wisdom. It was the type of look typical of someone who'd lived over five hundred years and gone through multiple hardships.

Sayid would often visit Ahmed and listen to all his life stories and parables. Sometimes Sayid had a hard time understanding which stories were real and which had been invented, because the real stories were often much more gripping than the parables. When Sayid turned sixteen years old, Ahmed gave him a gold coin. He said that it wasn't enough for a robust and burly man like Sayid to live a beggar's life and that he had arranged for Sayid to work with a trade caravan, first as a porter and then, after gaining a little experience, he could accompany them crossing the desert. Sayid rejoiced. He thanked Ahmed and promised him that it wasn't in vain. He assured Ahmed that he would never regret recommending him. After Sayid left, Ahmed prayed to Allah and asked him to make the boy's path straight and smooth.

The next morning, Sayid went to the place where caravan owners, sellers, and camel pullers usually gathered. They had many interesting stories to tell and fondly shared them in their free time. Sayid started working that same day. The job was not particularly hard; he was to load the camels before trips and unload the returning caravans. It wasn't long before he grasped the nuances of the job. He learned how to arrange the loads and, most importantly, how to secure them by tying the proper knots. He could easily estimate the carrying capacity of each camel and masterfully distribute the loads and arrange timely rest stops before each long trek.

A few months later, Sayid had already mastered all the skills of his first profession. One day, the head of the assembly point called him and said that one of the camel pullers had gotten married, become a permanent resident of another country and decided not to return from his trip. Another person was needed to accompany the caravan, which was to leave the next day. He suggested that Sayid should do the job. After hearing this, Sayid felt short of breath; he was elated. He viewed people who accompanied caravans as very important. Every time he finished loading a caravan, he would watch them departing and feel his heart pounding fiercely in his chest. He imagined all the exciting adventures that could happen along the way and the different countries the caravan would pass through. Of course, he agreed to take the job. Sayid was so excited that he didn't even ask how much he would be paid. He immediately gave his consent and rushed to Ahmed's place to tell him the news.

At first, Ahmed didn't understand why Sayid had burst through the door shouting, but he soon realized that it was related to the new job. When Sayid finally calmed down and could speak clearly, Ahmed gave him a hug with his old, skinny arms and kissed his forehead. He warned Sayid to remain disciplined and called for his prudence and caution. Opening the Holy Quran, Ahmed read out ayahs about moderation and deadly temptations, then he blessed Sayid and gave him two gold coins. Ahmed said that he wanted Sayid to bring him a gift from whatever distant town he was soon leaving for, but he didn't specify what gift he wanted to receive. In truth, Ahmed had given Sayid the money so that he could spend it only when necessary. He didn't want to just give it to him as a gift, lest it bring calamity. Ahmed knew that if Sayid bore in his mind that the money must be spent on his gift, then he wouldn't spend it unless it was absolutely necessary.

Sayid immediately started preparing for his first trip. After saying good-bye to old Ahmed, he went home, picked up his small bundle of belongings and rushed through the streets until he reached the caravan assembly point. He felt extraordinarily important to not be busy loading the camels as he usually did. Instead, he stood and watched how the other porters were doing it, knowing he was there as a camel puller. That was his new job. A feeling of pride filled Sayid as he realized it was the first promotion he had ever gotten in his life. The sun's sharp rays pierced his eyes and he looked forward to watching the slowly moving camels make their way toward infinity, to places still unknown to him.

Sayid couldn't wait to leave, but it seemed like the camels and porters were dawdling. Finally, the last tier of freight was loaded and tied up tightly.

The most experienced camel puller sorted the camels according to their loads and their behavior during past trips. After a few instructions by the caravan leader, they started to move slowly past the gates of Damascus and out into the desert. The camels were traveling again, having taken this trek a hundred times, and they were unaware of Sayid's impatience and haste, which was only increasing. Sayid kept asking questions to the experienced camel pullers, trying to understand how far they had traveled from Damascus. The experienced ones would respond to Sayid's questions with an indulgent smile.

There were also women in the caravan who were riding in the front. Sayid tried to understand the logic of such an arrangement. Usually women were only allocated seats where they would go unnoticed, but in the caravan, they were given the front seats where they were constantly seen by everyone. One of the experienced camel pullers explained that the desert was full of unexpected dangers, and therefore they needed to keep an eye on everything valuable.

Among the women travelers, there was a small, thin girl accompanied by two elderly women. As Sayid was fetching water from an oasis well, he saw her when she removed the sheila from her face. Only then did Sayid understood that there was a pretty girl in the caravan. Sayid had approached the well. Noticing him, the girl immediately stepped aside, pulling the sheila over her eyes. Sayid smiled and gestured with his hand for her to use the well. The girl gave a ringing laugh and, picking up the jug of water placed near the well, walked away. Sayid had seen her for just a few seconds, but that was enough to understand that there was a beauty in front of him. His heartbeat accelerated; he did not have much experience with love affairs. It was the first time he had felt something that he could not express in words. Later, this feeling changed into inexplicable sadness and melancholy. Sayid continued traveling, keeping his eye on the front of the caravan and constantly looking at the camels, trying to guess which of the women in black the pretty girl was he had met near the well.

Days passed, and on the tenth day the chief camel puller halted the caravan and said that strong winds were expected across the desert over the coming nights and that it would no longer be possible to continue during the nighttime; the caravan would have to stop as soon as it got dark. Moreover, the travelers would have to spend the night camping out in a new spot each night, and would only be able to continue on their way with the first rays of sun.

That night, the caravan stopped as soon as it got dark. All the men began erecting the tents. Half an hour later, they had formed two tents, one for the women and the other for the men. The majority of the caravan had gathered in the men's tent and were playing backgammon to kill time. The camel pullers had gathered in a corner where the chief was giving instructions. The novice camel pullers then asked the veterans for an interesting story, especially since they knew long nights were ahead of them.

"Let an old traveler tell us something interesting," the head of the caravan said, making himself comfortable in his seat.

"Have you ever heard the story of Bu Tahir Arrani?" the eldest camel puller asked. He had accompanied caravans from east to west, north to south. He was famous and respected all over.

"I have," one camel puller responded.

"I know you know it. Anyone else? Has anyone else heard it except him?"

The camel pullers sat around in a circle, silent.

"Since it won't be possible to make our way across the desert until daylight, and we've got some long desert nights ahead of us, I will tell a story to shorten the nights. Of course, only if you all want to hear it."

"Yes please," the newcomers shouted.

"Then listen..."

4. The Story of Bu Tahir Arrani: The First Religious Martyr

A sweets baker lived in one of the towns of Isfahan who was once very popular in and beyond the city. His fame had even reached the region's top officials and clergymen. It was said that the Chief Mufti of Isfahan wouldn't begin reading surahs unless he first ate some of the baker's sweets.

The baker was a well-respected man and lived a pious life. He observed the rules and hours of all holidays and prayer times, and it was in that spirit that he raised his only son. The baker, in addition to having strong religious convictions and living an austere lifestyle, was very kind hearted and would take candy out of his pocket and give it to any child he met on the street. He was the favorite of all the children in town and sometimes served as a patient and pleasant middle-man between the kids and their parents. It seemed as if Allah himself had blessed all his affairs. Everything was going well; his trade was flowing like the honey he sold.

The baker had a son whose name was Arrani. Arrani had been helping his father since his early childhood. He would gladly perform small tasks, helping to unload the camels with the spices his father had ordered or loading the donkeys with sweets to be sold. During the day, when there weren't many customers, he would take over behind the counter so his father could relax, smoke a hookah or sit on the store's front steps.

It is not known exactly why, but one day the baker's business began to decline. At trade stops, spice suppliers started demanding their money all at once, claiming that the great quantity of sweets had been spoiled in the heat. Soon, the baker began plummeting into bankruptcy. As a proud, secretive man, the baker concealed his failures from everyone, even from his own family.

The deterioration of his business was made worse by several small debts that kept increasing. Having waited some time, one day the creditors visited the baker's home and took all his valuable items. The baker, however, managed to hide the most valuable thing – a copper tray used for pilaf. The tray was handcrafted by the best Persian masters and was doubly valuable to the baker since it was a gift from one of the illustrious commanders of Persia, given to him as a sign of gratitude for producing sweets even sweeter than sorbet. When the business took off, that tray was hung on the wall of the living room amongst the decorations of his house, which consisted of many beautiful and gilded objects. Now, as the only piece of decoration left in the room, the tray only highlighted how barren his home had become.

Left in torment, the baker eventually decided to sell the only valuable item left in the house. He told Arrani to take the tray and follow him, only explaining why, once they arrived at the market in order to delay his embarrassment. This was humiliating for the baker. Everyone knew he was bankrupt, but people were so fond of him and didn't want to cause him extra pain when they saw him on the street that they would behave as if nothing had changed in his life and that his business was still running well.

Before leaving the house, the baker handed the tray to his son and started walking to the market. His son followed. At first, Arrani couldn't understand why his father was behaving so strange. On their way to the market, the baker ran into many of his acquaintances. He told everyone they were going to the market to make some deals, but they were really going to sell something. Having reached the market, the baker seated his son near one of the carpets on sale, then quickly walked a few meters away and began to watch his son trade. He did not want to be seen at the market near where they were selling the tray. Not many people approached Arrani. Actually, no one approached him, not even to ask the price of the tray.

In the evening, father and son returned home empty handed. Arrani understood that going to the market was tormenting for his father. He noticed that his father would break out in a sweat every time he ran into an acquaintance in the street. He thought about it all night, and after morning prayer he told his father that he would go to the market alone and try to sell the tray. There was no point in his father coming, as he would only watch from a distance anyway. At first, his father pretended to be angry, but after thinking it over for a while he agreed that from then on Arrani would take the tray to the market alone. Every morning after breakfast, he would carry the tray wrapped in paper and walk down the street toward the market. Arrani didn't know many people and he would hardly meet any acquaintances on his way who would ask him questions about his frequent trips to the market, so he didn't have to explain to anyone that he was trying to sell something that used to be precious to his father.

Though he would spend all day at the market, he always failed to sell the tray. Whenever Arrani returned home, he saw his father waiting for him on the porch. He would look at Arrani's hands first, and every time he saw that the tray was still there, he would feel both delighted that the most valuable item in his house was still there and sad because the money it was worth would have resolved many problems for a man in his circumstances. Days and weeks passed. Arrani still kept going to the market, while his father was busy looking for new ways to make a living.

One day, Hassan-i Sabbāh was passing through their town on the way to Egypt for a religious training. Hassan was the spiritual father of the Nizaris. He already had many followers with whom he travelled through different countries preaching the Nizari religion. Hassan-i Sabbāh was a powerful leader gifted with divine grace. Ismaili Muslims loved him like a father. His words were sweeter than honey and thicker than syrup. Anyone who listened to him could not remain indifferent or disobey his will because Allah himself was speaking through his mouth. Hassan had been wandering along with his allies for several years already. They had been visiting the Arab territories, which were under Seljuk rule, and preaching the Ismaili way of Islam. Hassan was now going to Egypt, where he would study for a few years to complete the last phase of his religious training under the supervision of the most prominent imams and scholars of that time.

Arrani, of course, didn't know anything about Hassan when his retinue approached him. It was hard to identify him at first glance. The main figure of the group had royal mannerisms, though he was moving on foot and was not accompanied by messengers like kings usually were. The figure, who stood out from the rest of the group, was wearing clothes that looked much more expensive than those being worn by the others. His beard was sleek, and his hair was trimmed neatly and formed into nice waves. The others followed him obediently. It was Hassan-i Sabbāh.

Hassan turned his attention to Arrani and approached him. He didn't even look at what Arrani was selling. Instead, he stared straight into his eyes. Arrani noticed the stranger's intense gaze and felt a tremor pass through his body.

"My child, how much are you asking for this beauty?" Hassan asked with a husky voice as he picked up the tray.

"Sir, I haven't set the price yet. I thought I would sell it to the person who could determine the real value of its beauty."

Hassan looked at the young merchant and smiled. Everything about Hassan's look suited him perfectly – his expensive velvet clothes, his wavy hair, his sleek beard – but not his smile. That seemed to be almost borrowed from someone else.

Hassan guessed Arrani's thoughts and, without hiding the joy on his face said, "Aren't you afraid that someone will name its true value and deceive you, paying less than it costs?"

"That's not a problem, sir. The most beautiful things in the world are free, aren't they? And they are the creations of the heavenly Lord."

Hassan put the tray on the ground and began to scrutinize Arrani. As it happened, Hassan was more interested in examining the merchant rather than his commodity.

"Young man," said Hassan, "the seal of Baghdad Mosque is put on this tray. It cannot be sold. It is a sin to sell the property of the mosque; it can only be given as a present."

Hassan was obviously testing Arrani's intelligence.

Arrani paused and then spoke. "One night, Caliph Umar made up his mind to leave his palace dressed like an ordinary man. He decided to walk the streets and see how ordinary people lived. While crossing the street, the caliph heard someone singing a song. He listened to the voice and realized it was coming from the neighboring house and, climbing over the fence, looked into the window of the house to see who was singing. The caliph spotted the landlord drinking heavily and singing, and he became so angry that he entered the house through the window and shouted, 'How dare you sin in excessive drinking? Don't you know it's forbidden?'"

'Oh, Caliph of the Believers,' the drunkard responded, 'I have committed a sin and I don't deny that, but I would like to know what punishment awaits me, because I have sinned thrice.' Slightly confused, Omar asked what he was guilty of. The man replied, 'The Prophet has forbidden eavesdropping and prying, which you have done. The Quran says, 'Enter a house only after having welcomed its inhabitants.' The third transgression is that all Orthodox Muslims enter their homes through the door, while you entered through the window.' Caliph Omar then admitted his sin."

Hassan looked at Arrani with admiration.

"I see you are knowledgeable of the sacred writings. How old are you?"

"People are his servants, even still unborn. I am fifteen."

That day, Arrani had a long talk with the stranger, who introduced himself during the course of their conversation. They talked about the Holy Quran while Hassan admired young Arrani's theological knowledge and depth of faith and devotion to Allah. At the very least, Arrani left an impression of a meek lamb. He had very masculine facial features; his tight muscles could be seen even under his clothes. His answers were clear, without excessive humility. He didn't show off his knowledge but gave clear answers to Hassan's confusing questions, sometimes even having the courage to disagree with him. Hassan clearly enjoyed the fellow's courageous words. Absorbed in conversation, they even forgot about the tray, which was the initial reason for the heated conversation. The tray was placed between Hassan and Arrani and separated them symbolically. Their conversation revolved around who was going to take the tray.

"My son, what do you do?" Hassan asked, caressing his white beard.

"Nothing so far."

"Your knowledge is what many officials lack."

"He who wants to rule must learn to obey first of all," Arrani interrupted.

Hassan stood there lost in his thoughts.

"I am travelling to Egypt to meet with local religious leaders, but I assure you that your devotion to Allah is great enough that you shouldn't be selling goods at this dusty, shabby market."

"I do not work at the market. I'm just selling this tray at my father's request. It is the tray of our house, sir Hassan."

"My son! I will buy this tray. Actually, I will pay for it, but I'll leave it with you, and I will take it on my return. But before that, I want to ask you to consider joining me. I will be passing through this town again in a few months. If you decide to deepen your knowledge of theology and devote yourself to the service of God, I will take you with me."

"Where are you going? When will you be back?" the young man asked, interested.

"When you make your decision, you will know," Hassan answered, ordering the man standing next to him to pay the price of the tray.

"I leave the tray to you. Protect it!"

"I will protect it until you come back," Arrani promised.

"The tray is a material thing and it is replaceable. Take care of yourself, my son! See you soon!"

After these words, Hassan turned around and left the market with his retinue.

Nearly four years had passed since that meeting. Arrani had given the money to his father and wrapped the tray in paper in preparation for when he would hand it over to Hassan. His father hadn't really understood what had happened; he didn't know who his son had met, or whether Hassan had good or evil intentions. Arrani had told his father that the stranger who had introduced himself as Hassan and bought the tray had also suggested that he should join him. Naturally, his father hadn't liked the idea, and he made sure that Arrani had no special plans to leave his family.

Everything continued as usual. Each new day began with morning prayer, and every family member minded their own business. Arrani helped his parents with household chores. A friend of his father would send them Egyptian teas, and they made a living selling them. The profit was not very much, but it was enough to satisfy the family's needs. Things weren't bad, but Arrani had become a little withdrawn. He kept silent for days. His silence didn't affect his work in any way, but it worried his mother. She would question her son often and when she didn't receive an answer, she decided that her son's mysterious silence was the result of falling in love, which usually happened to boys his age. His mother even tried to guess who had become the cause of her son's melancholy. She carefully watched all the girls who her son interacted with, but there weren't that many. Of the ones that came around, she couldn't figure out which one it could be.

Then something happened one morning in autumn that forever changed the quiet, peaceful atmosphere of their home. Arrani disappeared. Nobody knew where he had gone. His mother could not be comforted, and the worst things kept crossing her mind. She just kept crying, like any mother would do. His father completely lost touch with reality and felt powerless, left to just sit motionless and unable to explain his son's disappearance. The strangest thing was that the tray that Arrani had wrapped in paper and been keeping for its new owner had also disappeared.

It had already been over a month since Arrani started following Hassan. Having joined Hassan's retinue, he was chiefly busy preaching and engaging new believers from different countries. Arrani was not yet aware of their final destination, and perhaps one didn't even exist.

Once, during their overnight stay, Hassan assembled everyone and announced that he had important news to share. Having returned from Egypt, Hassan had clearly decided to create his own state where only Ismailism was to reign. Before that, he had sent his preachers to Alamut Castle, where they had successfully settled inside the castle and were busy preaching. Now, he had received happy news from his preachers staying in Alamut and wanted to share it with everyone who he had been traveling and preaching with throughout this long period.

"Dear brethren! We are going to join our brothers in Alamut Castle and establish a lifestyle favored by Allah. There is not and has never been anything more pleasant in the world than serving the almighty Lord, and when this service becomes a lifestyle, the Lord's love will descend on this settlement. We will not be busy praying or keeping the rules set down by the Lord, we will serve the Lord in our daily life. You will be surprised to see how we will liberate Alamut Castle, which is currently under the rule of infidels who keep oppressing our faithful brothers. I will liberate Alamut in a way no commander has ever liberated any other castle. Alamut will be liberated with the help of Allah and without bloodshed. Take heart, my brothers! Open your eyes and be careful, and you can see numerous miracles being performed by Allah."

Two weeks after Hassan's speech, the retinue reached the gates of Alamut Castle. Hassan's preachers had been sent to Alamut a month prior to make Alamut's dwellers convert to Nizari Ismailism. The castle commandant, who had been appointed by the Seljuk Sultan, tried to defy Hassan's call to surrender, but he had no power over his dwellers because almost everybody had adopted the Ismaili religion; they acknowledged Hassan-i Sabbāh as their spiritual leader and obeyed only his orders. After Hassan addressed the Alamut dwellers, the commandant had no choice but to surrender without resisting. Everyone, including the commandant of Alamut, acknowledged

Hassan as the spiritual authority. The dwellers took the initiative to open the castle gates and let Hassan and his supporters in. Hassan was being glorified and even deified. From that day forward, the castle was handed over, and Hassan and his supporters began their reign over Alamut.

Immediately after taking over, Hassan made the castle's ex-commandant sign an indenture requiring him to pay a fine of three thousand pieces of gold, and promptly dismissed him upon receiving the payment. The next day, Hassan-i Sabbāh announced the creation of a new Nizari state at Alamut Castle. In those times, when bloodshed and cruelty prevailed, this was a remarkable event. Hassan-i Sabbāh had conquered Alamut Castle without a single fight or life lost, using only his negotiation skills and Allah's word.

Nevertheless, the newly formed Nizari state couldn't escape the attention of the Seljuk Sultan, considering a new religious state had just emerged in the center of the land under his rule. Moreover, the citizens of the new state refused to acknowledge the sultan's authority and were carrying out aggressive propaganda across the entire region. The sultan's chief vizier, Nizam al-Mulk, who was responsible for preaching and spiritual security, was most concerned about this issue. Al-Mulk would often declare that Hassan's newly formed state couldn't last long, and he ordered others to be intolerant toward Hassan's preachers, treating them as disseminators of a denominational stream and causing them inconvenience by imposing sanctions on them at every opportunity. This caused the Assassins to act and move with extreme caution and observe the principle of confidentiality. They continued to travel from country to country, preaching the spiritual work performed by the great leader Hassan-i Sabbāh.

The Assassins claimed that Hassan was the only person in the entire world through whose mouth Allah was speaking. Hassan-i Sabbāh was believed to be God's envoy to earth. His job was just and his punishment was merciless. The Assassins would bribe the heralds, paying them to tell stories throughout the market squares about Hassan-i Sabbāh's wisdom, intelligence, equity and cruel punishments. Those stories would then find their way into ordinary people's homes, spreading like gossip and folklore. Every man considered it his duty to enrich Hassan's reputation by telling his acquaintances what he had heard about Hassan and his followers. Gossip, as you know, is the most ingenious and reliable means of disseminating information. If the information that needs to be disseminated does not need to be specified but needs to be spread far and be heard by everyone, or if the message needs to reach a level of being called a legend, then gossip and oral stories are the best methods; the aura of secrecy increases the pleasure of knowing the disseminated information. After all, possessing information that is not available to others gives a feeling of pleasure, and boasting about that secret knowledge in the presence of others gives double the pleasure.

"Sayid, you can try it yourself if you ever have time to," the caravan leader said. "Say something confidential to seven people in your circle and you will see that it will return to you in seven days – of course, in a more distorted, embellished, and artistic form. And if you want that information to spread ten times faster, then before you reveal it, ask people not to tell anyone about it. First, it will increase the listener's interest in the story, and second, a lie containing secrecy usually spreads faster than the simple and obvious truth."

"Do you mean that my friends will disclose my secret? Does that mean that it would be sheer folly to trust anyone and that my family would like to ruin me?"

"Not at all! A close friend who possesses your secret will never want to do you harm. Before disclosing your secret to anyone, they will modify it a little, comforting themselves that the way they told it was the safest way for you."

The leader motioned for him to continue the story.

"As I have already said, a decision was made in the upper level of the government to hinder the activity of Hassan's preachers in every possible way, but not in an overt manner. Official religious representatives dismissed Hassan's people, or the Assassins as they were called, from religious gatherings. Heralds were instructed to spread negative news about the activities of the Assassins everywhere they went and to call on people to beware of them. When dealing with government agencies, Nizaris faced difficulties. Negative attitudes were being formed toward them everywhere, which forced the Assassins to act in a secretive manner. They would gather in Nizari apartments and act cautiously, trying to avoid direct contact with outsiders. Consequently, a unique secret system of signs emerged by which the Assassins recognized each other among the crowd. Secret gathering places were established in all major towns where Assassins were given new assignments or simply needed to rest after a long trip.

Despite the unfavorable attitude toward the Assassins, the number of Nizaris was growing day by day. Because of the intolerant attitude enforced by Chief Vizier al-Mulk, and as a result of the Assassins' underground activities, it had become nearly impossible to determine the official number of Assassins that existed. They were doing everything possible to conceal their activities, and the chief vizier had no way of knowing that they had already gained such popularity and actually represented a serious threat for Seljuk power.

In the meantime, the center of the Assassins, Alamut Castle, was continuing to develop. Though Hassan had proclaimed Alamut a religious state, it was still just a small religious community in which a disciplined and ascetic lifestyle prevailed. Abstinence was encouraged, and any splendor was denied. Even wearing warm shoes in cold weather was considered a splendor. A Nizari believer was to devote his life to Allah and never think about his own life or welfare. Hassan would strictly suppress any deviation from religious dogmas. Flagellations, which were carried out almost every week, were the mildest punishment at Alamut. Residents, sharing the same religious orientation, treated each other as brothers. Together, they celebrated all religious holidays and organized both funeral ceremonies and weddings. Community members were guided by the principle of sharing their neighbors' concerns. Alamut residents were willing to help and support each other because that was the type of behavior favored by Allah. When it came to solving problems within the community, the people of Alamut would immediately join together and act as one. Hassan's only job was to rule over the community fairly and send his preachers to the boundless depths of the Arab world, where they glorified the achievements of the Nizari religious community and invited more and more new believers to Alamut.

Upon returning to Alamut from their preaching duties outside, the Assassins were replaced by new preachers who were sent to the outside world. Territories stretching thousands of miles, including all major states, were equally divided between Hassan's preachers.

Another important reason for the Assassins' covert activities was that, aside from spreading word about Hassan-i Sabbāh's fame, the Assassins would collect information about the countries where they preached and then convey this information to Hassan. Although he sat in an impenetrable fortress and was cut off from the world, he was eager to know every detail about the latest events and innovations happening outside. It was necessary for him to have a thorough understanding of the outside world. Thanks to the Assassins, Hassan was kept aware of the strengths and weaknesses of all rulers, their sexual preferences, if they had orgies organized for them, their favorite officials and the endless drama between those officials. Hassan would try not to intervene in those matters – he was simply collecting information. His people would neither help nor harm any side. They simply acquired information by any means necessary and sent it to Alamut by secret post. Neutrality was respected because Hassan didn't want his religious community to be involved in the intrigues and struggles of the outside.

However, even remaining neutral, the residents of Alamut Castle could not escape the attention of the political authorities. Religious officials dwelling in settlements under Seljuk rule disliked the Assassins, to put it mildly, and impeded their activities as much as possible. The Assassins, as was mentioned earlier already mentioned, liked to keep a low profile and had their private homes in different settlements, where they gathered secretly. Religious leadership had already begun to seriously worry about Hassan's activities and was jealous of Hassan's actions and the actions of his people. They used various channels to try to warn the sultan about a religious unit operating within his territory of which he had no power over, as the residents of Alamut Castle would obey only Hassan-i Sabbāh and ignored any other authority. They believed that Hassan was Allah's man on earth. That was why his position was much higher than that of any secular ruler, including the sultan. The situation was gradually deteriorating in the suburban towns where, due to their active preaching, the Assassins were treated normally by ordinary people, while the religious and secular authorities showed blatant disfavor to Hassan's people. This conflicting situation was just waiting to explode, and that day was not far away.

In the year 1092 (according to the non-believer's calendar), exactly twelve years after settling in Alamut, Bu Tahir Arrani, who was already the leader of the Assassin preachers, was leaving for the Seljuk town of Sava to meet with the head of the local Assassins' secret gathering place and deliver Hassan-i Sabbāh's new sermon to his spiritual brothers living there. People of their group, out of habit, entered Sava disguised as merchants. They must have either failed to conceal themselves properly or they were betrayed by someone, because Sava's muezzin noticed their movements.

The muezzin, of course, had repeatedly heard about the Assassins and their leader Hassan-i Sabbāh, but that day was the first time he had witnessed their activities in real life. He therefore decided to follow their tracks. Afterward, he was sure that he was dealing with a new, aggressive religious order. Together with his disciple, the muezzin began to oversee Arrani's group and their movements, making note of people they met with and sometimes eavesdropping on their conversations.

In the evening, the Assassins would gather at their secret spot, the entrance of which was only from the roof. During one gathering, the muezzin entered the Assassins' assembly room and started shouting and threatening them. Bu Tahir Arrani and the other Assassins understood that their secrecy was no longer aiding them. Arrani urged the muezzin to go away and forget about them altogether, but the muezzin threatened to go to the authorities right away and report the meeting. This made Arrani angry, and he attacked the muezzin and thrust his dagger straight into his heart. Arrani committed the murder so that they wouldn't have to break their principle of keeping the group private, although none of the Assassins in the room knew that the muezzin hadn't been alone; his disciple had been watching the whole scene through the window, inadvertently becoming a witness to the murder. The Assassins also had no idea that that same disciple, together with the muezzin, had been following them the whole day and were aware of their secret meetings and conversations. The body of the murdered muezzin was hidden in a well on the outskirts of town. At night, Arrani left Sava with his group and went underground for a while until everything became known and the situation had stabilized itself again.

In the morning, the muezzin's disciple approached the Sheikh and told him about what he witnessed the day before, including the muezzin's murder, and said that he knows where the body was hidden.

When the body of the murdered muezzin was found, the entire town erupted with rage. Some people immediately spread rumors that the muezzin had been murdered by Hassan-i Sabbāh's preachers. Apparently, the disciple had told everyone what he had seen. A wave of hatred and revenge arose in Sava. Mass riots started and unrest brewed. Some people began burning shops and making disobedience calls. Citizens were coming out onto the streets seeking fair vengeance for the death of their clergyman. Having prayed at the mosque, believers came out to the town square and made demands to immediately exterminate anyone who professed another religion. A few more enterprising people began enrolling Jews and Christians living in Sava. Craftsmen refused to go to work and chaos, panic and disobedience spread through the town of Sava. The management of the town was beyond the control of local authorities.

The situation became so acute that the Seljuk Sultan's Chief Vizier, Nizam al-Mulk, was informed about it. Assessing the situation, the chief vizier understood that the sultan's power in Sava had wavered and was already in doubt. Nizam al-Mulk ordered his men to immediately catch the leader of the local Assassins and execute him according to the principle of fair revenge. As a result, the Nizari leader was arrested and suffered a torturous death under the sentence of execution imposed by the command of Nizam al-Mulk. After the actual execution, the body of the Nizari religious preacher was dragged along the streets of Sava so that everybody could be sure that just retribution had been exacted and nothing could undermine the sultan's power and glory. The Assassin was also hung in the central market square so that his lacerated body appeared as evidence that justice had been maintained by the sultan by virtue of his authority as a ruler.

Having reached Alamut Castle, Arrani told Hassan about the events. Arrani was not aware of the after effects of the muezzin's murder because his group had left Sava early in the morning after hiding the muezzin's body. Therefore, at the time they arrived at Alamut, none of them knew that the muezzin's body had already been found, nor were they aware of the chief vizier's commands or the Assassin's death penalty.

Hassan reproached Arrani severely for his carelessness and lack of foresight. Being quite astute, Hassan understood that sooner or later the muezzin's murder would come to light, and this would significantly disrupt everything that was planned. Hassan was particularly annoyed by the fact that the balance had been irreversibly disturbed, and it would be impossible to maintain neutrality after the clergyman of the Sava community was killed. Hassan's anger intensified when a messenger entered and informed them about the tragic conclusion of the incident. Hassan expelled everyone from his room and ordered them to leave him alone. Nobody dared enter Hassan's room for three days and three nights. During that time, the news about their fellow brother's capital punishment quickly spreads across Alamut. The event was discussed by the castle residents nearly everywhere. Of course, there were no spontaneous protests since Alamut, unlike Sava, was a community of deeply religious people whose beliefs were guided by law and order. Instead of burning down buildings and calling for violence, the Assassins gathered in front of Hassan's house, voicing their only demand for requital for the murder of their brother in faith. They were most frustrated with the brutal details of the execution, particularly the part about the public humiliation of the lifeless body.

The indignant residents of Alamut Castle gathered in front of Hassan's house, demanding a fair and adequate retribution from those who had cruelly torn their friend to pieces. It was then announced to the protesters that Hassan-i Sabbāh was going to give a speech in connection with the deplorable events that took place. The Assassins were looking forward to the speech immensely. At the appointed time, Hassan climbed up onto the roof of his house so that everyone could hear his speech. He started with a prayer for eternal rest for the soul of their lost friend and asked the almighty Lord to place the murdered Assassin on his right side in the heavenly paradise as one of the most faithful followers of Allah that the world had ever seen. He expressed confidence that Allah would be merciful and would retribute him for all the pain and suffering he experienced until the moment of his death. Hassan declared the murdered Assassin a faith martyr, noting that he was killed for the sole reason of serving Allah. In other words, the deceased was Allah's soldier, and those who killed him would certainly become food for demons.

During those three days staying indoors, Hassan had been praying for the murdered soul, asking that he be granted the best destiny in the most beautiful corner of the heavenly paradise. Hassan prayed so long that an angel of the almighty Lord appeared to him and assured him that the lacerated Assassin was in the most beautiful part of the garden, enjoying the attention and favor of the Lord omnipotent. The angel said that the most beautiful hour is had gathered around the victim and were comforting the soldier of faith with their beautiful naked bodies every second. Besides giving details about the slain Assassin's afterlife, the angel gave Hassan instructions and told him to convey them to the residents of Alamut Castle. First, the heavenly Lord's appearance instructed all his soldiers and true believers not to fall apart because of the event; he urged them to come together and stand as one. Everyone knew that only such devotees would be merited his kingdom. Allah told Hassan that anger should not be directed toward the scoundrels who had personally committed the dastardly murder. They were non-entities and it was not proper for the soldiers of Allah to deal with filthy gnats. Nizam al-Mulk was the main Shaitan and he was to blame for the villainy. Those who personally committed the murder were instruments in Shaitan's hands and it was necessary to fight, not against Satan's instruments, but against Satan himself. That's why the soldier or the believer who managed to kill Nizam al-Mulk and send him to hell would go straight into the arms of Allah, regardless of if he survived the task or not. The name of that courageous Assassin would be forever inscribed in the history of humanity and his deed would become exemplary for others. Hassan told the heavenly Lord that he had gathered together all those at Alamut Castle who were willing to accept such a destiny, but Hassan would have to choose the right group of volunteers who would be eager to carry out the execution of Shaitan Nizam al-Mulk.

Hassan stood before the religious community, appealing to everyone who was destined to participate in the mission, and realized that it was the wish of all of Alamut. He then told his followers that he would like to hear from all those Assassins who were ready to achieve the desired retribution.

Having finished his speech, Hassan came down from the roof and approached the people gathered around. A murmur was heard among the Assassins, who had been listening to Hassan's speech attentively. The number of those wishing to carry out Al-Mulk's death penalty was not small. Of course, no one in the crowd knew how the murder would be committed. Al-Mulk was one of the most powerful figures of that time. No one knew where he lived, and if his house was found it would certainly be surrounded by high walls and hundreds of soldiers protecting it. Everyone had heard about the chief vizier and his activities, but no one in the crowd had ever actually seen Al-Mulk's face, so they had no idea how they would even identify him. Rumors about the mission were spreading like waves from one part of the crowd to the other.

"Old Man of the Mountain! I have a word to say," a voice said suddenly from out of the crowd.

Hassan squinted and, recognizing the speaker, stroked his beard with satisfaction.

"We are listening to you, Bu Tahir Arrani," Hassan cried out.

"If Allah sets such a task before us, he will illuminate our way toward completing that task with his divine light. His light is brighter than the sun and the moon together, isn't it? Of course, this is a difficult and complicated task, but I wonder if there is any way to the Heavenly Kingdom that is easy. Tell me how to get to the foot of Muhammad and I will take that way. No, there is no easy way to Allah. And this has a special meaning, since all those whose faith is not as solid as iron, whose love is not brighter than gold or diamonds, or whose hope fades sooner than a candle, are swept onto that road in this way."

"Old Man of the Mountain!" Arrani shouted louder, "The balance has been broken through a fault of mine and by my hands. I acted carelessly, endangering our fair job. I too am guilty, and there is no excuse for my behavior. Maybe I will live forever in the flames of hell, and devils will expose me to ridicule in the eternal fire. Maybe I should have become disheartened and lost my desire to live. After all, my last hope to meet the prophet in the heavens has been taken away from me. It is torture and humiliation, not the Heavenly Kingdom and walks in the garden of paradise that await me. However, maybe the almighty Lord has been merciful toward me, providing an unprecedented and unique chance to return to him. Slaughtering Shaitan al-Mulk is my last chance to return to our heavenly Lord, to atone for my sins in front of both Allah and his vicar on earth, the Old Man of the Mountain. Please, my brothers, do not deprive me of my last chance to atone for my sin. Old Man of the Mountain, please show mercy on me and let me carry out yours and Allah's will, sending Shaitan Nizam al-Mulk to hell."

As Arrani finished speaking, the crowd fell silent. Everyone held their breath as they waited for Hassan's decision. Hassan remained in deep thought, stroking his beard. It seemed as if he was in his own world and had not even heard Arrani's touching speech.

Having stood like that for several minutes, Hassan said, "Bu Tahir Arrani! There is truth in your words. You have only one chance to atone for your sin, and it wouldn't be fair of us to deprive you of that chance. My son! God loves all his children and doubles his love for those who sinned unwittingly but then left the path of sin and returned to him. I bless your work, your path and your goal. Goodbye, our beloved brother Bu Tahir Arrani, and let Allah accompany you in all your undertakings."

After these words, Arrani knelt down and kissed Hassan's hem and everyone else returned to their business.

Arrani spent a few more days in Alamut. First, he gathered a small group of eight people to help him accomplish his difficult task. Then, Hassan gave him all the information about the vizier that had been collected by the Assassins in recent years. There was quite a lot of information and it contained necessary details. Before Arrani left, Hassan called him over and handed him a dagger anointed with poison with which Arrani was to carry out the death penalty of the chief vizier. The next night, Arrani and his squad, divided into three groups, made their way to Sahna, where the Chief Vizier Abu Ali al-Hasan ibn al-Hasan ibn Ali ibn Ishaq al-Tusi, better known as Nizam al-Mulk, lived.

Arrani pretended to be a Sufi as he traveled. He had very good knowledge of the Quran and he managed to adjust his appearance to be disguised as a Muslim cleric. His years studying theology in Alamut had paid off; he had mastered the look so well that he presented himself as a Sufi without any fear.

Arrani separated himself from the squad, and they all agreed to meet in Sahna to join forces in carrying out the death penalty. Arrani had been traveling from town to town for months, exploring the opinions and attitudes of the residents under the sultan and his chief vizier. Ordinary people did not like the sultan, referring to him as a greedy, insatiable and unjust ruler. People cursed the chief vizier for his numerous incomprehensible taxes. Arrani's hatred and personal disgust against the chief vizier was gradually strengthening. He was becoming more and more convinced of Hassan's words that the chief vizier was a Shaitan who needed to be eliminated. Arrani's belief that he was performing Allah's will was also strengthening more and more. After all, there were so many people who hated the chief vizier and would get rid of their detested ruler with his help. It was with these thoughts in mind that Arrani approached Sahna where, according to the information provided by Hassan, the chief vizier's house was located.

When he arrived, Arrani first visited the secret gathering place of the local Assassins, where he was welcomed by their leader who was cleverly disguised as a tailor. It was expedient to do so, as various people would visit him during the day to get dresses, tablecloths and curtains sewn.

When taking orders, the tailor would press the customers for information, which they would willingly share, and then he would carefully collect that information and convey it to the Alamut fortress. The tailor wasn't particularly good at tailoring; he had actually hired a few real tailors who sewed clothes for him. Having been working this way, the tailor acquired a reputation as a good tailor, and everybody to whom he had once provided his services would come back to him.

The tailor hid Arrani in the attic of his house. As soon as it became dark, he let all his employees go home and went up to see Arrani with some food in his hands. Arrani said that he needed to find the chief vizier's house and orient himself both within the vicinity of the house and, more importantly, inside the house gates. The tailor promised to collect all information about the layout of the rooms inside the chief vizier's house and the frequency of people's movements inside. Arrani asked the tailor to describe what the chief vizier looked like, since he had never seen him. The tailor said that he also had never seen the chief vizier since he didn't often come out of his workshop in order to avoid attracting attention to himself, and he never risked roaming the streets in case he was accidentally noticed. The tailor promised Arrani that he would somehow find a solution to this problem. Arrani told him about his intention to dress like a beggar and walk around the chief vizier's house for a few days, but the tailor laughed at Arrani's naivety. All the beggars in town knew each other and if they saw an alien beggar, they would beat and banish him from the town at best, or in the worst case, they would report the stranger to the authorities and his arrest would be imminent.

"I do not know the purpose of your visit and I do not even want to know, but the fact that you wear Hassan-i Sabbāh's blessing ring on your finger makes me obliged to serve you and fulfill all your demands."

"There aren't too many of them!" Arrani snickered.

"Maybe, but what you want is too dangerous," the tailor said. "Take a rest for today, and I will try to solve your problems tomorrow."

"Thank you, but it would be better if they were solved quickly, because I haven't come here for sleeping."

"Do I look like a fool? I suppose, but I am not. I have guessed more or less why you have come here. May Allah bless your two hands! Save your youthful energy! I will arrange everything at the highest level."

Having said this, the tailor wished Arrani a good night and went downstairs. The next day, the tailor didn't show up. From the attic, Arrani could hear him meeting with customers and talking to them with an amiable tone of voice. Arrani could not hear exactly what the tailor was talking about, but he had an unconcerned tone, which irritated Arrani, as if he had forgotten all about him and had just returned to his normal life. He had even decided to reprove the tailor for his negligent and irresponsible attitude.

The voices coming from beneath stopped during the daytime prayer. Arrani tried not to hold back from it and started praying, using the sunlight penetrating through the attic vents to determine the sun's approximate position.

As soon as it grew dark, the tailor let his employees leave and, taking a plateful of food, went up to the attic to see Arrani. The tailor also held a map in his hand. As Arrani ate, the tailor explained the position of Sahna and the logic of the town's streets. When Arrani grasped the tailor's explanations, the tailor handed him the map of Sahna, which showed the chief vizier's house. At this point, the tailor left Arrani and promised that if he waited a few more days, he could provide complete information about the identity of the chief vizier. He gave Arrani a mysterious look as he left the attic, saying that the mystery might even be solved already and that he would tell him more later.

The next few days passed in the same way. During the day Arrani was alone, deep in thoughts and prayers, while the tailor managed his business. In the evenings the tailor would pay a visit to Arrani, give him the information acquired during the day, feed him, and leave him until the next day.

Four days later, the tailor went up to the attic in a particularly good mood. He said that all the major issues were resolved. He had talked to one of his customers and learned that there was a gap in the southern part of the wall around the chief vizier's house through which a tiny man could easily get in. A winter garden, filled with some of the most diverse plants and trees, was located just beyond that wall, in front of the gap. Another client had said that the chief vizier was in the habit of going for a short walk in the garden just after waking up in the morning and before going to bed in the evening. The customer had said this to emphasize the chief vizier's love of nature and also to show off his intimate knowledge of the chief vizier's everyday life.

"You were saying that you would help me recognize him. Is there any progress?" Arrani asked impatiently.

Now he was getting closer to his goal. A few more small details and everything would happen the way it had been planned.

"Of course! I could not have forgotten about that small but important detail," the tailor said with a sly smile. "By a happy chance the head of the chief vizier's armed guards visited me a week ago and ordered a precious cloak embroidered with gold thread. Tomorrow I am handing over the order. Apart from the cloak, I will present him thirty bright green cords for their shoes. I will say that it is a gift to the chief vizier's armed guards and that I would be happy to continue to serve that guard as a tailor. It's typical of traders to give such gifts to attract new and rich customers. When you see the chief vizier's retinue, remember two things: first, he loves to dress luxuriously, and the man dressed in the most expensive and brightest clothes is probably the chief vizier, and secondly, people accompanying him, namely his armed guards, will be wearing shoes with bright green cords, thus differentiating themselves from the chief vizier. This way you will be able to guess which of them is Nizam al-Mulk. Stay here today; tomorrow you can go on your mission. And may Allah bless you with success!"

The tailor hugged Arrani and said goodbye to him. The next day Arrani spent the whole morning preparing to leave the tailor's attic. He prepared the clothes he was going to wear, studied the map of the town by daylight once more and without hurrying, tried to picture the sequence of his actions. As soon as it became dark, Arrani jumped out of the attic and onto the ground and hastily disappeared into the streets.

There was a gap in one part of the south wall surrounding the chief vizier's house. It wasn't a very big hole, but Arrani carefully removed another plank from the wall and the gap became wide enough that he could easily enter the territory of the chief vizier's house. He waited a little longer and, certain that there was no one in the vicinity, entered through the hole in the wall. The tailor had not deceived him; the winter garden was only twenty steps away. Arrani sped through the garden quietly and quickly. He hid in the high bushes along the garden walkway and sat motionless. It seemed he was not even breathing. He remained motionless in the same position the whole night. During the night, only one guard came; he walked around the garden and then went away. According to Arrani's observations, the presence of the guards was not likely to ensure actual security, as they had a rather formal nature about them.

Everything was quiet in the morning, but lively voices could be heard in the afternoon. Arrani looked up; he asked Allah to forgive him for missing the hour of prayer, explaining that he had good reasons for it. Soon, Arrani could hear footsteps and a loud discussion coming from the garden. Two men were walking to the middle of the garden, talking. Arrani took a close look at their feet. The cords of their shoes were bright green. The chief vizier was surely not among them. The number of people in the garden increased quickly. They began to walk along the path of the garden. Arrani tried to examine their cords; everybody was wearing shoes with the bright green cords the tailor had given them – everybody except two men. The first person's shoes had no cords at all, while the other's shoes had black cords. Arrani tried to guess which of them might be the chief vizier. They were both almost the same age and both were dressed in expensive clothes. The two men were talking with each other as equals, but suddenly one of them, who wore shoes with black cords, smiled during the conversation and gave a slight bow to the one who wore no cords. Arrani realized that there was no point in delaying things.

"Go to hell, Shaitan!" Arrani shouted, and he thrust his dagger into the chief vizier's chest three times.

The bodyguards, deeply shocked, were looking at Arrani; everything was very unexpected for them. Arrani seemed to have fallen from the sky or emerged from beneath the ground. His soft face had even given the bodyguards cause for mystic contemplations. Some of them even threw up their arms and got down on their knees, thinking that they were witnessing Allah's punishment. Only two of the more experienced bodyguards made no fuss and immediately grabbed Arrani's arms, snatching the dagger out of his hand. But it was too late. The chief vizier's inanimate body was laying in the middle of the garden path, bleeding, and it was impossible to change what had happened.

Arrani laughed. The bodyguards tortured him for a long time. His body was beaten and torn apart and thrown off the property. Arrani looked happy and joyful until the end and said absolutely nothing. He just laughed.

A few hours later, the Assassins, having received a special signal, ran up to the chief vizier's house from different angles. They were already aware that the chief vizier had been murdered, and they also knew that Arrani had been killed and torn to pieces. They silently surrounded the chief vizier's house and set it on fire. The house burned down, and the flames reached higher and higher, making the night sky look blood red when viewed from the heights of the city. They say Hassan personally followed the whole course of the retribution operation from one part of the town and kept looking at the crimson sky as the chief vizier's house burnt down.

Jubilation and celebration broke out in Alamut as the news about the chief vizier's murder spread. Everyone was happy and thanked the Lord Almighty for his help. A month later, a large copper board with an inscription was fastened on Alamut's gates that read: "Bu Tahir Arrani, the fearless soldier of Allah, who killed the Sultan's Chief Vizier Shaitan Nizam al-Mulk and met Allah for that deed."

5. Faith or Love? (Paris, AD 2015)

"Ali, are we really alone? Won't someone suddenly come?" Liz asked, tearing herself away for a moment from the long and passionate kiss.

"Don't worry, my dear, no one will disturb us. Patrick promised to come home only in the evening. We are alone, absolutely alone, and no one will interrupt us," said Ali, feeling out of breath from kissing. Then he smothered any remaining words with another passionate kiss.

They kissed like crazy. A narrow ray of sun, penetrating through the window, was lighting the room and providing some heat. Even though the room was heated, there was the impression that the narrow ray of sun was ensuring its temperature. Ali pulled Liz into his arms, spinned her around in a circle, and then gently laid her back onto the bed. He used his lips to lift her pullover, revealing her girlish breasts and aroused nipples, which were not yet fully developed. Ali seemed to go crazy at the sight of her breasts. He began to feverishly kiss her lips, breasts, and belly button, as if he could not decide which part of her body he liked the most.

"Ali…" Liz groaned with pleasure. She wrapped her arms tightly around his neck and pressed him to her breast. Her eyes went dark.

They had been lying in bed for a long time already, looking at the ceiling. Ali felt that his life had acquired a new wonderful meaning, a meaning that hadn't existed before. His life also seemed to have acquired a new color. Actually, it would be more correct to say that his life used to lack color completely. Liz felt happy. Near Ali, the young, carefree girl became a sensual, mature woman. Though Liz had been in love before, her previous love affairs had mainly been confined to a few slobbery, unpleasant kisses, which always made her feel like she was teaching young children how to kiss. It was impossible to build a long-lasting relationship based on that kind of feeling. Liz was tired of that. Moreover, it didn't really matter what age the men she met were. They weren't younger than her, of course. Liz simply wanted a man who, regardless of his age, would be mature enough that a woman could get from him all the chromosomes or hormones that were missing in her.

With Ali, everything was different. He wasn't like the others. For one thing, he and Liz were the same age. Ali also looked like a prince from an eastern fairy tale; he was a broad-shouldered, dark-skinned man with black, sultry eyes. Liz was crazy about him. They were high school students and studied together. Liz initially pretended not to be interested in Ali's signs of attention. Coming from a completely different culture, Ali behaved like a British, aristocratic gentleman.

Liz lived with her aunt in Paris, while her parents lived in the south of France and were busy farming a small piece of land. Liz had moved to Paris to study and settled there. It didn't take long for her to erase all traces of her peasant origins and be considered a Parisian girl. Her aunt had lived in Paris all her life, and it could be assumed from some of her stories that she had lived a life full of many memorable episodes involving characters from Paris' well-known bohemian scene. She wasn't particularly strict with Liz. Actually, Liz was completely free to do what she wanted. For security reasons, her aunt would call her a few times a day to make sure everything was ok, but these calls gradually became fewer and fewer once Liz started to orientate herself with Paris so well that even her aunt was sometimes amazed to learn something new about Paris from her.

Ali and his family had left Syria and moved to Paris two years ago. Their hometown had been bombed many times, and Ali's father, having no other options, had decided to move his family to a European city far away from the explosions and seemingly endless bloodshed. Their family was large; Ali had four brothers and sister. Ali was the youngest of the family. Everyone treated him with special love and care, especially his mother and sister. Even though Ali was nineteen, his mother would still try to fix his hair with her hand before he left the house. She did it not so much to see her son clean and tidy, but to satisfy her maternal yearnings for just a few minutes. To his mother, Ali was always considered the baby of the family.

His father had his own expectations for Ali. He ardently wished to see his son become a priest. He dreamed about his son being devoted to Allah, so he would openly enforce strict methods of parenting, although somewhere inside him he also considered Ali a little boy who must constantly be guided to the right path and be kept away from secular temptations. Ali's father exhorted him to enter a university in one of the Parisian suburbs and major in Religious Studies. And since no French institute offered an advanced course on Islam, his father also decided to send Ali to Egypt to join Cairo University's Department of Islam so that he could start building a career as a highly qualified religious preacher after graduating. Of course, Ali's father made sure his son was unaware of these plans, choosing to leave everything to Allah's favor, but he was always strict when it came to Ali's upbringing and kept a close eye on him.

Ali was a high-performing student. He studied all religions with equal delight but of course kept to the rules of his faith, Islam. In his first year of study, he met Liz. Liz was not particularly fond of studying. She was not very interested in the different religions and religious movements. She considered her studies a hobby that prevented her from getting bored to death while in Paris.

After a while, Ali's offerings of attention proved successful. Liz began to smile at Ali more. After classes, they would spend their free time together. They saw each other so often that their relationship grew to a deeper level. They were walking by Notre-Dame de Paris one August evening when Liz, looking at Ali with a smile, said, "I don't actually like Paris in August."

Ali looked at Liz with confusion. She was wearing a simple chintz dress. That year, clothes with ordinary motifs were fashionable and it was a style that suited Liz best.

"I always thought you were in love with this city."

"Paris is an amazing and indescribable place, but it turns into a boring and unbearable city in August," Liz started to explain. "The locals leave the city and go to their summer houses or go further down to the south of France, or they travel to other countries. Meanwhile, Paris is attacked by provincials and foreign tourists.

"Are you against people coming to Paris?" Ali asked in a perplexed tone.

"No, of course not. But for them, Paris is a city caught on camera. They take photographs hugging the Eiffel Tower. They never see the real Paris. Actually, even the Eiffel Tower is different in their eyes. They don't even see the tower, they just take thousands of photos near the tower."

Ali did not understand Liz's words. Paris hadn't become his home yet, but certain feelings of attachment had grown inside him after having lived there for two years already.

"Liz, is there a place in Paris you love the most?" Ali asked.

"Of course, there is. Come on, I'll show you," she said, taking Ali's hand and leading him to the back of Notre-Dame.

They stopped in the middle of the yard, not far from the entrance.

"Here it is!" Liz declared, pointing to the ground.

"Here? What is this?" Ali noticed a round stone on the ground, which differed from the other tiles. It had an octagonal star in the center that was embedded in the concrete of the square.

"This is Point Zero. According to legend, the city began and expanded from here. This is the belly button of Paris."

Ali wasn't listening to Liz. Every time he looked at her, his breathing stopped. Now, his heart seemed to have gone furious and was about to fly out of his chest, leaving nothing but a hole in its place. He hugged Liz and kissed her lips. Now it was Liz's turn to feel dizzy. Although Liz had noticed that Ali was staring at her, his kiss was still really unexpected.

Everything became a blur in Liz's head: Point Zero, Notre-Dame, the kiss, Paris in August. Especially Paris in August. Liz caught herself thinking that she may even begin to love Paris in August, despite its foreign visitors. She also realized that, for the most part, she herself was a provincial girl who had come to settle in Paris and who was kissing her beloved at that moment. What's more, he was neither a Parisian or a French provincial; he was a young man who had quite another nationality, religion and culture, but who was very good looking. That man was kissing her in the center of Paris at that moment. For a second, even Liz thought that she was going crazy.

Almost a year had passed since that kiss. They met quite often during that year; together they would go to Notre-Dame's yard, where Point Zero was, and repeat their first kiss. Now, half a year later, they were lying in bed inside the small house of Ali's friend, Patrick, looking at the ceiling.

"What time is it?" asked Liz, still coming out of her dream.

Ali stretched out his hand toward the chair near the bed on which his trousers were carefully placed and took his phone out of his pocket. He looked at the screen.

"It's half past three."

"Oh my god," Liz jumped up. "That's terrible, it can't be so!"

Ali looked at Liz.

"Why do you look so surprised?" Liz said. "Have you forgotten that today is Sunday? I should have visited my grandpa Matteo half an hour ago."

Ali remembered. Yes, of course he had known about it. Every Sunday, Liz would visit her grandpa, who lived in a nursing home. She would take him fresh fruit and sweets. Her grandpa was very fond of sweets. Sometimes, when Liz was busy with important things or was getting ready for her university exams, Ali would visit her grandpa for her. Ali didn't mind it. Respecting and paying homage to elderly people was an accepted practice in the east. Ali would listen to Liz's grandfather for a few hours. Matteo was a very interesting storyteller; he would always find something interesting to say. It was impossible to determine what was true and what was invented, but the stories he told were really captivating.

But Matteo had a problem. He would sometimes fall into a deep oblivion, during which he couldn't recognize anyone, not even his own granddaughter, whom he adored the most. His bouts of memory loss would last a few minutes at most. Everything would fall into place after a while, and Matteo would begin to tell another interesting story that happened to him or his acquaintances. The problem of his memory loss had emerged recently in the last several years. Liz had already accepted it. After a couple of meetings, Ali also had stopped noticing her grandfather's lapses.

"If we stay here for at least another half an hour, I'll visit your grandpa for you, and you'll be able to go home and prepare for your exams."

How quickly time flies when you're lying in bed with the most beautiful girl in the world, looking at the ceiling cracks and dreaming. Even their extra half hour together disappeared and melted away as if they were a few seconds. Liz finally managed to sit up in bed, stretch herself like a cat, and stand up.

"Ali! Put on your clothes. We must go."

Ali hated partings. At those moments, he would realize how great his love for Liz was. Ali and Liz had even turned the simple act of leaving the house and closing the door into another opportunity to share a long and passionate kiss. As they reached the door to leave the house, Ali took the opportunity to give Liz another kiss goodbye. They would sometimes pretend to be ashamed to kiss in the street, but soon after they would forget all about conventional behavior and exchange kisses while older passersby would gaze at them with condemnation.

"Ok, I'm kissing you goodbye now. Take care, see you tomorrow," Liz said and left with light, swift steps.

Only then did Ali finally return to reality. He forgot about everything around him when Liz was beside him. Still, how could he have forgotten that today, before leaving home, his father had strictly warned him to be home by five o'clock, before the hour of evening prayer?

Ali realized that if he visited Liz's grandpa, he would definitely get home later than five. But it was too late; he had already promised Liz. "I need to call her and tell her about it," Ali thought. He took out his phone, dialed Liz's number, and heard her voice after a few rings. "I'm listening to you, my eastern prince," Liz joked on the other end of the phone.

"How are you?" Ali asked absentmindedly.

"Well, just about three minutes ago I was happy to be by your side. Has anything happened?"

Ali realized that he couldn't ask Liz for anything now. After all, Liz had been late because of him, and he himself had insisted on visiting her grandpa instead of her.

"No, everything is ok. I just called to say I missed you."

"Me too," said Liz. "Well, my dear, my bus has arrived. Call me when you leave my grandpa's, and please take oranges for him. He asked me last time. Kisses."

Liz hung up the phone. Deep in thought, Ali entered the supermarket. "Whatever will happen will happen," he thought. "After all, nobody will kill me at home. I will try to explain that I had some urgent business."

"Give me five oranges, please," Ali said to the shop assistant.

"Whatever will happen will happen," Ali thought again, standing in front of Matteo's nursing home. He entered the building, climbed to the second floor, and entered the familiar room of number 216.

6. Liz's Grandpa and Ali
(Paris, AD 2015)

"Hello grandpa Matteo!" said Ali as he entered the room. "I brought you some apples and oranges, as you ordered last time. Now I will peel them for you."

Matteo was sitting on the bed playing checkers with his roommate, Professor Moshe.

"Thank you, my son!" Matteo smiled. He turned away from his game and began to attentively examine Ali. "Please, tell me your name. I want to know who this kind young adult is."

"Grandpa! It's me, Ali! I have been visiting you every Sunday for two months already, don't you remember?"

"Ah! This damn memory. You used to come with a girl – is she your sister? She's very beautiful."

"Grandpa, that's your granddaughter, Liz, and I am her classmate. We study together."

"Really? I knew nothing about that," said Matteo, his eyes remaining on Ali.

Ali didn't answer. He put the fruit on the shelf and removed one apple and one orange. He peeled the apple and cut it into slices and placed it on the table. Even without its skin, the dark red apple kept its color.

"You have been so careful with me. I want to tell you a secret, but first promise me that you will not tell it to anyone else," Matteo said in a mysterious tone.

"I promise you that, grandpa," said Ali, looking at the clock on his phone as inconspicuously as he could.

Ali understood that it would take a man Matteo's age a long time to disclose a secret.

"America is preparing for a major war," Matteo announced, looking around suspiciously.

"What war?"

"Hush!" Matteo pressed his thin forefinger to his lips. "Someone may be eavesdropping on us. This is very confidential information. Do you remember M*A*S*H?"

Professor Moshe, realizing that Matteo didn't want to disclose his secret in the presence of others, left the room under the pretense of going for a walk.

"M*A*S*H?" Ali asked, peeling the orange with a knife. "To tell you the truth, this is the first time I am hearing about it."

"It used to be the most famous comedy, or more precisely, comedy television series. Oh, everybody used to watch M*A*S*H. How could you not know?"

"When was it broadcast?"

"From 1972 to 1982. In those years, the whole world was watching Pierce and McIntyre's cynical jokes in the military hospital's operating rooms. People tried to repeat the jokes in their everyday lives, but of course most people would fail."

"Grandpa Matteo! I wasn't even born then. Even my mother hadn't been born; she was born in 1973."

"You are too young. You wouldn't know what was going on in that mobile army surgical hospital, what furious passions were raging there. I am talking about the Korean War, which began in the early fifties."

"And what does it have in common with the impending war?"

"Impending war?" Matteo seemed to have forgotten about the secret he was going to tell Ali. "Oh, yes! The war...well, I will explain bit by bit. In order to understand my story, you must first know what M*A*S*H was about. They told the most anti-war story I had ever heard, seasoned with the sharpest jokes and most cynical humor. The events took place in North Korea in 1951. Although the number of casualties on both sides reached a few million during the war, it wasn't even called a war for propaganda purposes. The events were called a 'police operation.' Despite the militarism of that period, the military and the squaddies' 'in the box' thinking were mercilessly mocked in the film. The characters were too mellow. The main character was Captain Benjamin Franklin 'Hawkeye' Pierce, a tall, brunette, young, talented surgeon endowed with extraordinarily sharp and cynical humor. Pierce was fair-minded; he looked out for injustice everywhere he went and tried to fix it at all costs. He would support the blacks, the gays, the low-ranking soldiers, the women. No! Women were his weakness. Pierce had two weaknesses: women and drink. Throughout the show, Pierce's justifications for his behavior always came from the depths of alcoholism: 'I drink because it is realistically impossible to fight such a stupid war,' he said. The next character was Pierce's partner, Captain McIntyre, who was married with two beautiful daughters. Being a tall surgeon with blonde hair, he would chase every skirt and participate in pretty much any buffoonery started by Pierce. McIntyre was Pierce's partner in everything from winning over women to drinking alcohol and indulging in self-abandonment. Pierce and McIntyre were the salt of the hospital.

They were at the center of each memorable event taking place in M*A*S*H. These guys absolutely didn't care about military regulations and ranks. They seemed to have set a goal to mock the military at all costs as a way of showing everybody the fear and dread of war and to discredit those military men who made a career at the expense of young people's health and lives. They weren't just engaged in heavy drinking and chasing the hospital nurses, but also in operating on the young men who had passed through the chopper of war, sometimes for days at a time (as they claimed), collecting them in pieces.

Major Frank Burns and Major Margaret 'Hot Lips' Houlihan were their antitheses. Frank was also a surgeon, but he was lower middle class and had bought his medical license and married for money. In general, he was the most conservative, opportunistic, stingy person in the world. Frank took the war too seriously and wanted to excel and move ahead at any cost. He would reproach anyone who didn't show enough patriotism or love for America, preaching that they should be relentless against the enemy. For these reasons, Pierce and McIntyre reacted to him with constant derision and jeering. Pierce, McIntyre and Frank lived in the same camp, which meant Frank's life became a living hell. Frank would try to keep a balanced position, but bad things kept happening to him. Whenever he tried to speak about patriotism, the two drunkards immediately silenced him. In short,

Pierce and McIntyre mocked anyone, including Frank, who justified the war and the official position of their state.

The next character was Major Margaret Houlihan, a woman of astounding beauty who was a typical military officer. Her father was a retired colonel, and throughout the film, her many gifts for Frank Burns were presented with the following words: 'My father presented this to my mother on their wedding night.' Frank and Margaret had a romance, despite the fact that Frank was married, and Margaret was not a particularly inaccessible woman; she was always ready to spread her legs, especially before high-ranking military officers. She was an ordinary army prostitute who kept several lovers at the same time. However, the long, sad wartime nights brought Margaret and Frank close together, which only made Pierce and McIntyre pick on them even more. And the more Frank and Margaret tried to hide their romantic relationship, the more bad things kept happening to them.

The next character was Corporal Max Klinger, a hot-tempered resident of Toledo who, for some reason, fought on the front line in North Korea. Klinger was capable of doing absolutely anything to get rid of the damned army and be sent home. When I say anything, in Klinger's case, it should be taken literally. He was a hairy, masculine man with a big nose who would wear elegant feminine dresses and high heels so that the medical commission would expel him from the army for being a madman. To do this, he needed three doctors' signatures, which he failed to collect. So, he continued to fill his wardrobe with new dresses, which always got him into funny situations. Klinger symbolized the desperate hatred of the war and the army – so desperate that people like him would take such crazy and foolish steps to express it.

The head of these troublemakers was Colonel Henry, a civilian who was so far removed from military life that the word 'colonel' was used with great reservation. Despite being married, Henry was also fond of chasing women and getting drunk most of the day. He had no idea how to run the hospital, which was also a military unit. All of the hospital's paperwork was entrusted to Henry's assistant, Irish Corporal 'Radar' O'Reilly. Henry dreamed of a quick end to the war and looked forward to returning home to his family."

"You are describing it so nicely, grandpa! Now I even want to watch it. I think I can find it on the Internet. What did you say? What was it called?"

Ali took out his smartphone and connected it to the Internet, not forgetting to look at the clock inconspicuously.

Matteo took the phone from his hand and said, "The film was beautiful because peace and the mockery of war were lying in its basis. Then suddenly everything changed. First, Henry allegedly died in the beginning of the film; the screenwriters introduced Colonel Potter, Henry's antithesis, instead of him. He was an old army rat, dedicated to law and order. Later, McIntyre was demobilized, and B.J., who was McIntyre's antithesis, was introduced instead of him. B.J. was a married man who remained faithful to his wife throughout the Korean War. Can you imagine how disgusting it is? Next, the screenwriters expelled Frank Burns, and his antithesis, Winchester, a snob of noble descent living in Boston, was introduced into the film instead. Then Klinger gradually bid farewell to feminine clothes, and in the end, Pierce's jokes became stupid. The film went from being a work of art, mocking war and the U.S. army, to being a banality, carrying out an anti-violence campaign."

"And what can be assumed from all this?" Ali asked.

"Ali, in the USA, everything is based on propaganda. The Americans began to glorify their military operations everywhere. This can mean only one thing: they are preparing for a large-scale war." Matteo sighed. "Now life rather resembles a pornographic film."

"Do you mean the demoralization?"

"There has never been a lack of immorality. Today, life looks like a porn film because it is the only film genre where there are no positive or negative characters. Everyone is more or less involved in that dirty beastly activity. There are no innocents; everybody is waiting for the director's instructions."

"I don't really understand," Ali said, chewing an orange. "And as for war, they are usually declared out of necessity, as opposed to something that was prepared from decades of propaganda."

Matteo did not answer; another bout of memory loss had apparently begun. With a broad smile on his face, he looked out of the window and thought about something pleasant, known only to himself.

Turning back to the room, Matteo spotted the plate of oranges on the table, took a piece with childish joy, and began to eat blissfully.

"Did you know that Fernando, my next-door neighbor, died five days ago? We were very good friends."

"I am sorry for your loss, grandpa Matteo," Ali said, trying to finally leave Matteo's room.

"He was a very good accountant. Unfortunately, he wasn't buried with all the honors as befits a great commander."

Ali realized that if he asked Matteo another question, he would have to listen to the answer for a long time. However, he could not resist the temptation and asked, "And why do you think that an accountant should be buried with the honors of a commander?"

"He used to lead an entire country's troops. Few people know about it."

"As an accountant?"

"It's not a question of what he had been good at. He was mediocre as an accountant, but he had no equals as a military leader."

Matteo got up, went to the rocking chair at the other end of the room and, making himself comfortable, began his story. "About fifty years ago, accountant Fernando went on a business trip to a small African country. He was sent there as an accountant to carry out an audit in a local French enterprise. The company was engaged in the manufacturing of textiles and, in addition to other products, produced canvas tents. Their main customers were the national police and army. The company's accounting turned out to be extremely intricate. Now, when telling this part of the story, Fernando would always describe all the commercial details, and though I've heard this story a million times, I could never quite figure out what sort of accounting problem he had encountered. Then again, I am quite weak at accounting. Anyway, Fernando soon handled the problem completely by himself. The enterprise appeared on the verge of bankruptcy and passed into the possession of the police because of their accumulated debts. Fernando had finished his work and was about to return to his homeland when he received an offer from the police chief to continue working for the company as a police chief accountant, since without an experienced accountant the textile enterprise would certainly go bankrupt again, causing unnecessary troubles. Fernando was offered a high salary and a special status for staying in the country. He was also told that within two or three years, once all of the company's issues were resolved, he would be able to return to his homeland. Fernando didn't have any particularly important business in France and, enticed by the high salary and special status, decided to accept the offer. In the first six months, everything went fine. But after that, strange things started happening. Fernando received a letter from the head of the army, inviting him to participate in a military meeting. At first, Fernando thought that it was definitely a mistake, and ignored it until he received a second letter, in which the previous polite tone was replaced by a harsh and clear threat. Fernando had always been an extremely cautious and easily frightened person, so he quickly panicked and asked the police chief to explain what sort of gathering he had been invited to. It turned out that the invitation came as a result of Fernando's special status. According to local law, persons with special status, regardless of their citizenship, were directly responsible for the country's safety, along with the twelve high-ranking officials of the country. Since Fernando was the only person who had special status in the country, it was necessary for him to partake in all gatherings on issues related to the country's security. Fernando initially refused to participate in the Security Council meetings. He tried to explain that he was only an accountant at a textile factory and didn't even want to get engaged in the political or military issues of his homeland, let alone those of a foreign country.

He asked to terminate his special status, but it turned out that the status had been granted for one year, and early termination was impossible. Fernando threatened to leave the country but having studied the local law on the special status, he realized that persons granted with that status were only entitled to leave the country with the consent of the other twelve officials. Some of those officials were against Fernando's early return, as they believed he had much to do in their country. They were convinced that if he were to leave, he would never return. Fernando wanted to turn to the French Embassy, but they politely declined to intervene in any cases related to persons with special status. Eventually, Fernando decided to just put up with the law. The local authorities, trying to put themselves in Fernando's position, made the following decisions: Fernando was expelled from the mandatory Security Council meetings, or rather they agreed to turn a blind eye to his absence. Instead, he was to take on the responsibility for the operational duties every thirteen days. Fernando desperately agreed, cursing his naivety for leading him to agree to work in that country. He was comforted only by the fact that he had half a year left before he could go home and forget about both the damn country trying to engage him in obscure responsibilities and the whole African continent itself.

Every thirteen days, he would conscientiously carry out the country's operative duties. They did not particularly overload his daily routine. During the first three months, he reported about two or three major crimes committed in the country and immediately informed the police chief about them. His unwelcome responsibilities might have seemed successfully overcome, but then an unexpected event occurred. The event could have had a favorable impact on Fernando and could have become a chance for him to leave for his homeland, unless, by some unfortunate coincidence, it happened to be the thirteenth day. On that day, the opposition started an armed revolt, killing the president and strategically blockading important places, including the country's only airport. When he reported the events, Fernando hardly knew how to react. He tried to call the police chief, but the connection ultimately cut out, and it turned out that all communication was also under the opposition's control. Fernando couldn't connect with anyone for an hour.

After an hour, the country's generals came to him and swore their loyalty and dedication to his service till death. Fernando felt like he was losing his mind. The generals showed him the official list of the operative duty officer's responsibilities, on which it was plainly written that in the event of an armed conflict and the subsequent danger imposed, the operative duty officer is responsible for carrying out the management of the armed forces and the implementation of military action programs until a lawful situation is established in the country. Fernando became enraged. He realized that it was impossible to avoid these duties, which had become a scourge. He commanded the generals to liberate the airport from the rebels at all costs and to destroy all those who tried to hinder the flight of aircrafts. Later, the generals would recall Fernando's speech with admiration. Until the end of their lives, they remained convinced that Fernando had used his experience as a strategist to decide to first restore all air communication with the outside world, so that the country could receive military and other aid. It hadn't even occurred to anyone that Fernando's first command to liberate the airport was given out of hopelessness, and that saying 'destroy the rebels' meant anyone who dared prevent his return to his native country. The generals applauded Fernando for a long time and hurried to fulfill his command. After a full day of fighting, the airport was finally liberated. Of course, telephone stations needed to be restored next, because without them, planes would not be able to take off or come in to land. Since the telephone stations and post office were both located inside the Ministry of Communication, the post office was also liberated. Since the rebels had mainly targeted those areas, once they were neutralized, dozens of oppositionists surrendered and asked for forgiveness. In just two days, the rebellion had been fully suppressed. They later learned that the rebellion had been planned for many years.

Fernando was finally able to leave the country, except for a minor problem that still needed to be solved: the country's upcoming elections. Having witnessed Fernando's strategic decision making, the military was now rallying around him and did not recognize any authority other than Fernando. They eventually agreed to transfer the power to someone else, as long as Fernando himself nominated that person and managed the entire electoral process."

"And then what happened?" Ali was intently listening to Fernando's story. He was quite interested in the idea of an accountant becoming a military leader.

"Then the elections began. I think you can guess how they went. Fernando refused to rule the country, and anyway the law itself didn't particularly allow him to do so because his special status was about to expire. He chose one of the generals whose distinguished conduct during the suppression of the armed revolt had stood out to him and introduced him as a presidential candidate. The general started his campaign, and Fernando began to pack his suitcases. Everyone was left satisfied and, thankfully, unharmed. During one election campaign speech, the general gave a pledge to finally settle the decades-long territorial dispute with the neighboring country. The electorate was thrilled. People were celebrating in the streets. Finally, the decades-long dispute, which seemed unsolvable, would be settled. The general, of course, had said so in order to attract voters to his side, but the trick backfired within just a few days. People still only trusted Fernando with military issues. Newspapers began to report that the general was Fernando's false candidate, and that Fernando was preparing a great political and military event, known only to himself. Other news sources were saying that Fernando was ruthless and cruel and had commanded the military to kill everyone in order to suppress the rebellion, and that the generals had just shot the captive rebels out of fear. Fernando didn't know what to do. On one hand, he could escape unnoticed at night, but on the other hand, his special status didn't allow him to leave like that. He decided to postpone his return until the end of the elections. A week after the elections, the neighboring country's envoys asked Fernando for a reception. With their heads bowed, they admitted that their country was in a very difficult economic situation, and that a war would completely destroy them. The negotiators said they would agree to any resolution of the territorial dispute so that their people could avoid the disasters of war and of Fernando's merciless retribution in particular.

Fernando dictated the most severe conditions, all of which were met with grumbling acceptance. The neighboring country's messengers were forced to withdraw their troops from the disputed territories. Moreover, they were banned from having any troops or weapons for fifty years. Fernando ended up living in that country for a long time; he even managed to suppress two more rebellions, almost doubling the country's territory. The leaders of all the neighboring countries feared Fernando's name. They tried to come to terms with Fernando the potentate. Songs were even written about Fernando's mercilessness and heartlessness. People would tell stories of his reign. Fernando, who was already old, barely managed to escape to France after failing to prevent another uprising. He was declared wanted as a war criminal in Africa. By that time, he had no one. He was found in the street and brought into this nursing home by police officers, who had taken him for a vagrant. Five days later, he died in obscurity."

Ali was thinking about what he had been listening to when Professor Moshe came in. He had allegedly gone for a walk so that Ali and Matteo could be alone.

"Allah loves brave warriors. I think Fernando will have a lot to tell during Allah's trial!"

"Are you a Muslim?" Professor Moshe asked in surprise. "It's interesting. I've never had the chance to ask."

"Yes, but it is Allah, not me, who will decide to what extent I am a good Muslim," said Ali.

"Interesting," Professor Moshe kept saying. "Have you read the Quran and what can you tell us about it?"

"Of course, I have. My father is Mustafa, the Mufti in the eastern part of Paris. Therefore, my knowledge of the Quran is rich, but I don't think that it is necessary to study the holy book in order to believe. Faith should come from here," Ali touched his chest with his fist.

"Do you think that one can believe without studying, without seeing and understanding?"

"Yes, true faith must be like that."

"Interesting." The professor was deep in thought. "And have you ever heard about Akhenaten?"

"No, who is Akhenaten?"

Professor Moshe began pacing back and forth across the room as if he were trying to decide whether or not it was worth it to disclose Akhenaten's secret to Ali. After a few minutes, he relaxed and sat on the bed.

"Listen, my son. I will tell you Akhenaten's story, and then I think you will understand what true faith is."

7. Professor Moshe Tells Akhenaten's Story (Blind Faith)

Amenhotep IV's reign was not marked in any particular way. The new pharaoh didn't stand out for any specific reason, with the exception of his appearance, especially the elongated shape of his head. Much like the coronation of the previous pharaoh, celebrations were accompanied by numerous sacrificial offerings that lasted several days.

Celebrations were typically held along the coast of the Nile River, stretching the entire length of Egypt's northern border. They began early in the morning when the local priest, with his rod stretched toward the heavens, welcomed the sunrise with his prayer. Immediately after, the priest would kneel down before the statue of the sacred beetle that was attached to the pedestal and express his gratitude. The sacred beetle was considered the sun's mother; at the end of every evening, as soon as the sun would set and life on earth would slow down, the sacred beetle would curl up with the pains of childbirth to the sun, and the sun would then give life to earth once again. Every morning, people and animals were born again together with the sun, to which the sacred beetle had given life. Every morning, the priest would thank the sun's mother for a new day. He would promise the sacred beetle that people would fervently sacrifice to the God of the Sun as a sign of their gratitude for the warmth that the sun had promised to give them. After expressing his gratitude, the priest, according to ritual, would turn to the sun, which had already risen and was looking toward the north, south, east and west, and make sure it was equally lighting all sides of the world. After the ritual washing in the sacred basin, the priest would walk toward the coast of the Nile River. Four or five servants, laden with fruit, would follow him. Before reaching the Nile's coast, the priest would stop at seven random houses. The hosts of those houses were supposed to add something to the servants' load. Since the homes were selected randomly, the whole settlement had to be prepared to accept guests who were fulfilling the holy mission. By the seventh house, the servants would be so cramped that they could hardly move. The priest would slowly approach the Nile and ask for an abundance of water and canals and, getting down on his knees, he would pray with his face to the sun. After the prayer, the servants would discharge their loads into the sacred river. While they did that, the priest, looking up to the heavens, would call out.

"Oh, Gods! Accept these gifts from mortals and turn a kind eye to the earth."

Amenhotep IV was the youngest son of Amenhotep III; therefor he didn't have particular pretensions to his father's throne. During the last years of his father's life, Amenhotep IV had been helping his father run the country, and after the sudden death of his elder brother, Amenhotep III increased his son's involvement in the palace and transferred his power as pharaoh to him. The priests, whose positions within the palace would usually strengthen with each new pharaoh, could hardly hide their delight. Amenhotep IV's reign coincided with the richest and most grandiose era of the Egyptian kingdom; the treasury was full, canals were deep, the lands were fertile, and people were replete. Rulers of neighboring countries were also afraid of the Egyptian army and would seize every opportunity to improve their relations with the pharaoh.

The priests thought up a new ritual for the pharaoh's coronation; they would praise all the Gods, who were led by Amun, seeking approval and patronage for Amenhotep IV. They believed that Amenhotep IV had become a pharaoh mostly due to divine providence since, according to the principles of inheritance, the likelihood of his crowning was small. According to law, following Amenhotep III's death, the eldest son was to become the pharaoh, but he died before Amenhotep III and the pharaoh's youngest son ended up inheriting the throne, being proclaimed Amenhotep IV. Even after being given this gift of fortune by the Gods, Amenhotep IV did not seem in a hurry to offer sacrifices to them. After his anointment, his behavior became more and more strange, and his attitude toward the priests was gradually becoming more hostile. The priests could not understand the reason for his attitude, nor did they understand why the pharaoh avoided meeting with them, using the excuse that he had governing matters to deal with.

Moreover, he would always change the topic of conversation whenever the priests brought up the ritual of offering sacrifices. Even direct warnings about how his frivolous attitude could irritate the Gods, especially Amun, had no impact on him.

One of the priests even dared to suggest that if Amun became dissatisfied, he would immediately change the ruler of the country, causing discontent and widespread unrest. Having heard the priests' complaints, Amenhotep thought deeply and finally announced, "I will conclusively unravel this tangle in the near future. I am sure that the solution will leave no unanswered questions for you or the Gods."

The priests did not understand what Amenhotep IV meant. Nevertheless, they believed that all pharaohs were Amun's suns on earth, and it was pointless and sometimes even dangerous to mind them. They left the palace as a group, trying to guess what the pharaoh had meant by promising to unravel the tangle.

After that day, the pharaoh remained in complete isolation inside his palace for several months. The reports from the priests were beginning to cause anxiety among the people. The pharaoh's behavior was gradually becoming incomprehensible, and sometimes even unacceptable, to them. People were beginning to show signs of concern, especially those who got their news about the ruling elite from the priests. People were afraid that the Gods would turn their backs on Egypt because of the pharaoh's questionable behavior, and that drought, famine, and disease would strike the country. Ordinary people, of course, would suffer the most because of the pharaoh's actions. They were the ones who would perform all the rituals, regularly offering sacrifices and praying to all one hundred and nine Gods.

Soon after, Amenhotep IV's heralds visited the priests. They said that the pharaoh had something important to say and invited the priests to visit the palace in three days' time. The form of the invitation seemed quite strange to the priests; no pharaoh had ever invited them by sending heralds. All the previous pharaohs had always called the priests personally, sometimes having discussed the meeting date with them beforehand. After all, if not the priests, who else was aware of what the most suitable date for each event was or when the Gods would be in favor of starting or stopping wars? Even sowing days were set with the help of the priests, and now Amenhotep IV had decided to go against ancestral tradition, choosing to determine himself when the suitable time was for inviting the priests to the palace to say some-thing important. There was something strange in the invitation wording as well. Usually, the pharaoh would emphasize his name, origin, and devotion to Amun and all the other Gods. The priests had a bad feeling about this. The Gods would claim with outrage that Amenhotep IV's protocol violations had already gone beyond the bounds of the permissible.

Egypt's three high priests were so displeased that they put aside their usual disagreements for the first time in their lives and decided in unison to act against the pharaoh's religious policy. They agreed to be uncompro-mising and to not avoid harsh punishments. The rest of the priests were instructed to unconditionally defend the high priests' viewpoint during the meeting.

On the specified date, the priests, dressed in festive attire, went to the pharaoh's palace. As they approached, they could hardly conceal their sur-prise when they saw a crowd of people, all representing Egypt's different social ranks. There were Egyptian nobles, merchants and even homeless Egyptians, and all of them had been invited to the palace on the same day. The priests were stunned and outraged; how could the pharaoh have invit-ed this motley crew to discuss the most important spiritual issues? There seemed to be no logic in the list of invitees. Of course, the priests didn't mind the pharaoh meeting with representatives of the secular society, but inviting the spiritual elite there as well was an absolute misjudgment. The Gods would certainly be angry. And who was going to mitigate the anger of the Gods? The priests, of course.

Having consulted with each other for a moment, they reiterated their dissatisfaction and went up the stairs swiftly. A large crowd had gathered in the upper hall of the palace, which had been decorated with colorful festive handkerchiefs and flags. The musicians were standing in the corner, waiting for their command to start playing. It was quite noisy in the hall. Everyone was trying to understand the meaning of the strange event, but no one had any concrete information to verify their suspicions.

Some people claimed that the pharaoh was planning to launch a military expedition to the south, while others claimed the pharaoh had fallen in love with a woman. Some people were even whispering that she was a simple woman without origin. Others were confidently stating that the pharaoh was going to announce the birth of his new child or the name of the heir to the throne. Many possibilities were discussed, but all of them were speculation. Each new version of the truth spread through the hall with a buzz.

Suddenly, the musicians began to play loudly, and Pharaoh Amenhotep IV's retinue entered the hall. First, the military members of the pharaoh's guard came in and lined up along the walls of the hall in their specified corners. Then the pharaoh's wives entered; they took their places at the rear side of the palanquin. Next, Nefertiti, the pharaoh's beloved queen, entered. The guests froze. Nefertiti had always fascinated everyone. Her beauty was divine. No mortal woman was endowed with such beauty. Nefertiti was not Egyptian; she was the daughter of an eastern king. There was so much delicacy in her mannerisms that she enchanted everyone around her, regardless of their gender. Nefertiti's elongated and delicate neck made her look like a deer. She always walked with her head proudly held high, representing her noble origins and emphasizing her height and delicate white neck. Everyone in the hall, without blinking an eye, was watching the queen, and no one seemed to have noticed Pharaoh Amenhotep IV enter. He sat on the throne and motioned to the master of ceremonies to command the musicians to start playing.

The master of ceremonies lifted his rod, at the end of which a red flag was attached; this was the musicians' signal. From that moment, no one had the right to speak unless the pharaoh spoke to them. The musicians, understanding the signal, began to play with such enthusiasm that it seemed they were about to break their instruments.

The pharaoh was anxious; he didn't pay much attention to the music or the buzz of excitement throughout the hall. He was absorbed in his thoughts, contemplating what he was going to say. It was obvious that his thoughts were not in harmony with the joyful music that was being played. Suddenly, as if he had been jerked awake, the pharaoh stood up. The musicians immediately stopped playing. The pharaoh turned to look at the hall, and everyone stopped dead. The pharaoh's stare was cold, and his eyes had a blank, glassy expression.

"After the untimely death of my brother, my earthly father, bright ruler Amenhotep III, passed on to me the right and obligation to rule the most beautiful country under the auspices of the sun," the pharaoh began. "Sacrificial rituals were held, as has been the tradition for all of time. Our people, my subjects, were expressing their joy over my coronation. Numerous rulers sent congratulatory letters, some of which I didn't respond to out of political expediency, while others I am planning to form various alliances with. Today I have gathered you here because I have something important to say. A pharaoh's every word, every statement, is important, of course, but the message I want to deliver today will mark a turning point for our country. Today you will witness the beginning of a new era. Before passing to the main part of my speech, a poem of mine, dedicated to my wife Nefertiti, will be read."

"Mistress of my dreams, Queen Nefertiti!
You are a sweet source of nourishment.
No one will offend you anymore,
Since your guardians are the Sun God and me.
We will together measure our life with steps
And stretch our hands to the sun.
At nights, we will believe in immortality,
Sweeping off the time-grains of sand.
From now on, we are one body, Queen Nefertiti.
We will either rise or be lost together.
I am the ruler, but the sun is the witness.
Now, there is another ruler over me."

When the master of ceremonies finished reading, everyone bowed down to show their approval. The master then motioned to the orchestra and they began to play softly. Nefertiti's mistress of ceremonies came forward and read out a short response poem from a handmade papyrus.

"You are the master of my yearnings,
I am blinded by you; I do not see the sun,
Since every wife of a ruler is a queen,
But not every queen's husband is a ruler."

The music stopped and complete silence fell on the hall. The pharaoh stood up again.

"Amenhotep IV has died today," he said.

The crowd, unaware of what was going on, made exclamations of surprise.

"As of today, Pharaoh Amenhotep IV is dead. There are no longer any Gods who have been worshiped and offered sacrifices from time immemorial until now. From now on, much will change in the life of Egypt, and many things will no longer be the way they used to. The power of the priests will be limited; religious rituals will be headed not by the high priests, but by seven landless, literate people with no origin, chosen by me from among the people present here. A divine light fell on me from the sky and informed me that there is only one God, and it is Aton, the God of the Sun, who caresses his people with his ray-hands every day, giving strength and wisdom to rulers, love and warmth to women, and playful entertainment to children. The worship of Aton will bring love and harmony to our lives, because there is nothing more pleasing in the world than to see how Aton's hands, the rays of the sun, play with colorful flowers, how fruit grows sweeter from the sun's warmth and Aton's love, and to see how the sun is born every day, bringing life to the world. And there is nothing sadder than at night, when the sun leaves the sky, leaving the world in darkness. Even blonde desert sands turn red when meeting with the sun, and as the sun disappears, they turn black and die yearning for it to return. Aton sends us his love through his rays and never gets tired of doing it every day. From now on, for the sake of our one and only true God, Aton, I forbid the worship of any other idol. I repeat, Aton is the only true God."

Everyone in the hall was silent. It seemed like the pharaoh was playing a joke. Maybe the pharaoh was performing a play in front of the diverse and spotted society members to arouse interest in theater. No one could understand what was happening. No one could imagine how it was possible to renounce all the Gods and worship only one God, especially one who was a man-God under the auspices of Amun. After all, Aton, as old writings testify, was once a pharaoh who had risen as a god to the heavens through rays of the sun, uniting with Amun-Ra. How would Aton be worshiped? Would all the sacrifices be devoted to him only? And would they incur the wrath of the other Gods? Not only Egypt would suffer then, but all of humanity. No one had ever been able to avoid the wrath of the Gods. And if this was true, then thousands of questions were arising. The pharaoh's speech defied any reasonable logic. To worship only one God? That was impossible. Such a thing could never happen! Even to joke about it would bother the Gods. No, the pharaoh was definitely not in his right mind, and he was playing a very dangerous game. The Gods would not forgive him.

"Pharaoh Amenhotep IV, ruler of Egypt, earthly son of Amun, dear child of Gods, your decisions are the wisdom of heaven, but don't you think that this decision will stir up the wrath of the Gods?" the high priest asked. He realized that the situation didn't promise a favorable outcome for the priests, and he tried to gather up the courage to object to the pharaoh – something that had never been done throughout history. It had been quite the contrary; throughout the centuries, priests had always preached humility toward pharaohs. In any other circumstance, the high priest's speech might have been viewed as an obvious rebellion.

"Amenhotep has died today!" The pharaoh shouted from his seat. "There is no more Amenhotep! You might not have been listening to me attentively. I am not Amenhotep! Amenhotep has died, and Akhenaten was born today. I am Pharaoh Akhenaten, a ruler whose name means 'effective to Aton'. From now on, all those who call me by another name will be subject to imprisonment, and the same will happen to anyone who speaks out against the religious reforms initiated by me. Guards! Arrest the priest!"

The pharaoh had hardly finished getting the words out when the guards took the priest out of the hall. Complete silence fell over the hall. People were confused and nervous. They stood with their heads hung low, avoiding the gaze of the pharaoh and Nefertiti. The silence was only getting stronger.

"Long live Akhenaten! Long live the ruler of Egypt! Long live Aton's son," the master of ceremonies shouted, and everyone in the hall began to repeat the words in praise of Akhenaten, first mechanically and then more clearly and confidently.

A few months after the palace gathering, unprecedented events took place in Egypt. First, by the pharaoh's order, all the Gods' temples were abandoned and shut down. Temples that had been built across the whole country, dedicated to Osiris, Amun, Ra and all the other Gods, were left alone to become places which were never visited. Anyone who visited a temple other than that of Aton was threatened to be put in a dungeon or killed, if necessary.

Aton, before becoming the subject of a fanatic cult for Akhenaten, was not famous at all. Aton was usually depicted as a sun disk with rays extending as long arms with tiny human hands at each end, as if wanting to caress the whole world. The solar Aton was worshipped as a God even before Akhenaten's religious reform; only he used to have a very insignificant role. Osiris, the ruler of the afterlife, the underworld, and the dead, was considered much more important. Egyptians had been preparing to meet with him their entire lives. After all, Osiris was the ruler of immortality, and people were to be under his eternal domination after their short lives on earth. That was why the religious reform was initially happening so slowly and unwillingly. At first, people did not support Akhenaten's religious reforms; they believed that Osiris would get angry for having been ignored, and that his curse and wrath would fall on them. Of course, the priests, who had been inculcating polytheism for centuries and therefore strengthening their own positions of power were also contributing to the spread of such rumors. They had found their stable place in the ruling class, adding secular influence on their already unlimited spiritual power. And now, after Akhenaten's famous gathering, the priests actually lost their influence and their jobs. This change mostly affected the lower level priests. Most of them could no longer receive donations from people and faced starvation. Mighty temples lost their primordial shine. They no longer gave off their aromatic smell of smoke and you could no longer hear the rhythmic sounds of cymbals or whispered prayers. It looked like the Gods had abandoned their own temples and turned away from the ungrateful people.

High-ranking priests were also in bad condition. Many of them were selling the gold they had accumulated over time in order to procure means of livelihood. Of course, the high-ranking priests were certainly not starving to death, but having gotten used to a luxurious lifestyle, they had some difficulties securing the same kind of comforts without any source of income. It was becoming more and more impossible with each day, and the priests were forced to start saving what they had. They gradually used less gold, replacing it with silver, which was cheaper and increasingly being used more in their finery. The number of walks through the town square, accompanied by chariots and numerous slaves, had decreased, as could be expected. The priests were angry and kept busy trying to think of ways to correct the situation.

Now a month after the meeting at which the start of the religious reforms was announced, Akhenaten made a new statement, informing all the people of Egypt that a new capital was going to be constructed. The new capital was to be in a deserted area and would be called Akhenaten, in honor of the only God of Egypt, Aton. Pharaoh Akhenaten's palace was to be built in the center of the capital, and it was to surpass in size and shape any building ever built in the world for any living human being. The capital was to be built exclusively from white alabaster, so that Aton could caress and warm the town built in his honor. A huge temple of the only true God, Aton, was to be built from white alabaster in the heart of the capital.

With Akhenaten's command, the large-scale construction of Aton's temples began across the country. Places of worship of various sizes were built, made mostly of white alabaster stones. Small chapels, resembling cells, and huge buildings were built. Akhenaten would personally choose the priests serving in the temples and would mainly show preference to free and landless young men with no origin. This seemed to deepen the former clergymen's hostility toward the pharaoh and his reforms. The priests, touring on golden chariots, were being replaced by uneducated street people who not only had no basic knowledge of geometry and couldn't differentiate north from south, but also had difficulty reading; many of them could not write, and they lacked the skills needed for prayer. The former priests would deprecatingly call their alternates "zuhuds." They were sure that the zuhuds would soon destroy the life they had built and that the Gods would eventually get angry at their foolish deeds and dreadful punishments would be inflicted on them.

Of course, divine wrath on the zuhuds was not the priests' only hope. The former priests spent their time regularly discussing the issue of regaining their lost positions. Many of them were of the opinion that the pharaoh was an anti-God henchman. Supporters of this version of events claimed that the pharaoh wasn't actually Amenhotep III's own child, but no one could recall exactly when Akhenaten had appeared in Amenhotep III's family. Akhenaten's mysterious origins only made this version seem more likely. He didn't look like any of his family members; he had an elongated head, strangely large, almond-shaped eyes that lacked any expression, feminine features and body shape, and delicate white skin, which most Egyptian men lacked. Others kept bringing up the argument that Akhenaten's elder brother was meant to be crowned instead of him, but that he had died a few months before the coronation and left the throne to Akhenaten, which he then completely took advantage of. Some would insist that Akhenaten's wife, Nefertiti, was a witch sent by enemies and had evil magical powers. Nefertiti was said to have enchanted the pharaoh and that, under her spell, he had fallen under the influence of evil powers. The priests claimed that Nefertiti, not being a native Egyptian, had been sent by one of the hostile states and wanted to destroy Egypt's power through her influence on her husband. There were multiple stories, all of which were dark and disconcerting. Even the priests supporting different versions were unanimous on one thing: they had been treated unfairly, so it was necessary to restore the previous order of things as soon as possible. The idea of conspiracy was hovering in the air: the only thing they had to do was to specify their plans and coordinate future actions.

Akhenaten, having locked himself in his palace, would come out only on rare occasions. He mostly stayed indoors, only going for a walk in the palace garden for a few hours a day. While walking, he would dictate his poems to the palace scribe. They were full of subtle exquisite lyrical arrangements, and all contained some sort of prayer or romantic quartet dedicated to Nefertiti, a military call, or glorification of the sun. The interesting thing was that his poems were not just about Aton, the God of the Sun, who Akhenaten proclaimed the only true God, but about the sun itself as a luminary. Akhenaten would describe how nice and bright the sun is, how it awakens nature and brings colorful flowers to life, how it caresses people with its warm rays, and how it fills the spikes with wheat, paints desert sands reddish-yellow, and how sad and bleak life becomes when it leaves at night, shrouding the world in darkness. In his poems, Akhenaten would thoroughly describe the sun's positive impact on the world. His pure love for the sun was so clearly laid out in his poems that it obviously stemmed from years of ritual worship. Akhenaten loved the sun, or rather, he was in love with the sun. Those who knew him would sometimes even doubt whom Akhenaten loved most – Nefertiti, his beloved and exceptionally beautiful wife, or the sun. Nefertiti would wait for Akhenaten in the park every day to hear his new poems. There was a sense of sadness in Nefertiti's manners, behavior and words, although she rarely spoke. No one had ever seen her smiling. Only when she listened to Akhenaten's poems, leaning on her palanquin in the park, would she sometimes smile with satisfaction, and then quickly hide her face as if afraid someone would notice.

One day, Akhenaten was standing in front of his white palace. Nefertiti stood nearby with her head held high and her gracefully long neck exposed. They both had smiles of satisfaction on their faces. Their clean, white clothes waved in the desert wind, as if they had fallen straight from the sky.

The Egyptians had gathered to admire the new buildings of the capital, which were all public facilities. Akhenaten's palace was the only residential house and had a seven hundred-meter facade. As the sun spread its rays over the city, a divine view opened; it was a dreamlike city, seemingly unreal, resembling a sparkling white oasis in the blonde desert sands. Akhenaten had described the city of Akhenaten in his poems before it was built. He wrote that Aton was hugging the city tightly. He wanted to convey his warmth to the people by warming and caressing the white capital. Aside from Akhenaten's palace, there was one other large building in the center of the city, and that was the temple of Aton. The entrance to the temple was guarded by two large sacred beetles. Aton, the sun disk with sunrays transformed into hands, was depicted overhead.

The construction of the temple, which had been carried out by ten thousand slaves, took five years. Their work had been supervised by three hundred architects who managed to turn the sloppy work performed by the slaves into an exquisite structure. The temple's ornaments told the story of the God Aton and how he used to reign on Earth as a fair and clever pharaoh. Military invasions and hunting scenes were also depicted. On one of the ornaments, Aton was depicted wearing a blindfold, holding a newborn infant in his arms. A large crocodile lay under Aton's feet with its mouth opened wide, as if it were waiting for Aton to feed the infant to him. On other ornaments, Aton was depicted rising to the sky. He had risen as a God to the heavens through the rays of the sun and united with the sun disk to become the sun itself. The sun disk was so happy to be meeting with Aton that it no longer sent disasters to the people, and it started caressing the earth from above through its rays. This was the idea the architects had tried to convey through the inner ornaments of the temple. Aside from a few images having magical significance (like the sculpture of the newborn infant and the crocodile), all the other sculptures were so beautiful and their presence so natural that they did not even need further explanation. Those structures with magical significance were not even subject to an explanation, as their meaning was already known to the priests.

There was, however, an interesting peculiarity in the ornaments. None of them depicted scenes describing how the pharaoh, the builder of the temple, behaved in the battlefield. There were no pictures depicting Akhenaten hunting or offering sacrifices to the Gods. Actually, there were absolutely no Gods depicted in the temple.

The priests, mostly newly appointed, stood in a semicircle burning aromatic incense inside the palace. They made their way through each room of the palace, sanctifying it with their prayers. In their prayers, they said they were dedicating all the big and small buildings to Aton. They were glorifying Aton, asking him to turn a kind eye to Pharaoh Akhenaten so that he, faithful to his name, could be helpful to the God of the Sun in every way.

Having circled through the palace in the opposite direction of the sun's journey seven times, the priests began the temple's consecration ceremony. A stone bridge connected Akhenaten's palace to Aton's temple. The ceremonial balcony, from where the pharaoh was to appear and address his people, was in the middle section of the bridge.

The temple's consecration was performed room by room. The smell of the aromatic smoke spread through the whole temple, filling each corner and driving out the evil forces. Two drummers beat their drums with all their strength, creating an interesting rhythm to go with the ceremony. The cymbals crashed together, giving a voice to Aton residing somewhere high in the cosmos. From afar, the scene was beautiful and interesting. People danced to the rhythm of the drum beat, praying with their arms outstretched to the sky.

Three hundred people had gathered from different parts of Egypt for the opening of the new capital. Their women's breasts were exposed, displaying various tattoos of beautiful ornaments on their bodies. The men were delightedly watching the women writhing as they danced; they symbolized all the beauty that lives in the sun, under the auspices of Aton, enjoying the warmth of his hands. Akhenaten and Nefertiti, surrounded by numerous slaves and servants, were walking arm in arm along with their entire retinue. They passed through rows of dancers, prayers, musicians and priests, greeting everyone equally. Akhenaten was holding Nefertiti's arm so close that it almost seemed like he was carrying her in his arms. Everyone watched and stood in awe of their love. The pharaoh was not an ordinary mortal to them, and therefore his feelings toward his wife were thought to be divine.

The pharaoh and his beautiful wife, with her elongated neck, continued to walk and embrace each other, occasionally welcoming people with a nod of their heads. It was quite a harmonious scene.

Seven long years passed, during which Phoebe, the former capital, completely emptied. It was quite the opposite in Akhenaten: people would come to find spiritual harmony, expecting a quiet and peaceful life.

People of various professions were living in the city, but the majority of the population was composed of artists. They found a certain inspiration in Akhenaten. All branches of applied arts flourished in the city.

During these years, the pharaoh's family suffered several losses. Queen Nefertiti died from an unknown disease and Akhenaten withdrew into loneliness; it was too difficult for him to cope with the loss of his wife. He would stay indoors for days at a time, and although he had never been particularly involved in royal affairs before, they had now reached a state of total neglect. Many unresolved state problems had accumulated, which of course caused new ones, and as a result Egypt's state power had decreased in the eyes of foreign rulers. The Syrian king not only refused to pay taxes to Egypt, but he would also openly ridicule Akhenaten in his letters. The Hittites, for their part, were trying to spread conspiracies. In his letter, their king had reminded Akhenaten that no one from the Hittite Kingdom had been invited either to Akhenaten's enthronement ritual or to his and Nefertiti's wedding ceremony. Military alliances, which had actually concluded during Amenhotep III's reign, were collapsing one after another. The Egyptian state's power was waning. Akhenaten seemed to have given up and was not trying to fix things in any way.

One day, the master of ceremonies reported to Akhenaten that Fidekh, one of the former priests, wanted to see him. He was told to convey to the pharaoh that it was about a very important matter. After much consideration, the pharaoh decided to let Fidekh in. Initially, Akhenaten did not want to meet with anyone, especially someone who reminded him of his past life as Amenhotep, when the capital was Phoebe and there were numerous Gods. But there had been a lot of monotony and weariness in his life recently, so he agreed to see Fidekh at least for a change of pace, even though he had once imprisoned him for speaking out against his religious reform.

"He probably has something interesting to say," the pharaoh thought. He sent an order to allow Fidekh into the palace the following day after dinner.

The next day, the palace was getting ready for dinner. A group of musicians were invited from a distant country and, although they were playing a style of music that was very new to the guests, it was still very pleasing to the ear and it was known that the musicians were skilled experts in their country. The food displayed on the royal table was not particularly diverse, but it was abundant. The cupbearers poured wine from their pitchers into the guests' glasses.

During dinner, the pharaoh ate almost nothing except a small piece of bread, and his table companions also did not particularly seem to be in a feasting mood. Everyone drank at least two glasses of wine and ate only a few pieces of food throughout the entire meal.

Akhenaten motioned to the master of ceremonies and the music stopped. The master of ceremonies approached the table and, opening the papyrus scroll, began to read aloud one of Akhenaten's poems dedicated to Aton.

"Wonderful, you wake up at sunrise,
Aton, creator of life, living forever.
Rising in the east,
You fill the whole country with your beauty.
You're awesome and powerful, you shine.
When you go down to the west,
The earth becomes shrouded in darkness, like at death's door.
All the lions come out of their dens;
All the snakes begin to sting.
Under night's dominion, the earth becomes silent,
As long as the creator rests in darkness."

Everyone gathered in the hall immediately bowed to show respect and gratitude for the amazing experience they had as the poem was being read.

"Speak, Fidekh! I am listening to you. What has brought you here?" the pharaoh said, without turning to the former priest.

Fidekh gave a bow and, kneeling down in front of the pharaoh, began to speak.

"Ruler of Egypt! It is a great privilege for my eyes to see you! It is a supreme pleasure for my ears to listen to your poems. But I have come for another purpose. I have something quite interesting to tell you. An Egyptian official is trying to undermine the basis of our state. He has made the destruction of our country the main purpose of his activities. In all probability, the scoundrel has formed a criminal, traitorous relationship with a hostile country and is carrying out their orders to destroy and undermine mighty Egypt."

"Who are you speaking about? Who is the traitor?" the pharaoh asked quietly.

"Pharaoh! My ruler! I am talking about a high-ranking official. His ties reach all the way to your palace, so I can't speak about it openly. It's possible that someone here knows him or, even worse, they are the traitor's spy. Akhenaten, the apple of my eye! My message is of great importance to the state. For your own safety, I would like to talk about it privately, with Aton and his fair rays by our side."

The musicians were the first to quietly leave the hall, leaving their instruments in the corner of the room. The master of ceremonies ordered the slaves to start their cleaning duties and clear away the remnants of dinner. About half an hour later, Akhenaten and Fidekh were left alone. They sat in silence for a few minutes; it seemed as if the pharaoh wanted to make sure that there was nobody else in the room except them.

"Well, now that we are alone, you may begin. Who is the renegade official who dares to darken the glory of Egypt with his actions?"

There was a long silence. Then Fidekh spoke calmly and quietly. "That person is you, Akhenaten!"

"What? Are you crazy? How can you dare to say that?"

"Keep calm!" Fidekh interrupted. "I know your secret, and if something happens to me, my friends will spread it all over the world in one day."

"What? What secret? What are you talking about? You have gone mad! I will call my guards now and they will arrest you immediately."

Fidekh smiled. "You won't do that. Again, I know your secret. You'd better start talking. You'll have time to call the guards later."

Akhenaten was red with anger. Fidekh's impertinent behavior went beyond all boundaries. Not only was he informally addressing the pharaoh, the child of God Aton, he was also trying to dictate terms to him. Akhenaten, restraining himself, finally spoke. "Let's assume, Fidekh, that you really know something. What do you want? Why did you come here?"

"I knew that you would make the right decision and listen to me until the end. What do I want? Fifteen years have passed since you came to power. But today is an even more remarkable day than that of your coronation. Today, for the first time, you have to be interested in what somebody else wants. You have reigned this country for fifteen years already without ever doing that. You have just been doing what your heart wants."

Fidekh laughed. "Listen, Amenhotep, who calls himself Akhenaten! I have known you since your early childhood. I know all your family members. I used to be your father's most favorite priest. There was a time when Phoebe, the real capital of Egypt, flourished and prospered thanks to your father. The temple of God Amun, built in the city, was full of visitors. Ordinary people, merchants and soldiers, were offering sacrifices in the temple of Amun. After each military victory, your father would present the priesthood with five hundred prisoners of war. Thousands of priests would hold gratitude rituals every day in the temples of Phoebe. Amun, like all the other Gods, was satisfied. Egypt was flourishing."

Fidekh took out a small papyrus from his pocket and began to read. "Sixty kilos of gold, one thousand kilos of silver, two thousand five hundred kilos of copper, twenty-five thousand jugs of wine, three hundred bales of velvet fabric and twelve thousand acres of land. This was your father's last donation to the temple of Amun. He gave so many sacrificial offerings to the Gods during the last year of his life. This was the last offering. The people of Egypt were waiting for their next pharaoh, Thutmose, your brother, who was serving as a priest in the temple. But Thutmose died unexpectedly, and since he had only one brother, the throne of Egypt was passed to you."

"What you are saying is true, yes. But I can't understand the reason for your discontent. Fidekh, what is bothering you so much? Why have you endangered your life coming here and standing before me today? You are speaking so boldly."

"Everything was going normally," Fidekh continued. "The Gods were rejoicing and blessing our country, fertilizing our lands and making our soldiers stronger, until you became a pharaoh. You even refused to bear the name your father gave to you. That is enough for you to be cursed by the Gods and your people, but your crimes don't even end there. Actually, that's just where they start. You refused to offer sacrifices to the Egyptian Gods, making them angry. You refused to live in the capital your father constructed and repaired. You built a new capital that only you enjoy. You secluded yourself there, abandoning the once vast and powerful empire. After all that, you proclaimed yourself the son of the God of Sun, Aton, and established monotheistic worship, ignoring all the other Gods. You announced to the people that there is only one true God, Aton, and that the others are false."

Akhenaten listened attentively to Fidekh without interrupting. He wondered what the former high priest would say at the end of his speech. Fidekh was actually one of his father's closest companions and would often visit him. Akhenaten had lived an isolated life since childhood and wouldn't often partake in his father's public rituals and events, but he was still aware of Fidekh and his father's close relationship. Fidekh had a great influence on Amenhotep III. He had even been involved in making the decision to name Akhenaten as the next pharaoh. It was almost impossible to do that without Fidekh's consent. Initially, Fidekh didn't treat Akhenaten seriously. When he began his religious reforms, Fidekh was understandably angry, but hoped that deep down the pharaoh's religious wanderings were only temporary, and that after a little time everything would fall back into place.

"And what am I accused of? Replacing the archaic polytheistic nonsense, followed in the name of religion for centuries, with a bright and new idea? Or was it that I showed people the light about their ridiculous images of animal heads and human bodies? Or maybe that I left thousands of dependent priests jobless?"

"Not just priests were left jobless," Fidekh said angrily, clearly offended by the words "dependent priests." "Numerous craftsmen, incense traders and many other people who were serving in the temples all became poor. They cursed you and your religious lunacy. Your father's capital, Phoebe, became empty. People left Egypt. It became an evil place for them. Akhenaten, are you aware of the military situation in Egypt? Are you aware that our neighboring countries haven't been paying taxes for two years already and the Hittites are preparing an expedition against Egypt? Do you know that we have lost two castles in Syria? Do you think that after all this the priests are dependent, and not somebody else? You locked yourself in your invented city, Akhenaten, and refuse to participate in ruling your country. The Gods have cursed you! If you continue to rule like this, Egypt will finally be destroyed."

Akhenaten was silent. In the past, he would have immediately called his soldiers and ordered them to arrest the priest, who had so much audacity to accuse the pharaoh of such things.

Every time he opened his mouth, Fidekh pushed the limits of his words further. Unfortunately, after Nefertiti's death, Akhenaten had lost interest in everything, even fighting back. Now he sat there listening to Fidekh's judgments and silently tolerating them. He could actually even see some truth in them.

When he announced his religious reforms, Akhenaten knew what he was getting into. He realized that it wouldn't be easy, and he understood that people would not be able to immediately accept the truth. He knew there would be people who would suffer from the changes. Naturally, the pharaoh would receive daily correspondence from all the Egyptian castles and was well aware of military affairs, but the solution he saw was quite different from what the former priest imagined. There was nothing shocking or new in Fidekh's words. Everything was old news, just like the Gods worshiped by Fidekh himself.

"For this and many other reasons, and in order to prevent any further destruction, I, as the highest and chief priest of Egypt who is blessed by the real Egyptian Gods, am depriving you of the right to the throne. I am exiling you from Egypt together with your supporters. You and the residents of Akhenaten, regardless of sex, age or occupation, are forever cursed. You are doomed to many long years' wanderings in the desert. Your clan is cursed, and people will forever try to harass and attack you at every given opportunity. You have come out against the whole world and the traditions practiced by people for thousands of years. People will never forgive you for being different from them. Your only son, Tut, will be appointed as pharaoh instead of you, and I will anoint him a king and give him the name Tut-ankhamun, which means "living image of Amun." It's true, he is still just five years old, but as soon as he is anointed a pharaoh, the other priests and I will help him until he becomes an adult, and he will rule Egypt much better than you. Phoebe will again be the capital, and Akhenaten, the capital you have built, will be eternally cursed and doomed to desolation and destruction.

Akhenaten was silent; he was listening to Fidekh with his head hung low and did not even try to contradict him.

Fidekh, lowering his voice, continued. "But you know, there is one thing that I have been trying to understand, but I haven't succeeded so far."

"What?" Akhenaten asked.

"Your poems. For example, the one that was read at dinner: 'Forever living Aton, the creator of life, rising in the east, you fill the whole country with your beauty. You're awesome and powerful, you shine.' How could you write such poems? You established the worship of the sun, founded a city dedicated to the sun, built a temple dedicated to the sun, and you describe the beauty of the sun in your poems. How, Akhenaten? How can you describe something you have never seen? You have never seen the city you built, or the temples you have built, or the beauty of your wife, Nefertiti. You have never seen the sun that you describe in your poems. How did you manage to keep your secret from everyone all this time? Akhenaten, your secret is that you were born blind."

8. Urban II Studies the Public Opinion (Clermont, AD 1095)

Pope Urban II was sitting at his worktable, absorbed in studying a large map of eastern kingdoms. The royal cartographer had painted it specifically for the high priest, along with a few others. One of the maps depicted the eastern states, their borders and detailed notes about them, as well as the current religious situation, while another depicted all the relatively safe roads through the kingdoms. The last map contained information on the well-being of the population. All the data had been collected by the pope's Secret Intelligence Service.

Urban was studying the maps, sometimes making notes on a piece of parchment or on the map itself. He was so absorbed in his work that he didn't even notice that Odo had entered the room. He stood in the corner, silently watching Urban. Nobody could say how long he had been standing there in the pope's study. That was Odo; he was the only person in the palace to have free access to the pope's rooms, even the bedroom. No guard could stop Odo. At times, he seemed like the pope's shadow. No one even noticed his movement within the palace anymore.

"Oh, it's you. Sit down. I'm finishing already."

Odo settled himself down at the other end of the table.

"I wanted to ask you about something, but I forgot what it was," said Urban, still staring at the map. "Ah, yes, the royal cartographer told me today that you have been instructed to recruit two hundred artists and that you are going to give those artists some important orders on my behalf."

Odo gave a sly smile. "I am carrying out preparatory work before the campaign stage. The two hundred artists are to paint icons depicting scenes where the Muslim infidels are slaying and plundering Christian pilgrims on their way to the Holy Land."

"Have there been such cases? Why haven't I been reported to about it?" Urban asked. "Is the head of the intelligence service an idiot? Why has he hidden news of such atrocities from me? Call him here right now!"

"There haven't been such cases so far," Odo said. "Muslims, of course, are behaving aggressively in some places, but mostly to each other, not to Christians. Conflicts occur mainly among the Turks and the Arabs in the form of small clashes over local matters. Don't worry, the head of the intelligence service hasn't deceived you. No one is slaying the Christians. At least not for now."

"Then what are these icons for?" Urban said hesitantly.

"The icons are to be hung in churches all over Europe. We want believers to pay attention to them, study them, and then become enraged toward the non-believers while taking part in their liturgies, very similarly to just now when you couldn't suppress your anger from hearing about Christians slaughtered. You, having one of the world's most powerful intelligence networks and being informed about even the smallest events taking place in distant countries, accepted my words on faith. Just imagine how easily the deeply ignorant and uninformed people will believe it."

Urban paced back and forth through the room. Even after Odo assured him that his words weren't real, he couldn't get rid of his anger.

"I do not understand the purpose," said Urban. "We agreed that we still need to discuss the idea of launching a Holy War, didn't we? You promised me that you would do some research and report back to me. We didn't make any concrete decisions concerning the war, and yet you've already begun spreading hatred through religious icons."

"One thing will not interfere with the other. The impact of the creation of these pictures and their placement in churches will only be for a couple months. This is preparatory work. If we make a decision not to start a war, which I highly doubt we will, then we'll remove the pictures from the churches and this topic will be forgotten in a few days. But if we do decide to go to war, we will already have set a foundation and people will already be angry, so the only thing we would have to do would be to organize it."

Urban considered this. "In any case, I don't like that you've jumped the gun without my knowledge."

"Well, let me ask you this – if there were still any lingering doubts in your mind about the war, then why are you studying the map of the Muslim world? And why did you order five copies of that map?"

"With or without the campaign, it's necessary to study this. I am not going to report to you about every move I make. You're starting to push your limits. Yes, I am studying them, but it does not mean anything yet. I am doing it to understand just how crazy and foolish your undertaking is."

"Well, similarly, a few extra icons in some churches still do not mean anything at this stage; we can hang them and take them down whenever we want," Odo replied.

Urban went back to looking at the map.

"There are places that are almost impassable. I can't imagine how the army would pass through those parts."

"No, you don't even try to imagine," Odo said cynically. "What really matters is that the army will get to Constantinople. From there, it is Emperor Alexander's task to assist the forces and guide them to the Holy Land the right way. He is our only ally in the east, and after all the hostilities are over, he'll be in a very powerful and desirable position. Throwing Muslims out of the Holy Land will really increase his power in the region. One way or another, all the liberated cities will bow to Alexander and be in the grip of Byzantium."

"You are speaking as if we are undertaking this for Alexander. Throwing Muslims out will actually strengthen our position in the east. Even if I agree to this, Odo, I will only do it with the expectation that Christianity, as the true religion, will spread in the east."

"Christianity or the papal power?" Odo said with a grin. "Though, by and large, there is no difference. You had better think hard about who to spread that power to. You haven't decided to move to Constantinople, have you? Either way, the papal power will be exercised by Alexander, but we will also be enhancing our influence in the east. At this point, I do not see any other alternative."

Urban walked to the window. The palace garden was filled with multi-colored fragrant flowers, and the pope's study window looked right out onto it. Indeed, everything created by God was beautiful and had God's blessing.

"For me, it is important to spread the teachings of Christ in the east. I want to bring God's light to those who are in darkness."

Odo was not listening to Urban. He was busy looking at the maps lying on the table, measuring things with a ruler and muttering incoherently under his breath.

"In the end, what is my mission?" Urban asked, turning to Odo. "It's to protect the Christian flock from evil and from Satan by reinforcing it with newly rescued lambs, isn't it? Even if there's one lost lamb, I am prepared to roam the earth to bring him back. Non-believers will have to save themselves."

"Of course, they will," Odo said with a smile. "By all means."

"Didn't you want to report something to me?" Urban asked.

Odo reached into his bag, took out some papers with notes on them, and arranged them on the table.

"First, I would like to say that, up until now, no one has ever carried out such an extensive study of any one place. In general, this is the largest study of public opinion that we know of at this time. Of course, I borrowed the methodology from a few books at the Notre Dame Cathedral in Paris, including a Hermetism textbook, but I myself have added several subtle elements, which have never been applied before, and which have made our study complete. I have tried to adapt it slightly to our situation. The icons depicting Muslim atrocities are the result of the research conducted, and the actual research has been carried out in several stages. I tried to get a sense of the public mood in Germany and France through heralds, pub owners, retailers and hairdressers. This turned out to be quite a complex algorithmic procedure; I will not weary you with its unnecessary mathematical details. I can only say that the areas researched, and the number of participants involved were as large as possible so that I could gather the most accurate information. But of course, all this research wouldn't have been so precise and accurate if I hadn't taken advantage of one of the most reliable resources at the church's disposal for studying public opinion – confession booths. Thousands of people confess their sins every day."

"Odo, I hope you have not forgotten about the secrecy of confession."

"No, of course not. Don't worry. Confessions will remain a secret, just as they always have. No one has dared to violate the principle of the secrecy of confession. But apart from its religious significance, a confession is an extremely sincere dialogue between a confessee and a confessor. The range of issues that I wanted to find out about in order to get a sense of the public mood required that I had candid questions and answers. So, I just included them in the list of the confessors' questions and voilà! I got the real picture of public opinion."

Odo took out one of the papers and began to read. "The majority of the public is dissatisfied with the burden of state taxes, the monotony and weariness of their own lives, and lack of entertainment. This discontent has led to an increasing volume of people going to church, and, at the same time, an increase in lack of faith. Most people go to church not with religious or spiritual intentions, but because they don't know how else to spend their free time. People pay their taxes to the church and then they feel obligated to attend, just as if they were going to watch a performance they had already paid for. The number of fairs in Germany has increased, which actually turn into episodes of mass drunkenness. People exercise their strength and fighting skills during these fairs, which usually leads to a mass brawl by the end. Essentially, they are looking for a suitable occasion to show off their strength in a way that's considered legal and acceptable by the church in order to have a little fun."

"What do you mean? Do you mean to say that people do not go to church with love and faith?" Urban asked, skeptical about Odo's research.

"Love and faith have lessened in the hearts of the people, and the church is also to blame. After all, the church is just a building. It is the people who make up the church. Despite being gilded, temples will lose their shine if people stop visiting them. The church comes alive because of the people and it dies without them. This observation, of course, has nothing to do with the results of our research, but it is no less important. The church itself needs to reform. However, let's not get off track. According to public opinion, the campaign could be carried out successfully if society's expectations are met." Odo placed one of the pieces of papers on Urban's table. "The society's requirements are as follows: material and spiritual gifts, to be given at the start of the campaign to those involved in its implementation, and a promise that additional gifts will be given in the future, especially since the campaign could last many years and it is necessary to maintain the morale of the participants. If these requirements are met, we'll be able to implement a social movement that will help carry out the campaign to the east and spread your power to that region."

Urban took the paper and began to study it carefully. Odo's points did not particularly mean much to him, but he understood that they were only the first step and that the solutions would come later. Urban was used to Odo presenting such grand plans in his reports.

"By the way, let me remind you that the campaign's goal is not to spread my power, but to spread the light of Christianity in the east," Urban stated.

"In that case, I'll remind you that Christianity, which you aspire to spread in the east, actually originated there and then came to us. Maybe you have forgotten, but our plan is to take back the rich historic heritage of Christianity from the non-believers. So, maybe it is too early to say from where that light will be spreading."

Urban turned a deaf ear to Odo's remarks. He kept thinking about the points he had made earlier. Urban was convinced that Odo had already thought about all the next steps and that he had his own approaches in mind. Odo was just gaining time; he wanted Urban to ask him about plans for further actions before he started to talk about them. That was the kind of man he was. If he thought of any brilliant (in his opinion) solutions, he would purposely delay its announcement until his opinion was forced out.

"I think you already have some solutions in mind," Urban said. "Present them. What suggestions do you have?"

Odo, flattered, gave a smile. He was always prepared before going to see Urban. Of course, he already had solutions in mind. How else could he have carried out such difficult research?

"The first point refers to the material gift. I think we need to completely exempt the participants of the campaign from paying taxes, fees and fines. The burden of paying taxes is already so heavy, releasing people of that burden will become an encouraging material prize that will motivate people to get involved in our undertaking. Anyone who has problems paying their taxes, and there are a lot of people, will rejoice at this news. It will also be an excellent opportunity to implement the part of the Lord's Prayer that says, 'forgive us our debts, as we also have forgiven our debtors.'

At first, the amount of unpaid taxes will seem great, but only at first. I will come back to the settlement of the financial issues during my enumeration of the other points. The next point is the spiritual gift. The participants of the campaign should be guaranteed admittance to paradise as a result of the devotion of their lives to God's cause. Participation in the liberation of the Holy Sepulcher is the greatest martyrdom that a person can obtain in his life. I think they deserve to be released from all their sins by a special encyclical of the pope and should stand before the judgment of God with pure souls. What could be more favorable to God than warriors fighting and dying in his name?"

"I agree with the first two points with only a few reservations," said Urban. "First of all, I would like to hear the solutions for alternative financial sources as a result of the mass exemption from taxes, since this will make a huge dent in an already unhealthy financial system. We have many plans for the future, all of which require abundant financial resources. The papal treasury will empty without taxes within a few months. I do not see any problems associated with the remission of sins, but for the taxes issue I hope you have already thought of some solutions."

"Of course, I have," Odo said with a grin. "Would I come to you and suggest an incomplete plan? That's what my third point is about. The material rewards that people will receive in the future will be gathered during the campaign. Eastern towns are rich, full of gold, silver and other treasures. The treasures of the occupied city will immediately be placed at the disposal of pilgrims and will become their property. The patron of the pilgrimages is the church. Therefore, to make the transfer of property of the liberated areas acceptable for the church, fees will be imposed on the pilgrims in the amount of twenty percent of their trophies. As for the liberated cities, a separate fee will be imposed on the commander who has liberated the city and establishes his power there. These sums, in my estimation, will be several times bigger than the taxes that we are currently receiving from people through suppression and oppression. By and large, this resolution will lead not to a decrease in financial resources, but to an increase. Thus, after the start of the pilgrimages, the papal treasury's revenues will increase by several times, and the problem of legitimizing the plunder will also be solved this way. People want to be sure that plundering their enemy is not a sin."

"Well, let's suppose that works. How will the control of the resolution be carried out?" Urban asked. "How will the entire process be managed?"

"Very simply," Odo answered quickly. "The entire course of the pilgrimage will be overseen by the pope's special envoy, who will govern the spiritual aspect of the pilgrimage and monitor financial transactions. You can assign one of the priests who is most faithful to you to the post and, should that clergyman not have a high rank, you can immediately ordain him as a bishop. Everything is in your hands."

"And the fourth point?"

"The fourth point has to do with the material gift that a man gets in the future. The pilgrimage is a very dangerous undertaking. There will be many people, who, for whatever reason, will not reach the end. They will become victims in battle, die of diseases, be involved in accidents, etcetera. It's important that everyone remains confident that even if they die during the pilgrimage, their soul will still go to heaven. This is the promise that will accompany them during the whole campaign. It is this confidence that will motivate people to perform brave acts. That's all. I have finished."

It was clear that Odo had said everything he needed to say. Urban was absorbed in his thoughts. Odo had presented a very well thought out and planned campaign. Of course, the success of such an undertaking was largely, if not entirely, dependent on the mercy of God, but Odo's plan was so carefully assembled that there was no doubt it would work well. In any case, Urban had often fallen under the weight of responsibilities, and this was a very difficult and lengthy undertaking. The responsibility was too great for him. No one had ever implemented such a campaign. Of course, there were many instances in history when a papal army had participated in fighting to various degrees, but not a single pope had initiated a full-scale military campaign by himself, despite the fact that Odo was calling the campaign a pilgrimage and they would be relying on the zeal of believers, rather than a professional army.

Urban, of course, appreciated Odo's perseverance and his ability to completely take care of all the details, but he realized that the responsibility of the campaign would fall solely on his shoulders. Suddenly he remembered something and couldn't help but frown. He took the papers lying on his worktable and looked through them again.

"Odo," Urban said, raising his head from the papers. "The work you have done is very significant, there is no doubting that. Your plan might prove quite effective. As far as I can see, you spent lots of time and money on your research. However, even though you are a layman, I think you should at least know the Ten Commandments. Do you remember the Sixth Commandment?"

"Of course I remember. 'Thou shalt not kill,'" said Odo.

"Yes, 'Thou shalt not kill.' And how am I going to justify the call of the Christian Church's leader to completely violate God's Sixth Commandment?"

"Urban, we're about to start a global undertaking, and you're thinking about trifle obstacles like that?" Odo tried to sound more understanding. "Of course, I have taken that into consideration too. Yes, we need the commandments, but some of them are extremely controversial. Before answering your question, I myself have a question. I am certain you know the Ninth Commandment, which says, 'Do not give false testimony against your neighbor.' At first, it seems like a very commendable commandment. And really, how could anyone give a false testimony against their neighbor? But here a question arises: if false testimony against your neighbor is considered inadmissible, and it is even written in the Bible, can't we assume that you can give false testimony against someone who is not your neighbor?"

"There is no such thing," Urban objected.

"Of course there isn't. That's what I'm saying. There is a commandment that forbids you to bear false witness against your neighbor, while a Christian is free to bear false witness against a person living two villages away. If it were forbidden, the commandment would have stipulated that it is forbidden to bear false witness in general, not just against one's neighbor. Everything that is not forbidden is allowed. It turns out that bearing false witness as a phenomenon is not condemned, but rather its concrete use against one's own neighbor which is denounced. You have absolute freedom to bear false witness against other people."

"Let's not get off topic. Please answer the question about the non-compliance of the Sixth Commandment. In this case, it's obvious: do not kill. How can I, as the Christian Church's leader, as St. Peter's successor on earth, as the high priest, call on believers to break the Sixth Commandment of God, calling it a sacred mission. Yes, I can't deny that up to now, the Holy See has shown support or assistance in a few wars in one way or another, but there has still never been a single case where the church itself took the initiative to start a large-scale war or, even worse, approve military killings. What you're saying is very interesting and tempting, but it is still incompatible with Christian values. A Christian can't receive the church's blessing for committing murder."

"People have always killed, and they will continue to kill, regardless of the church's approval or disapproval. People kill animals and birds while hunting; they kill to sate their hunger. They aren't thinking about the Sixth

Commandment then. Urban, you, as the leader of the Christian Church, have tasted the meat of partridges killed yesterday evening. You did not kill them, but you became a part of that murder."

"The example of animals and birds doesn't work. The Sixth Commandment applies to people, not cows or hens."

"And who said that this commandment applies only to people? It is not specified in the commandment. In the Ninth Commandment, the object is clearly specified: Bearing false witness against your neighbor. But there is no clarity in the Sixth Commandment. Who can or can't be killed? Can you tell me?"

"I don't think there is any need to clarify the Sixth Commandment," Urban explained.

"Of all the commandments, this one needs specification the most. And I think that the responsibility of clarifying this commandment should fall on your shoulders since you are the earthly vicar of St. Peter the Apostle. Interpreting the living word of God is the main function of the church. We must put an end to this uncertainty and clarify that commandment. As I have already said, it seems that there is no objection to killing animals and birds. As creatures lacking reasoning, their lives are devoid of purpose and spirituality. You can fish in the sea and then fry and eat the fish with no sense of sinning, and it won't be considered a murder. By the way, let me remind you that St. Peter was a fisherman too."

Odo approached the window of the study. It was already sunset, and the red sun rays had merged into the colors of the flower garden, making it look even more beautiful. Odo admired the view for a moment and again tried to convince Urban of his plan, knowing full well that Urban would not say yes easily.

"Can you explain to me the difference between animals and non-believers?" Odo said while still looking out onto the garden. "After all, a man is a man to the extent that he is close to God. What is the meaning of a non-believer's life? What is the difference between non-believers and the fish in the sea that were caught and killed by St. Peter? I will answer for you: there is no difference!"

Urban listened to Odo and felt deep embarrassment. He had always considered Odo a secular man who was far removed from theology, but for the first time in his life Urban was listening to his secular adviser make spiritual claims that were substantiated with a profound knowledge of theology and solid counter arguments.

"The Sixth Commandment shouldn't have been 'Do not kill,' but 'Do not kill Christians.' Only the murder of a Christian man can be considered a sin. The murder of a Muslim infidel or a Pagan is an extreme necessity and not a murder, especially when it comes to performing such a pious act like liberating the Holy Land. This necessity is even greater than that of sating hunger, for which the blessed murder of animals, birds and fish is committed. As a Christian, I would rather stay hungry and starve to death than put up with the current reality. I refuse to leave the Lord's Sepulcher in the hands of the infidels so that they can continue to constantly desecrate Christian holy places."

Urban did not know what to say. There was truth in Odo's words, and it was extremely difficult to find a counter argument to match his. Whether the pope liked it or not, Odo was right. The content of the holy book concerned only those who accepted that book. Since the non-believers have turned away from God and, unlike animals, they did so by their own reason and will, they must be considered useless and anti-God creatures. The non-believers' useless existence became even more convincing when Urban recalled the fact that the Holy Land was occupied by them. Whatever Urban answered now, he would unwillingly become a defender of the infidels.

"Do not kill a Christian!" Urban said. "Not bad."

9. Pilgrims of Urban II's Call (Europe, AD 1095)

Immediately after the liturgy, a commotion began among the aristocratic landowners. Everyone was trying to decide the form and extent of their participation in the sacred pilgrimage. Mark's noble master handed him a bundle of papers and ordered him to immediately take it to Germany. The knight then explained to him that the bundle contained Pope Urban II's sermon, delivered at the latest Mass, and said that it was necessary to convey the contents to the inhabitants of all the German settlements. Mark took the papers and pocketed the small amount of money that was given to him for covering travel expenses. Saddling the sturdiest horse he could find, Mark set out north to Germany.

Unfortunately, his money ran out before he reached his destination. He went into one of the pubs along the road with pockets already empty and no clue of what was in store for him. He ordered wine and got comfortable at one of the tables. The pub was full of people and had a loud and lively atmosphere. After some time, a man approached Mark and settled himself at his table without even asking for permission.

"It's interesting, isn't it?" the man said.

"What do you mean?" Mark said reluctantly.

He looked at the stranger from head to toe. He was a man of medium height, with a beard and blue eyes. Something about the man's eyes told Mark that he was a resourceful man by nature.

"Well, all this mess. Everyone seems to have gone crazy. They want to go and liberate the Holy Land from non-believers. They're leaving their homes and moving to Jerusalem. Don't you find it strange?"

Mark grew cautious. He had heard that the pubs were full of the pope's undercover agents who were looking to arrest and jail all traitors.

"I do not see anything strange," Mark said. "People love Pope Urban and they're going to Holy War to obey his word. We should have recaptured the Lord's Sepulcher from the infidels a long time ago. After all, the right to pray there belongs to us Bible-loving Christians."

"It's good that people obey the pope's words, whereas in Germany, whoever says anything people will obey him. Scoundrels, thieves and homeless people began to gain power that way. There was recently even a case where a crowd of people were led by a domesticated duck."

"A duck?" Mark said in amazement. "How can a duck lead a crowd of people?"

"You see, it's easier to lead a crowd than one individual. It is much more difficult to lead separate people. Sometimes a crowd of people can be so stupid that even domesticated ducks can lead it."

"But how? You must be joking."

"Not at all. The crowd of people had decided that if they handed their will over to the unconscious bird, it would be easier for God to rule them through the duck. In this case, the duck played the role of intermediary between the people and God. But here a question arises: who was more unconscious, the duck or the people following it and trying to make God's cause easier?"

"And then?" Mark wondered. "What happened to the leader duck?"

"The duck was prancing around everywhere, and people were following him. The crowd started to kill the residents of whichever settlement the duck entered, claiming that it was God's will. The crowd, led by the duck, walked hundreds of miles until nearly four thousand people died in a big quarrel in one of the towns, and those who survived were cast out of the town along with the duck."

"Yes, these are hard times," Mark said frankly. He had already forgotten about the anxiety that initially plagued him when the man had sat down.

"And where are you going?" the stranger asked.

"I am traveling to Germany, to the north," Mark replied.

"You are also weird," the stranger smiled. "Everybody is going to the south now, to the Holy Land, whereas you are going in the opposite direction."

"I have important things to do," Mark said under his breath.

"We all have something to do," the stranger muttered to himself.

Mark took the glass of wine and, drinking it to the last drop, sighed deeply. He remembered that he had no money and no idea how he was going to pay for the wine, and that it was pointless to consider continuing on his way.

"Listen, is that horsie that's tied in the stall yours?" the stranger interrupted.

"Yes, it's my master's horse. Why did you call it a horsie? Do you know how much that steed cost? You've probably never seen that much money in your wildest dreams."

"Well, it depends how you sleep and what dreams you see," the stranger smiled. "Sell me the horse."

Mark was taken aback by the offer. Sell his master's horse?

"You will tell your master that you have been robbed on your way. We're facing troubling times now and it's quite a common occurrence. What will he do? Will he whip you? You will give him money instead."

"And how will I go the rest of the way?"

"There is almost nothing left to reach Germany. I can give you a donkey. You will be far less likely to attract attention. Remember, we are facing troubling times and there are robbers all around us. If only they were ordinary robbers, then they would have only caused half the amount of trouble. But these are robbers who believe they are doing God's will. There is nothing more dangerous. The most dangerous person is the robber who thinks he has God's blessings."

Mark sat deep in thought. The stranger was right; the nobleman wouldn't do anything to him. At most, he would punish him with a beating. And right now, he needed money like he needed air and water. Mark had also noticed that the closer he got to his final goal, the stranger people he kept seeing around him. The people surrounding him or even the casual passersby were becoming more aggressive. There was a strange coldness and cruelty in people's eyes. Of course, if someone decided to seize his horse and kill him, then he would immediately do his divine deed. Mark realized that sooner or later it would occur to somebody to kill him and take possession of his horse. Anyway, he couldn't expect anything good from a crowd who would obey a duck.

The stranger yawned lazily, giving off the impression that he didn't care much about Mark's decision.

"How much will you give me for the horse?" Mark asked.

"Well, thirty pieces of gold is the maximum I can offer, and that's taking into account your miserable condition."

"Thirty pieces of gold?" Mark shouted angrily.

"Shut up!" the stranger exclaimed, looking around him in fear. "You don't want to attract unnecessary attention, do you? There are robbers and plunderers all around us. If one of them hears us talking about gold, they'll kill us both."

"Well, your offer was rather pathetic. Last week I paid five pieces of gold just for outfitting it, plus seven pieces of gold for the leather saddle, and now you're offering me only thirty pieces of gold to give you the whole horse?"

"My maximum is forty, and nowadays you will hardly find anyone who will pay more. Besides, I'm giving you a donkey. Think about it – if you have forty pieces of gold, you'll spend twenty pieces on your way to Germany and back and you'll be able to keep the other twenty for yourself. I'll also pay for all your drinks tonight just for being an interesting conversationalist. Anyone else would just seize your horse rather than paying you so much money."

Mark thought that forty pieces of gold was really quite a large sum. He would tell his master that he had been robbed and keep the donkey to himself.

"Bring me some more wine!" Mark shouted, looking toward the bar. "You said that you'll pay for my drinks, didn't you?

The stranger gave a weak smile.

In the morning, Mark saddled the donkey, loaded it with all the products he had bought, and gave one last look at his steed tied up in the stable. Walking alongside his new donkey, he began his way north.

As he passed through different settlements, he noticed an interesting peculiarity; people would come out into the street and stare at him. Mark couldn't understand why they were so interested. Maybe it was his long beard, which made him look wild and disheveled, or maybe it was because a big burly man riding a donkey looked suspicious, or perhaps it was the look of his ripped, dirty clothes, which didn't match anything that was being worn in the German settlements.

Whatever it was, Mark got the sense that people were confused by him and could not decide whether to treat him as a beggar, a village retailer, a self-proclaimed knight (of which there were many in those days) or perhaps a prophet who had come to lead them. Judging from people's reactions, the latter was the most likely. People had begun to see God's envoys in every stranger. The stereotypical bearded stranger riding into town on a donkey created an image of a biblical savior. Rumors had started to spread that the man on the donkey was God's angel, sent by God to implement his word. He would travel on his donkey from town to town with a special assignment. Of course, that's what people would claim.

Mark's fame surpassed him. He was already known even in the towns he hadn't reached. People would lay out their clothes in the middle of the roads he passed through as a way of communicating with him. But Mark was unaware of all of this. His only concern was to fulfill his master's assignment quickly and return to France, while spending as little money as possible. That's why he would not stop at roadside pubs, and whenever he did stop it was only out of absolute necessity, for instance picking up some cheap food or spending the night in a cheap room. People would ascribe his miserable appearance to divine abstinence and modesty. Legends told about him had already gone beyond the boundaries of logic, entering the realm of miracle. People would say that he could heal an incurable disease just with a look. It wasn't apparent how long Mark's fame would last, but one day, as he was passing through town, some strange old men stopped him.

"Hello Mark!" one of the old men greeted him. Mark stopped and looked at the old men in surprise.

"Who are you and how do you know my name?" Mark asked. They had probably heard of him from one of the cheap shelters where he had stopped for a rest.

"We know who you are and on whose assignment you are here. We admire you. Forgive us, but we are kneeling down on our knees asking you to stay in our town today, and if you lead our small army to the Holy Land, we will be overcome with happiness."

Upon saying this, the old men knelt down before the donkey and bowed their heads, waiting for Mark to speak.

Mark was perplexed. He had clearly been confused with someone else. He had never received any sort of similar treatment, nor had anyone ever spoken to him with such fear and respect or knelt down before him or his donkey. Then Mark thought, why not take advantage of this? What did he have to lose? Mark suddenly got so lost in the fantasy of honoring himself that he momentarily forgot where he was. As a so-called "hick," coming from a "hick" family, he had never dreamed of having such honors. The only living creatures over which he had ever had any power were his master's horses. Even if he had been confused with someone else, he wanted to see where this would lead him, even if he ended up being found out and shamed for his lies. "It doesn't matter," he thought. "I will somehow run away."

"First, let's see how you have prepared to greet me," Mark said to the old men. He held his chest out proudly. "We shall discuss issues of the leadership of the military army and other affairs later. I am tired from my journey. Guide me to my shelter."

The old men exchanged pleased looks. They were happy that their courage in greeting Mark had yielded such positive results. A big argument had been had among the town councilors before Mark's arrival. Some claimed that it was best to approach Mark, talk to him and offer him some food and a place to rest, and then ask him to lead the five hundred enlisted people to Jerusalem to liberate the Lord's Sepulcher. Others were more cautious and didn't believe that taking on such a mission would bring any good to them. They claimed that they must not intervene in God's affairs and that they didn't need to turn to Mark for anything. The old men who approached Mark were some of the brave citizens who saw him as the head of their army. They were so thrilled that Mark, after only a little bit of persuading, had accepted their offer to stay. The old men knew how disheartened the other councilors would be because they were against the idea of speaking to Mark, which only made their happiness even greater. Thus, with their heads held high, the old men guided Mark's donkey to the most splendid shelter in town, where a table was laid for him within a few minutes, abundant with delicious snacks and wine. Being very hungry and tired from his journey, Mark immediately attacked the food. His table companions considered this behavior much more favorable than what they had expected for their unworthy community. The table companions, who were exclusively aldermen, did not dare touch any of the dishes. They waited for Mark's instructions with their heads bowed in reverence.

"Eat! Why do you despise God's gift?" Mark said to them to break the silence.

The table companions perceived Mark's words as an order and immediately began to help themselves. After supper, Mark wanted to relax and delay any business conversations until the next day. His wish was immediately granted.

Alone in his room, Mark tried to analyze the strange events that had happened to him. Of course, it was obvious that they had confused him with someone else. Everybody obeyed his will, but they clearly also had some expectations of him. First of all, as far as he understood, they expected him to lead the pilgrims of their settlement to the Holy Land. Mark couldn't imagine himself as a commander, but after thinking about it he realized he had nothing to lose. His status in society was not very favorable, so any change would be better than what he had, especially when he thought about the prospect of being whipped by his master for having lost the horse.

"May everything be the way it should be," Mark thought. He emptied his head of heavy thoughts and immediately fell asleep.

In fact, he was so exhausted that he didn't so much fall asleep as completely lose consciousness immediately after laying down. He could not remember the last time he had had such a deep and tranquil sleep, nor could he even remember the last time he had been laying on a normal bed. Mark used to sleep in his master's stable on a hard bed, and now a feather mattress was embracing his tired, sore body from all sides. This was the most blissful moment of his life.

Mark woke up the next day around noon. He began to remember everything that had happened to him the previous day, reassuring himself that it hadn't been a dream. The first thing he noticed upon opening his eyes were the new, clean clothes that had been put on the chair near his bed, as well as a jorum full of warm water for washing. He quickly forgot about any suspicions that it had all been a dream, put on the clothes laid out for him, and came out of the room. A lavish breakfast was already awaiting him. Next to the table, the Aldermen were standing and waiting for him, again with their heads hung low. Mark, paying no attention to them, began to eat his breakfast, this time not even bothering to invite them to join. This lifestyle was just so different from anything he had ever experienced before.

"They haven't confused me with someone else. I am the person they have been waiting for, and I am ready to lead them, even to hell. It's time to move forward," Mark thought to himself, and emptied the glass of wine.

"Dear leader, first of all we would like to wish you good morning," one of the old men said.

"Good morning," Mark responded.

The curtness of his greeting made the old man lose all courage and he stopped speaking, although it was clear he had something else to say.

"Did you want to say something else or did you just want to greet me?"

"I wanted to wish you a good morning," the old man said. "We have a few questions regarding going to the Holy Land. We need to provide a report, Your Holiness."

"'Your Holiness.' Not bad," Mark thought. Then he remembered that people only address the pope that way.

"Do not call me 'Your Holiness' any longer," Mark said.

The old man lowered his head.

"Speak. I am listening to you attentively," Mark continued.

"If you agree to personally lead the pilgrims of our town to the Holy Land, it would be a great honor for us. Also, aldermen from five neighboring towns have asked to convey a request to you. They are begging you to please not set the pilgrims adrift."

"Do they also want me to lead them?" Mark asked.

"Yes, they are asking humbly," the old man said quickly. "But if that will cause inconvenience to you..."

"I will announce my decision in three days," Mark said, interrupting the old man. "In the meantime, try to specify the number of pilgrims who want to go to the Holy Land and report to me by evening. This applies to those five towns as well."

The old men, getting their first assignment from their future leader, bowed down before him and left.

In the evening, the old men reported to Mark that the number of those wishing to partake in the pilgrimage was not small. From six different settlements, ten thousand four hundred fifty one people had expressed their desire to join the pilgrimage. Mark had already made a decision, but it had not even occurred to him that he would have to deal with so many people. He feared that he would fail to control the crowd, but he remembered the words of the stranger who bought his horse: "The will of a crowd is far weaker than that of a single individual."

One way or another, he had to lead these people away, if only because the city was getting too dangerous to stay in much longer. People would soon guess that he was not an angel or a soldier, but a former groom, and the probability of them reacting violently was growing more likely.

One evening, three days later, Mark came out to the yard where everyone who had expressed interest in participating in the pilgrimage had gathered.

"You are all chosen," Mark said to them, "and many are called, but few are chosen." He had memorized a few words from the Bible to make an impression.

"I will lead all chosen people to the Holy Land. We will achieve our goal because it is a holy goal. Now, go back to your homes to contemplate and analyze this journey. If you're ready for the test and will agree to unconditionally follow all my commands, gather at this same spot early tomorrow morning. Should you have even the slightest doubt or skepticism, it is better to stay in your homes because you cannot turn around until we have reached the end triumphantly. It would be better to not start the pilgrimage at all, than to abandon it halfway. I urge everyone again to think this over, make a decision, and then come back to this spot. Our pilgrimage to the Holy Land starts tomorrow morning."

Mark returned to his shelter and did not come out again until morning. People told each other that he had gone to consult the heavenly angels. In the morning, crowds of people were readily waiting for their leader. Mark smiled with satisfaction, made a series of hand movements as a blessing, and walked in front of the crowd. Everyone followed him. The pilgrimage had begun.

10. Sayid's Escape to Alamut (Damascus, AD 1115)

Sayid safely returned from his first trip to Damascus. It wasn't such a long trip – only forty days. He bought a beautiful hookah for Ahmed with the two pieces of gold he had given him to spend. Ahmed was so touched by the gift. He liked the boy's honesty very much, but sometimes Ahmed would worry about Sayid's strict dedication to following the rules and his overly trustful nature. Sayid was advancing very quickly in his career. In just three months, he went from a porter to a guide because everyone was so pleased with his conscientious and devotion to work.

Sayid accompanied caravans across the desert. In two years of doing that work, he already knew the language of the desert by heart. He knew when the wind would start, and when it would be hot multiple days in a row. He knew all the safe routes and paths. The desert, which may have seemed monotonously yellow and endless to an ordinary man, was a complex city with numerous signs and streets for Sayid. After making several trips, no one could argue with him about matters concerning the desert. Every time he returned from a trip, Sayid would bring a small gift for old Ahmed. The gifts were not particularly big: a new flavor of hookah, a rare tea, or a small prayer rug with unique patterns. Every time he received a new gift, Ahmed would hug Sayid and kiss his forehead. Then he would bend down to his hookah to adjust the fire, but in reality, he was hiding his tears from Sayid. Ahmed owned several sweet shops in Damascus and was not poor. Sayid's small gifts didn't particularly make him happy, but rather Ahmed was proud that he was able to keep an orphaned, homeless boy from unlawful conduct, directing him in the right path and teaching him to be a law-abiding worker. The presents were simply tangible evidence that Sayid had pursued a good path. Ahmed was convinced that he had done something good and was viewed favorable in the eyes of God. He would burst with pride when Sayid, returning home from this or that country, would tell him interesting stories from his journeys.

"May Allah be merciful," Ahmed thought.

Everything was going in a way that was pleasing to Allah, but then one fateful night changed it all. It was past midnight and Ahmed was sleeping in his bed as usual when he awoke and heard someone trying to quietly open the door to his house. "Thieves," the old man thought immediately. He looked up and muttered, "Give me strength, Lord Almighty." He went downstairs, where he could see the dark shape and outline of a person.

"Who are you? What are you doing in my house?" Ahmed shouted.

"It's me. Sayid," answered a voice.

"Sayid, what are you doing in my house?" Ahmed asked in surprise. He tried to light the lamp that was hanging from the ceiling.

"Ahmed, please! Don't turn the light on."

Ahmed approached Sayid. His whole body was shaking.

"What has happened? Can you tell me?"

"The caravan, the one I was accompanying, has been robbed."

"Sayid, caravans are often subject to robbery attempts."

"But I am the main suspect. I am being accused of organizing the robbery. I am being chased! I barely escaped."

"You? Sayid, why should they suspect you? Look into my eyes!"

There was a look of disgrace and shame in Sayid's eyes.

"Why do they suspect you?" Ahmed asked.

"I am the only person who survived the robbery. Also, I didn't take the caravan along the previously planned route, but rather the one that I thought would be safer. I did not know that there would be robbers. They attacked and massacred everyone and robbed the caravan. I barely managed to escape! After wandering in the desert for a few days, I finally reached Damascus."

"The fact that you're alive isn't a sufficient basis to accuse you."

"Ahmed, the caravan deviated from its path because of my command."

Ahmed was lost deep in thought. In these cases, the death penalty was inevitable. Though Sayid was not directly to blame for the caravan robbery, it was impossible to explain any deviation from the path of the caravan in favor of his innocence. If Sayid was caught, he would be accused of deliberately leading the caravan to robbers and would be sentenced to death almost without trial. The situation was extremely complicated, and Ahmed saw very little chance of being able to pull Sayid out of it. Another problem was that Ahmed had once interceded for Sayid already, but he had a reputation for being such an immaculate believer that there was hardly anyone who could accuse him of complicity.

Ahmed turned on the hookah and began to smoke. It helped him relax and collect his thoughts. Only then could Ahmed make a decision.

"Sayid, I'll give you an accompanying letter and send you to Alamut before dawn."

Two months after that crucial night, Sayid was standing before the gates of Alamut Castle. He cast one last look over the view opening from above and turned toward the castle gates. He had been traveling for two months. His experience as a refugee taught him to travel at night, when people were sleeping, and to sleep in the mornings, finding shelter far from settlements. Ahmed had given him some money to get by.

The night he left Ahmed's house and set out for Alamut Castle, located on the top of one of the most impassable mountains in Persia, Ahmed had told him the story of the castle in detail. Sayid had heard the story about Alamut and its bravest soldier, Bu Tahir Arrani, in the desert from the camel-puller, but he realized that he couldn't entirely rely on the information provided by the old caravan man since road stories were sometimes so exaggerated that they often lost touch with reality.

And now Alamut, in all its charm, was in front of Sayid. The mountain path to Alamut was too difficult and inaccessible. There was just a trail that wrapped around the mountain like a snake, leading to the castle gates, and a deep abyss surrounding the castle from the other three sides. The high walls were built right on the lip of the cliff, and it was hard to understand just where the rock ended and where the castle wall began. Alamut seemed to be the natural continuation of the rock. Sentinels were carrying out service inside the castle in the four citadels. They were people with cold stone eyes, unaware of surrounding events and changes in climate. Their facial expressions were always the same. Nothing could escape their sharp eyes. They were said to be the best archers of those times, and there was no way to get rid of their arrows. No other living soul was seen beyond the gates inside the castle. It was impossible to determine what events were taking place there. Sometimes various sounds of metal striking metal could be heard from inside during the daytime, which led people to conclude that sword fighting, and combat exercises were taking place.

A copper plate was attached to the castle gate on which was written, "May your fame be eternal, Allah's true son Bu Tahir Arrani, who sent to hell Shaitan Nizam al-Mulk and met Allah for this action."

On the night of seeing Sayid off, when Ahmed told him the story of Alamut Castle, he mentioned that specific copperplate as well. Ahmed, blowing out hookah smoke into the living room of his house in Damascus, had asked, "Sayid, have you ever heard about Alamut?"

"A caravan man told me about it once. Isn't it the castle where Hassan-i Sabbāh, the Old Man of the Mountain, lives?"

"Hush," Ahmed shouted, suddenly jumping up from his seat. "Don't say his name out loud. Here the walls also have ears."

Ahmed appeared to be seriously concerned. He got up from his seat and looked out the window, lowered the light, and finally sat back down on the couch.

"You are a child, a total child! That is why you get into trouble," Ahmed said. "Tell me what you know about it but speak in a low voice."

Sayid reproduced every detail of what he had heard that night in the desert. The story had impressed him so much that he remembered it word for word. After finishing his retelling, he paused and looked out the window. The son would rise in about an hour.

"I would like to tell you a few parables, since you will surely need a little wisdom on your long journey," Ahmed said. "What you just told me is the plain truth. I guess that camel puller had some connections with Alamut. But this story has two versions, and it would be better to tell you the second version so that you can have a complete view."

Ahmed fixed the hookah coals and continued. "There were also rumors, which may not be groundless, that Sava's muezzin was actually killed not by Hassan's people, the Nizari preachers, as everyone was told, but by Chief Vizier Al Mulk's people to cause a wave of hate against the Assassins. The reality is as follows: Chief Vizier Nizam al-Mulk, being informed that Ismaili preachers had achieved serious results and that ordinary people had started to love and believe them, gave a secret command to kill Sava's muezzin and blame Hassan's people for the murder, inciting religious hatred against Hassan and the Assassins. Which means the chief vizier himself provoked retaliation against the Assassins. Of course, no one knows and will ever know the real truth. Only Allah can judge, since only he knows the truth."

Ahmed's story was so detailed and captivating that it almost seemed like he had been there. It was entirely possible, since the events had taken place twenty-five years before. Ahmed not only could have been present, but he also could have actively participated. But Ahmed's story sounded more like a philosophical tale resembling a parable than actual reality. There were no miracles or supernatural phenomenon in the story, but it was so beautiful, and the characters were so exemplary that it was difficult to listen and think of it as pure reality.

"Ahmed, this is a very interesting story. Are you sure that it is real?"

Sayid was listening intently. For a moment, he forgot that he was on the run.

Ahmed continued. "After the very public and humiliating execution of the Nizari religious preacher, tempers grew hotter. The chief vizier's murder was an unprecedented event in the Muslim world, and it led Hassan-i Sabbāh to create a very interesting and simple concept of creating a state defense that would allow them to keep an efficient army without any costs and without having to bully people and punish them with demonstrative killings. Hassan realized that this was possible only if the core of the pending special service was religion. Only a believer would kill for free and would not fear death. Neither a high wall nor an army of guards could save the next victim.

The first thing Hassan-i Sabbāh did was create a powerful agent network. They were preachers of Ismaili doctrine who were scattered all over the world. Hassan was the first to apply a strategic mechanism of agent recruitment. Recruiting priests and imams had a huge impact on the agents. An imam's word was not discussed, it was welcomed as Allah's wish. Nizaris involved in the agent network believed that they had Allah's mercy. Agents were told that they were born for a great mission, and that all worldly pleasures meant nothing compared to the reward that they would receive after fulfilling their mission. Because they had such dedicated agents, Hassan-i Sabbāh was constantly aware of every detail concerning the lives of the eastern rulers – Shiraz, Bukhara, Balha, Isfahan, Cairo, Samarkand, and others.

The last element of the structure was the army, an army of professional killers who were not only supreme masters and experts in killing people, but who also were indifferent to their own lives; not only were they not afraid of death, but they also yearned to die."

After saying this, Ahmed turned to the boy. "Sayid, it is already getting light. They will search for you in the city. It's time to leave. Travel to Alamut. You will be welcomed there."

Giving his last instructions, Ahmed gave Sayid the letter of recommendation, which asked for a favor from Allah, and saw him off in secret.

11. Alamut (Persia, AD 1115)

There were numerous young men crouched under the castle walls. They all desired to convert to the beliefs of the Old Man of the Mountain and become an Assassin. Hundreds of young men had been waiting for their chance to enter Alamut Castle for weeks. All those waiting there were in uncertainty because no one knew how or when they would be let into the castle courtyard. Instead, soldiers carrying out their duty on the walls would ridicule the young men gathered outside. They tried to humiliate the young men in every possible way, from pouring waste water on them to uttering curses against them. The young men didn't even realize that this was their first test. It was a trial of patience. After all, only the most patient ones, for whom their faith in Allah was much more precious than their own comfort, were to be given the right to enter Alamut.

Thus, the young men went through their first trial while they were still standing outside the castle walls. There wasn't a single form of comfort – no bed, no toilet, no food. Absolutely nothing. No one had any idea how long they were going to spend outside the castle walls under the scorching sun, lying in the dirt.

Sayid had overcome a tough childhood. He used to wander along the narrow streets of Damascus begging, but still the deplorable state he witnessed at Alamut's gates really shocked him. Approaching one of the young men sitting on the ground, he tried to find out some information.

"As-salamu alaykum," Sayid greeted him.

"Wa alaykumu as-salam," the stranger answered. He turned his head to Sayid and began to examine him. He was a slim young man between eighteen and twenty years old with inquisitive, black eyes.

"When do the castle gates open?" Sayid asked.

"Only Allah knows. It has been ten days since I have been here; so far, the gates have been opened only once and only two people were let in. By the way, I am Almualim."

"Sayid," Sayid said, stretching out his hand to the stranger. "Does that mean that nobody is being told when the gates will open?"

"The tower bells usually ring five minutes before the gates open. Once they open, a few people come out and choose whom to let in and whom not to let in."

"Well, what if someone has something urgent, like a letter or a message?"

"Can you see the other end of the castle wall?" Almualim pointed at another part of the wall, far from the gates. "There's a door over there through which Assassins go in and out. They leave for assignments and come back, or as you said, bring letters, but only Assassins have the right to access that door. Don't even dare approach it!"

"Why? What will happen?"

"Archers are on duty above the door. They know by heart who has the right to enter or leave through that door, and they will shoot their arrows at any other people without even thinking."

"But what if I have to hand something over? What should I do? I have traveled a long way to get here. I've been walking for about two months."

"If you think that those who are gathered here have come from neighboring fields, you are sadly mistaken. There are people here who have walked for more than a year before they reached the castle. They are still quietly waiting for their turn," Almualim said.

"Well, well! Don't get heated! I have some fresh unleavened bread. Come on, let's eat together. Share a little about yourself."

The boys sat under the shade of the castle wall. Sayid took out the loaf of bread from his bag, divided it into equal parts with his hands and gave a piece to Almualim.

"Who knows when the last time you ate fresh bread was," Sayid said.

"I do not even remember when I ate bread last." Almualim grabbed the bread from Sayid's hand without hesitating. "There have been days when we ate nothing at all. Once, it was announced that the gates would be opening soon, and we all gathered nearby. We stood there for several days in a row and exhausted our food supply. We were all hungry and emaciated."

"Why didn't any of you go to fetch some food?"

"Those who go would leave us forever. Here, the conditions are very strict. You must withstand everything; if you leave, you leave forever, and you always have the chance to leave until you enter the castle. There is only one way to leave Alamut from the inside."

"How?" Sayid asked, chewing.

"Dead," Almualim said. "So far, no one has been able to escape from the Old Man of the Mountain alive."

Sayid and Almualim had a long talk. Almualim told him that before coming there he used to live a nomadic life; he didn't even know who his parents were. He had heard about Hassan-i Sabbāh by chance and realized that he was Allah's locum tenens on earth.

"I am already fed up with the mullahs' false sanctimonious sermons. Afterwards, they just forget about their faith. They really only use their faith to advance themselves."

"Do you think everyone behaves like that?" Sayid asked.

He had never heard of a mullah doing anti-God things, but he had met many people who liked to spread those types of rumors.

"'Well, maybe not everyone, but the majority of them definitely do," Almualim said.

Sayid listened carefully as Almualim continued his story.

"After many years of being lost, I made the decision to dedicate my life to Allah. I will go through all the trials necessary and become Allah's deserving son."

Suddenly, the sound of the tower bell rang out in the silence of the dawn. Everyone became flustered. The young boys, who had been sharing their bread and taking care of each other, were now rushing to take their positions in front of the gates, pushing each other in desperation.

"Sayid, now is your chance to deliver your message," Almualim exclaimed with joy. "They might let me in today!"

"How will you deliver my letter?"

"Once the gates are opened, three people will come out. They will go around to everyone and choose who they want to take with them. When they pass by you, stretch out your hand with the letter and say that you have a very important message. Are you sure that you're bringing good news? They aren't too fond of bad news."

"Bad news is never welcome," Sayid said.

"I agree, but the difference is that the reward for bringing bad news here is a strike from a sword," Almualim replied. "Come on, let's go! Hurry up! We will be late."

The boys ran toward the gates. As soon as they reached them, the door opened, and three burly men came out of the castle dressed in white hooded gowns. The men slowly walked past the recruits, looking at their faces one by one. They chose two people and started to go back to the castle without even having approached Sayid and Almualim. Almualim felt like the Assassins had just taken away all hope of ever entering the castle.

"Hey!" Almualim shouted aloud. "There is an important message for you!"

The Assassins rushed over to Almualim.

"Is it you who was calling us?"

"Yes sir! Since it might be a while before you come back again, I thought it would be best to let you know about it."

The Assassin immediately took out his dagger from under his clothes and put it against Almualim's throat.

"Where is the message, cipher?"

Almualim slowly raised his hand and pointed a trembling finger at Sayid. Sayid quickly took the letter out of his breast pocket and held it out to the Assassin before he had a chance to pull his knife on him. The Assassin took the envelope and, seeing its triangular seal, suddenly went pale. He motioned to his friend to remove the dagger from Almualim's throat. The three Assassins quickly re-entered the castle, taking the selected recruits along with them and leaving Almualim and Sayid outside. The gates closed with a squeak. The boys gathered in front of the gates remained standing in shock for a few minutes. Everything had happened so fast that no one really understood what had happened.

"Listen, are you crazy? Why did you speak on my behalf?" Sayid yelled at Almualim. "You were almost killed!"

"Then it would be Allah's will. Everything is in his hands. Look, they didn't kill me. Did you notice the way they reacted to your letter? What was in it, if it's not a secret?"

"I myself don't know," said Sayid. "Perhaps a message from a very important person."

Sayid had hardly finished speaking when Alamut's gates opened once more. This time, the tower bells didn't ring beforehand, and everyone was taken by surprise. An Assassin emerged from the gates and approached Sayid and Almualim. "Follow me!"

With no explanation, the boys silently followed the Assassin. They entered the Alamut gates, leaving behind the envious looks of those who had been waiting their turn for months.

Inside the castle, everything looked exactly the same way as other castles. The residents of Alamut were living ordinary lives without any strange activity going on, except for someone who was being whipped in the town square as a form of punishment. After every strike of the whip, the person would shout "Allah Akbar" at the top of his lungs.

When the Assassin leading them turned to walk toward the large house in the center of Alamut, which looked like a castle within the castle, the boys noticed several Assassins who were busy training. They were practicing dagger fighting. "This is how they refine their skills," Almualim thought, scratching his neck where the Assassin's dagger had previously touched. The Assassin accompanied the boys to the entrance of the house, but he did not enter the building. Inside, they were met by another burly man who took the boys to the second floor in silence.

The stranger invited Sayid into the room and motioned to Almualim to wait outside. Sayid entered the room, which resembled a large library. He had never seen so many books in his life. There were stacks of books written in an unfamiliar language. Of course, he wasn't very extensively educated in languages. He could barely read, and that was because Ahmed had taught him.

An old man, also muscular, was standing near the window of the library. He had a long, white beard and his thick, white eyebrows gave his eyes a mean, dangerous look. He was dressed entirely in white.

"Come in, Allah's misguided child," the old man said. His voice was deep but barely audible. "What is it that have you lost in here and what are you looking for?"

"I don't even know how to tell you, my Lord! My words have lost their power."

"Words are very important. With the right language structure, one can pray to the Lord and glorify him, while the wrong structure can easily turn a man into a servant of Shaitan. There was once a ruler who dreamt his teeth were falling out one after another. When he woke up in the morning, he tried to figure out the meaning of his dream. He spent all day feeling uneasy and anxious. That evening, he commanded his servants to find dream readers who could interpret his dream. The servants brought two people. The first dream reader, having heard the ruler's dream, shook his head and said that the dream had an ominous meaning and asked for permission not to speak. After negotiating with him for a long time, the ruler somehow convinced the dream reader to speak. He claimed that the teeth the ruler saw in his dream were his relatives, who were going to die one by one, leaving the ruler all alone. Upon hearing this, the ruler got very angry and gave orders to whip and imprison the dream reader. Afterward, the ruler invited the second dream reader to interpret his dream. He listened to the ruler's dream and said that it meant the ruler would live longer than all his relatives. The ruler rejoiced at this news and generously compensated the dream reader. The courtiers were astonished. Both dream readers had essentially said the same thing, so why did the ruler order that one of them be whipped and imprisoned while the other was rewarded? When the couriers asked the second dream reader about this, he said that people tend to attach importance to what they are saying to others, but it is just as important to know how to say something."

After finishing his story, the old man approached Sayid. Sayid suddenly felt the urge to kneel down. The old man put his hand on Sayid's head and said, "May Allah's blessing be upon you and the person who sent you here. I hadn't heard from my brother Ahmed for many years. My heart is rejoicing. I know that Ahmed would only recommend a person of eminent worth. He could never be forced to write a single line in favor of someone unworthy. Sayid, from today on, you do not have any other parent. I am your parent. You do not have any other home. This is your home. You do not have any other goal. Your goal is to serve Allah. From now on, you are dead to the world. You are only alive in Alamut. I, Hassan-i Sabbāh, the Old Man of the Mountain, Allah's vicar on earth, is saying this to you. Become a servant worthy of Allah, transform from a cipher into a slave worthy of Allah. Reject the futility of earthly life and you will receive eternal pleasures in heaven! Earn Allah's favor! You have entered Alamut; the rest is in your hands. Go, my son. Go and serve the Lord faithfully!"

Sayid bowed down and left the room. An Assassin was waiting for him to escort him to his shelter. The shelter was a poorly furnished room; its four narrow stone beds were the only pieces of furniture, and they looked very hard and uncomfortable. Only later, when he reached the end of his trainings, would he consider the stone bed softer than a fluffy mattress. But for now, he didn't know all that was waiting ahead of him in Alamut. He was still getting used to the new environment when Almualim walked in, his face full of joy.

"Sayid, I was chosen, and I will become an Assassin!" he said. He began to pretend to fight with an imaginary sword. "I can hardly wait to start practicing. You see Sayid, my presumptuousness finally yielded results. Sometimes you just need to be bold. Life sends its most generous gifts when you ignore the fear of death. Sayid, I'm so happy."

"Me too, Almualim. Me too." Sayid gave a smile and hugged his friend.

The life of the recruits in Alamut was very strict. They could not spend a single second of their time alone. Every Assassin was assigned four recruits, and it was their job to tell them what to do, from trainings to eating dinner to satisfying natural needs. During the first seven days, the recruits were adjusting to their new lives. They were given three minutes for breakfast, seven minutes for dinner and four minutes for supper. Once a day, they were given the opportunity to satisfy any natural needs. They would learn prayers every day. Any recruits who repeatedly violated the assigned schedule would be excluded from further classes and put in isolation. The Assassins explained that anyone who had a weak body or mind had no right to be called a soldier of Allah because they wouldn't have the strength to fully honor Allah's name.

Sayid and Almualim had almost no opportunity to speak or communicate with each other. Even the act of conversing was prohibited unless you received special permission. In those first seven days, they learned the rules and regulations of Alamut, and on the seventh day the actual trainings began.

Education played the largest role in life at Alamut. Hassan had a very serious approach to the Assassins' learning, and he invited various specialists who would teach the recruits using a strict, previously planned curriculum. The specialists were of different nationalities and many spoke foreign languages, so there were also special translators there who would help with communication. The trainers were very diverse in their appearance. Some of them were squinty-eyed short people with yellow skin and heads totally shaved, except for the hair in the center of their heads which was tied up into a ponytail. Then there were trainers whose skin was as black as night.

Others were missing limbs or eyes or had disfiguring scars on their faces. They had suffered those mutilations on battlefields, and they were proud of it. The recruits secretly admired those disabled people and dreamed that one day they could have similar injuries or even get to die for the sake of the heavenly Lord's name.

The learning process mainly consisted of four stages, each lasting three months. First, the recruits were taught martial arts skills, including how to use a dagger. By the final lesson, the recruits had already mastered using a dagger so skillfully that it was almost like an extension of their body.

At their first lesson, they were taught to stab with a dagger; a complete master would eventually be able to throw it. After mastering that skill, they were taught to snatch the dagger out of the enemy's hand. During these daily trainings, the recruits were taught to think of the dagger as a poisonous cobra tooth in their hands that they had to treat with care.

A small, round square was designated in the central part of the castle for the recruits to train during daylight hours. They started with simple blows and then moved on to prevention of dagger attacks, a striking sequence of serial blows to the vital points and applying the enemy's dagger. Every day, except on holidays, the sounds of daggers clanging together could be heard all over Alamut.

The recruits also learned the martial art of strokes. For that, specialists had been invited from the far east. The recruits then learned the rules of unarmed combat by heart during the dagger trainings. They learned to climb walls, lift weights, walk on their hands, crawl long distances, do long distance squat walks, and run.

This was just an incomplete list of the recruits' daily trainings. Three months later, when the first stage of the training yielded its results, their physical activity was decreased in compliance with the curriculum. Instead of doing physical training daily, it was done once every two days so that the recruits could at least keep up a somewhat active lifestyle.

The next stage of the learning process was called "lesson of patience." It began with the following assignment: each Assassin-in-training was given a large piece of ore that was to be broken into pieces with a crowbar. It was not an easy task at all. At first, it might have seemed like an interesting assignment, but some of the recruits were striking at the ore for hours or even days. Their lives revolved around it – they took the ore with them everywhere they went and spied on the progress of their fellow recruits out of the corner of their eyes. Once the recruits finally broke the ore into pieces, they were given another ore of the same size. This surprised the recruits, and they didn't understand the purpose or goal of the assignment, but they had to continue anyway.

An increasing feeling of emptiness was growing inside them. They hated their work, but felt obliged to crush the rock into pieces and continue to train without losing any of their enthusiasm. They worked for days in a row. The recruit who had already broken three stones was in just as much agony as the one who was still trying to break their first one. It was impossible to determine how much each of them had worked.

This disheartened many of the recruits. Some refused to work, but only the most patient ones continued their seemingly meaningless work in tranquility and kept trying to break more rocks without showing any emotion.

The next stage was called "lesson on temptations and endurance." The recruits' endurance was tested through a variety of assignments. They were told to remain completely and indefinitely immovable in a squatted position. This trial could last for days. They froze like statues, suppressing their body's natural urges. Naturally, not everyone managed to succeed. Many of them ended up urinating in their positions. Small ponds would form at the feet of the men as they stood frozen. They weren't ashamed of this, since their squinty-eyed trainer had told them that a camouflaged soldier who had already taken up his position must not be ashamed of urinating on himself, but of changing his position and being revealed. Doing that was just as bad as leaving the assignment unfinished, because you would be dying a shameful death not while fighting, but while urinating. Dying for urinating while battling for faith was the real shame.

The assignment was followed by a one week fast and refusal to drink water for two days. At this stage, speaking was strictly forbidden. Recruits would spend three months having no verbal communication with each other. In cases of extreme necessity, they would communicate through active gesturing. The final assignment of their training was that they were to be buried alive. The recruits spent three days buried in special boxes where they were only supplied with air through a narrow, thin pipe. Three days later, they were taken out of the boxes. This last assignment, apart from being part of their training, had a ritual meaning. Being buried and then disinterred symbolized their death and rebirth as an Assassin. They were able to be called an Assassin only after successfully completing this assignment. Before that, they had many names: cipher, brainless creature, sinner buried in sin. However, once they were disinterred, nobody could use insulting words against them. They were already Assassins.

The next stage of learning was preceded by five days of rest, during which the Assassins, already exhausted from their previous trials, were given an opportunity to regain their strength. After those five days, the trial of faith would begin. During this stage, the Assassins were divided into small groups to listen to preachers of various religions. Several preachers of Christianity, Sunni Islam, Judaism, and Eastern philosophy worked with the Assassins every day for three months. The Assassins were obliged to participate in all religious events, liturgies, services, prayers, and rituals. The preachers would do absolutely everything they could to convert the Assassins. They would tell fables from religious books, promise everlasting life or rebirth on earth, promise mental and spiritual peace, and read aloud enticing texts. For days, the preachers would try to convince the Assassins that their religious orientation was the only true religion and was superior to all other religions. The interesting thing was that there was also a preacher who was teaching atheism who tried to find a scientific explanation for each phenomenon to convince the Assassins that there was no supernatural force in the universe and that theology was made up as a way to make people look like fools in the name of religion.

Immediately after the trial of faith, something strange happened to Sayid. One night, just after his conversation with the inquisitor, Sayid had a dream. Sayid had seen many dreams, of course, but this one was the most beautiful and, at the same time, the strangest he had ever seen. Sayid was asleep on his hard bed as usual when he suddenly awoke, unable to understand what it was he just experienced. He didn't know whether he was still dreaming or if he was back inreality. Although his eyes were still foggy from sleep, he could see that he was not inside his usual room. By some miracle, Sayid was in an unknown but very beautiful garden. The permanent stink of Alamut had disappeared; instead, the fragrance of flowers had spread all around.

He was blanketed by the gentle shadows of the beautiful trees that surrounded him. A table stood under one of the trees, decorated with an abundance of food and beverages. He approached the table and started to eat. Everything seemed to be real: the taste of the food, the refreshing, cool drinks. Suddenly, someone hugged Sayid from behind. He turned around and saw a beautiful girl. She was completely naked, wearing only a transparent veil that only highlighted her nudity. As he looked lower, the shameful parts of her beautiful female body were visible. Sayid closed his eyes. He realized that he must be in paradise, and that the smiling beauty standing in front of him wasn't an ordinary human being, but a houri.

"Have I died and gone to paradise?" Sayid thought.

The beautiful girl laughed and ran away. Sayid was enchanted by her and decided to follow. The houri stopped under a tree and waited for Sayid. When he reached her, she gave him a passionate kiss. Sayid closed his eyes in bliss. Suddenly, he felt the houri's hands on the most important part of his masculinity. The houri held Sayid's penis, admiring its beauty. Sayid had never experienced such a feeling, or anything close to it. Waves of bliss went through his body. Sayid couldn't help but just lie down in the grass, and the houri lay down beside him. He didn't care about anything anymore. He just wanted to stay in that park forever, lying in the grass next to the houri and looking at the sky.

Suddenly, Sayid heard another voice. A woman was laughing, but it wasn't the houri; she was lying quietly beside him. Sayid raised his head. His vision was still blurry, but he managed to see another female silhouette at the end of the park. This girl was much younger. She came up to him and also started shooting admiring glances at Sayid's penis. He felt something warm, wet and maddeningly pleasing under his belly. He couldn't look down. The second houri was kissing the most delicate parts of his body. Sayid groaned and his eyes grew dim. When the girl lay down next to him, he suddenly recognized her. She was the girl he had once met in the desert when he was escorting a caravan. It had happened so long ago, but he still recognized her, and she seemed to recognize him. She pressed her lips against Sayid's ear and whispered, "Habibi, my name is Habibi."

Sayid jerked awake. As he got up, he realized everything he had seen was a dream. He wanted to talk to the inquisitor about it and ask him to interpret the dream, but he decided not to. In the months that followed, he would remember the dream, closing his eyes so that he could enjoy the memory as much as possible.

The next morning, a new trial was awaiting Sayid. The Assassins were taken out of Alamut and transported to a flat terrain not far from the castle, where there were several pits dug far from each other. The pits were deeper than an average man's height, and their width and length would allow a man to freely spread his arms. The inquisitor commanded the Assassins to enter the pits and pray to Allah. It did not matter what specific prayer they said. The major condition was that the prayer had to be said in the pits for three days and three nights. One bucket of water was distributed to each Assassin. They were allowed to stop praying only while drinking water. The sound of their prayers was to be heard for the next three days.

Sayid began to pray. During the first day, he prayed with ease. When it grew dark, Sayid felt that his throat was getting dry and he started to cough. Water helped temporarily, but the problem would just come back after a little while. His coughing and dry mouth began to disrupt his prayer. In the morning, Sayid had lost his voice; he could barely utter any words. Every time he tried to speak it caused him terrible pain. Words were like sharp nails, piercing and cutting his swollen throat. By the second night, it was already impossible for him to pray. Sayid didn't care anymore whether he was praying out loud or praying silently in his head. He was exhausted and was forcing himself to pray. He tried to do it quickly, but every word he uttered felt like a piece of his body was being torn off with great difficulty and pain.

Suddenly, Sayid felt an exhilarating relief. He was praying again, although very quietly. He couldn't say when or how it happened, but he was praying. It seemed that the only thing that got rid of the terrible pain in his mouth was prayer. It softened his throat like oil. He continued praying until the pain completely stopped. Sayid felt nothing but bliss. He saw Allah's light and heard Allah's voice. It was calling him to heaven. Sayid began to dream of the moment when he would be able to approach the light. He was no longer interested in earthly matters. In fact, he felt awkward and uncomfortable inside the mold of earthly life, like a traveler in a foreign land. He dreamed of reaching the light, experiencing that blessedness, getting to the paradise garden and living there as the lowest servant to the garden owner. Earthly life began to disturb him. He wanted to live beside Habibi. The houri had captured Sayid's heart. He started to hate the ground he was walking on.

Sayid opened his eyes. He was lying in Alamut's hospice. The doctor, who had also been invited by Hassan, was an expert. He was putting compresses on Sayid's throat. Sayid tried to ask how long he had been lying there, but instead of words, a wheezing sound came out of his throat.

"Be quiet. You can't speak for at least ten days. It will calm you to know that you have passed the trial of prayer. Now, relax and lie down. You should stay in bed for a few days and drink infusions."

Sayid smiled with satisfaction and closed his eyes. He had entered a state of total bliss upon hearing that he had passed the trial of prayer. His soul was floating somewhere high up in the sky and he didn't care about what was happening to his body. One day his body was just going to rot under the ground, anyway. Sayid saw the way of his soul. He was a happy man.

The learning stage, which included the trial of faith, lasted three months. At the end, the Nizari priest met with everyone for a private talk. He listened to the Assassins' questions attentively to find out who had deviated from their true faith. The last ten days of the three-month learning stage was aimed at building immunity against other religious sermons. The degree of each Assassin's dedication to faith was determined during this trial. This was one of the most important trials each soldier was to overcome on their thorny and difficult path to Allah.

After the trial of faith, the Assassins were to rest for three days. During those three days, they essentially did nothing, although they were allowed to freely communicate with each other. After their rest, the intellectual education of the Assassins was to begin.

Almualim and Sayid had a chance to communicate with each other and share their impressions for the first time since they entered Alamut. Almualim excitedly talked about all his training achievements, although he didn't have too many. Unlike Sayid, Almualim had failed a large number of trials. He wasn't very good at physical exercises. His body was not particularly strong, and he tired easily. The trainers were not very satisfied with him. Fortunately, Almualim passed the spiritual portion of the trials. In this regard, the trainers had few complaints. Almualim mentioned that the spiritual teacher had a special assignment for him and that he was looking forward to it.

Sayid decided to share his strange dream with Almualim. Up until then, he hadn't told anyone about his paradise garden dream. After hearing the story, Almualim looked at Sayid with slight envy and said nothing. At this point, the conversation ended when an Assassin came over and separated them, giving them different assignments.

The next and final stage of the training program was the longest of all. The Assassins were given a chance to develop their language skills or learn a new language. They also attended lectures on poisons, learned about their impacts and antidotes, and practiced applying them. The Assassins were also taught to bandage wounds and to use herbs to quickly stop bleeding. Allah's soldiers were also required to be able to sew and cook a few simple meals.

At the end of this stage, the Assassins learned the last and most important lesson, which was called the "Lesson of Truth." The meaning of this lesson was actually quite the opposite. The Assassins were taught everything related to lies: how to detect lies, how to lie without being caught, how to unmask a liar, how to detect a lie from a speaker's facial expression and look. This was one of the more unique parts of the training. The lessons were given by the teacher of the truth. He would quote parables and passages from the holy scriptures, which were interesting to listen to because of his rich vocabulary.

"When the Prophet Muhammad was persecuted and was being searched for to be arrested," the teacher explained, "a very interesting idea occurred to his father-in-law, Ali. He hid the prophet in a high basket, placed the heavy basket on his shoulders, and tried to pass by the town's guard soldiers. 'What is in that basket?' one of the soldiers asked. 'The Prophet Muhammad,' Ali replied. The guards laughed and let Ali pass. The truth holds much more power than you can imagine. People are not ready to hear the truth and are usually taken aback when meeting with it."

After the lesson of truth, the Assassins had to take an exam on the subject by staging a situation. The performance lasted until the Assembly of Elders considered the exam accomplished.

An Assassin would transform into a Christian preacher, a retail merchant or any other character, and begin to live in Alamut according to the nature of that character. Meanwhile, the Assembly of Elders would follow him around and fix his mistakes. This usually lasted from seven to fifteen days.

When they felt it was time, the Assembly of Elders would hand the Assassin his dagger to signify that he had completed the last stage of study and was finally a soldier of Allah.

From that moment on, the Assassin's life didn't belong to him. He was wholly Allah's property, and if he died under any circumstances, even from an illness or an accident, he was to go to heaven to meet the virgins. From that moment, an Assassin had only one desire in life – to die.

12. Conversations Between Father and Son (Paris, AD 2015)

Ali's father tried in vain to hide his emotions. His hands were shaking, and his face was red with anger. Shuffling around in his house slippers, he paced from one corner of the room to the other. His sons had gathered in one of the rooms and were discussing the night's major family event in a whisper, while his daughter and wife had locked themselves in another room to cry.

"What a calamity!" his wife cried.

"Mom, everything will be ok. Allah is almighty," Aisha said, trying to console her.

"I don't know...I feel sorry for your dad. He is suffering now."

"We are all suffering, Mother."

"No, not Ali! Everything would have been much easier if your brothers had done it." Her mother continued to cry. "I do not know what hardships Allah has in store for our family."

"Mom, it would be better if you were next to dad. His suffering has no size or limits."

"Yes, you are right. Let me try to console him."

Ali's mother left the room quietly and approached her husband. Mustafa turned around and saw his wife standing in her grey nightgown with her head hung low, wiping away tears with a handkerchief.

"You're to blame for all this!" he said angrily.

"Honey, may Allah punish me if I knew..."

"If you knew? I did not say you knew. This is the result of pampering him. It turned out that not only have we left our homeland, but we are also drifting away from our traditions and, even worse, our religion."

His wife did not answer. She just collapsed on the sofa and continued to sob.

"I do not know why you are blaming me. I have always been a lawful wife to you and an exemplary mother for your children. I embedded them with religious piety through my breast milk."

"I shouldn't have let him go to university here," Ali's father said. "I should have immediately sent him to Cairo."

At that moment, they heard the door open and someone try to enter as quietly as possible. It was Ali. Realizing that his father would be unhappy that he was late, he tried not to make any noise and hoped that everyone would already be sleeping. Ali entered the living room, placed his foot on the Persian carpet and froze like a thief that had been caught red-handed.

"Has something happened?" Ali asked.

His mother began to sob even louder. Mustafa said nothing. He turned to his wife and ordered her to leave them in the room alone.

She left and joined the rest of the family members who had locked themselves in their rooms but were listening intently with their ears pressed up against their doors.

"Where have you been?" Ali's father asked.

"A classmate of mine asked me to visit her sick grandfather for her. I couldn't refuse."

"Ah, you couldn't refuse. And can I know why not?"

Ali was confused and did not answer. He couldn't understand why his father was so agitated.

"Why couldn't you refuse your classmate, but you easily refused your family?" his father asked. "Why did you break your promise to come to family dinner? What did you have to do that was more important than being with your family?"

"Her grandfather is ill and lives in a nursing home," Ali said.

"This is a catastrophe!" Mustafa shouted suddenly. "A total catastrophe!"

Ali had never seen his father so intensely agitated before, and he certainly had never been the cause of it. He looked at his father with surprise, unable to understand why he was acting like this. He felt guilty, even though he never imagined that being late for the dinner could make his father so angry.

"You are destroying your life, Ali. Maybe when I get a bit older you will also take me to a nursing home. It seems to be the acceptable behavior in this country to throw old people away like useless things. Maybe then, when I'm in a nursing home, your friends will visit me instead of you."

These words touched Ali and he immediately stretched out his arms and tried to hug his father.

"What are you saying, Dad?"

Mustafa pushed him away.

"What am I saying? I am telling you the truth. I am predicting the future, Ali. Since when did the words 'nursing home' become normal for you?"

"Dad, I feel the same way about this issue as you do, but it was my class-mate's request."

"Ali, whose grandfather did you visit? What is the name of your class-mate?"

Ali hung his head.

"Her name is Liz. We have been seeing each other for a few months."

"Ah, here is the real matter!" Mustafa said loudly. "Of course, it's because you are seeing a girl, who I'm sure is not even Muslim. Here we have a more important problem. Ali, don't you know that seeing a girl, dishonoring her name and not marrying her is against our faith? A man has no right to treat a girl that way, even if she is an infidel."

Ali hung his head. Without looking at his father's face, he said quietly, "Dad, I'm not dishonoring her. I really love her."

Mustafa collapsed onto the sofa.

"Ali, my son, do you love us? Your father, your mother, your brothers, Aisha?"

"Father, you are the dearest people to me in this world."

"Ali, a man's actions speak for him. Your actions have proved quite the opposite. You do not love us. You have hurt us. You have brought the curse of Allah onto your family. When a person deviates from their true faith and turns his back to the Lord, the punishment of Allah descends not only upon him, but also upon his family and all his relatives."

Ali remained quiet. He didn't want to argue about theology with his father.

"Now listen to me," Mustafa said, getting out of the armchair. "From now on, you are indefinitely forbidden to leave this house. You will not leave the house even under the pretense of going for a walk, to the mosque or even to university. You will not leave the house until you wise up and realize that there can be nothing in common between you and this girl. Also, I forbid you to use the Internet or your cell phone. You have entered into a dangerous temptation and we are going to fight against it together. Now, give me your phone and go to your room and sleep."

Ali wanted to argue with his father, but he looked so angry that Ali just gave up and went to his room silently. He sat on his bed and began to think. His father's reaction was expected. He had always taken care of his family and he was accustomed to controlling everything and making sure that everything went his way.

Perhaps when Ali got married, he'd also try to control everything in his family. Who knows? But this time, his father had punished him very severely. Ali decided he would let Liz know what happened through Patrick. It would only last a few weeks; he could survive. He was already thinking about how much Liz would miss him, but it was too late to change anything that had happened.

Ali lay down with a heavy heart and fell asleep.

13. Ali's Dream (Paris, AD 2015)

Ali had no idea what time it was when he managed to fall asleep, but the dream he had that night was unusually interesting and strange.

In the dream, Ali opened his eyes. He was in Egypt, or more precisely, in the Egyptian Pharaoh's palace, which was situated right in the middle of the desert. Ali was standing in a crowd of people who had gathered in front of the palace to attend a ceremony. The motley crew of people were clearly looking forward to the event; he could sense their excited energy.

Alongside the sounds of trumpets, Pharaoh Akhenaten came out onto the balcony, which sat on the bridge connecting the palace to the temple and greeted people with a wave. The crowd reacted to his presence with joy. Oddly enough, Professor Moshe was standing next to the pharaoh. He wore a blue suit and yellow tie, which made him stand out from the rest of the people around him. He whispered something to Akhenaten and the pharaoh nodded in consent and turned to his people.

"Aton has ordered me to say something important to my people. He wants us to turn to our only God with this prayer." Akhenaten began praying aloud and the crowd began to repeat the prayer line for line:

"Our Father, invisible but real,
May your name be forever illuminated for us!
May it be the rule of your law!
It gives light to the world of stars and our lives.
Give us this day our daily bread
And forgive us our mortal debts,
As we forgive before the sky.
Keep us away from temptation and evil.
Let's repeat the name of our God at the end: Aton."
"Aton!" the crowd shouted.

Professor Moshe was watching the prayer with a smile of satisfaction on his face. Suddenly, the professor's eyes rested on Ali and he waved to him. The professor called over one of the soldiers and told him something as he pointed to Ali.

A few minutes later, two burly men approached Ali and informed him that he was being waited for in the palace. They escorted him to the door and showed him the entryway. Ali suddenly realized that he was actually expected to enter the hall. Inside, Akhenaten was sitting on the throne. He looked exactly the way he was usually depicted on statues. His eyes had no pupils; they were simply white balls, so that it was impossible to determine which direction he was looking.

"Ali, dear, come here," came the voice of Professor Moshe. "Pharaoh, I was telling you about this boy. He is a very devout, pious boy."

Akhenaten said nothing. He didn't even turn around to look at Ali. Professor Moshe approached Ali, linked arms with him, and brought him closer to Akhenaten.

"Moshe, does the boy worship Aton?" Akhenaten asked.

"Yes," said Professor Moshe.

"No," Ali objected. "I worship the only true God, Allah, and his Prophet Muhammad."

Professor Moshe and Akhenaten burst into laughter, and everyone else in the room joined in. Ali looked at them in confusion. "Fine, keep on laughing. Two thousand years from now nobody will remember your Aton, and everyone will be on the side of the truth."

Everyone there began to laugh even harder. Akhenaten even held his belly as if he couldn't contain himself. Professor Moshe was laughing and rolling around on the carpet in his suit.

"Your naivety has no limits," Akhenaten said. "You tasted the fruit of the trees we have planted and now you dare to criticize the tree."

"There is only one truth, and it will be the same even one thousand years later."

"Truth?" Akhenaten said.

"Truth is a disease," Professor Moshe said. "Five years ago, a man named Didie was hospitalized in our clinic for a month. He had almost drowned while swimming in the river and was pronounced clinically dead. Didie made the headlines in all the tabloid newspapers. But once Didie recovered, strange things began to happen to him. For some reason, he suddenly couldn't tell a lie. He got into trouble with his family because he started responding to his wife's questions with the truth. For example, his wife learned that on the day of the accident, Didie wasn't having a barbecue with his friends, as he had said he was, but was having fun with one of his mistresses on the bank of the river. Didie had four mistresses; he would regularly disappear with them. After his betrayal turned into a huge scandal, his wife tried to reconcile herself with the situation and forgive her husband for the sake of their children. But then, in response to one of his wife's questions, Didie announced truthfully that she was ugly, fat and noisy and he would always be in search of other lovers. It turns out that Didie, suddenly stricken with the ability to only tell the truth, couldn't even give compliments, which are really only a gentler type of lie. His wife, upon hearing the unpleasant truth, left Didie and took their children with her. During the divorce trial, Didie was accused of being a sociopath. He claimed to the court that his wife was no longer attractive to him and that he had been betraying his wife by sleeping with several women at the same time. When the judge asked Didie what his wife's major drawback was, Didie replied that his wife didn't have any particular drawback, which made her different from other women. The judge then asked Didie to specify the major drawbacks of other women, and Didie said that they live too long. He said that it would be fair if women only lived twenty or thirty years because that's as long as they can be tolerated. The judge had been looking at Didie's wife compassionately during the whole hearing, and as soon as Didie uttered those last thoughts, the judge hammered on the table and announced his verdict. Didie got a quick divorce. He was accused of being a sociopath and his apartment was seized, sold and the sum handed over to his wife. Shortly after that, Didie's mistresses all left him because he told all of them the truth about the existence of the others.

Didie thought maybe his misfortunes would end there, but they were really just beginning. One day at work, in response to a customer's question about the reason for the delay of an order, he revealed that he had been smoking marijuana that day and that's why he didn't come to work, and that the day before that he had been busy masturbating to Kim Kardashian's photo. The customer was so shocked by his response that he had to be hospitalized from suffering a heart attack and Didie was fired from his job. He started to look for a new job, but his veraciousness would always hamper him. He couldn't write any false information on his CV. He could only say and write things that were the absolute truth. His life had become full of so many different problems that it was impossible to cope with all of them. Even interacting with an innocent beggar would turn into a big fight. One by one, Didie's friends began to leave him. Even his sister started avoiding him; she never called him and rarely answered the phone when he called.

Then Didie told one of his neighbors that she was too fat, and a big fight started in the elevator. He tried to justify his words, saying that he had only said it because he was concerned about the safety of the elevator, assuming that it would be difficult for the elevator to carry such a fat person. Didie then had a conflict with his doctor, telling him that he smelled awful and should shower more frequently. The doctor carefully examined Didie and said nothing. He was a bit confused by Didie's words. The doctor was intelligent enough to understand what his patient was saying, but he was shocked at how the patient was right three times in a row! Didie was telling the truth – only he was telling it not the way others usually did by suddenly blurting it out in response to being insulted. He was telling the truth because he honestly felt that it was right.

Didie was tired of telling the truth. He would love to be able to tell a lie to solve at least one of the problems in his life, but he couldn't. Anything that wasn't somehow related to the truth ceased to enter his head. His brain refused to utter a lie. The doctor looked at Didie with bewilderment. Under normal circumstances, he would be offended by anyone who said such vulgar and rude things. But the doctor couldn't suspect Didie of intentionally insulting him; neither could he doubt the truth of Didie's words. After all, Didie had come to him with that problem. He could not lie; therefore he would always tell the truth. It was the first time anyone had told the doctor that he smelled bad. In fact, he had smelled bad for a long time and no one else around him had even hinted anything to him about it, even out of courtesy. Actually, the doctor suddenly recalled that during regular meetings his colleagues would ask him about the shower gel he used and he would give lengthy explanations like a simpleton. The doctor began to consider that he had been being mocked.

'How long have you had this problem?' the doctor asked Didie.

'For about a year,' said Didie. 'I have lost everything: my family, my job, my friends. I lost them all because I have been telling them the truth, and people hate the truth.'

The doctor stared at Didie in stupefied amazement.

'Do you think people like being lied to?' the doctor asked.

'Let me be clearer, doctor. The problem is not so much in the effect of a lie as it is in the absence of the truth. People hide the truth. Certain social conventions act as a veil behind which the truth is concealed. Please, admit that even you didn't like what I said, and you already have a negative opinion of me.'

The doctor said that he was used to hearing more terrible things from his patients. Didie sighed and turned to the window. 'I don't know what bad things you have heard from other patients, but judging by the fact that you were taken aback by my directness, you hadn't heard the truth until now. The truth is the hardest thing; it is too thick to swallow. Doctor, can you help me? Will I ever be healed?' The doctor said that every disease stems from a deeper problem. It all has to do with consciousness and subconsciousness, and he would have been lying if he said that he had ever encountered such a case. After a few seconds of silence, the doctor said, 'You're ill. Terminally ill.'"

As he concluded his story, Professor Moshe said that the doctors had already proven that the truth was a disease. At that moment, a herald's voice could be heard.

"Queen Nefertiti is coming."

Everybody stepped aside to let the queen through. Nefertiti entered the hall with her majestic gait. Ali froze. Nefertiti was Liz.

"Liz!" Ali shouted. "What are you doing here? Are you Akhenaten's wife?"

"Yes!" Liz exclaimed. "Akhenaten loves me just the way that I am. Your parents were against our marriage, and I agreed to become Akhenaten's wife."

Akhenaten, getting to his feet, opened his wings and flew out through the window toward the sun. The room filled with royal beetles. Liz looked at Ali for a few seconds and flew out the window after Akhenaten.

Ali woke up in a cold sweat.

In the morning, Ali asked his sister to call Patrick on his behalf and ask for a visit. At first, Aisha refused to help him, but when Ali explained that he needed to borrow books from him, Aisha got permission from her mother and made the call.

His mother was setting the table for tea that morning, shaking her head and discussing the previous night's events with Aisha. "Ali shouldn't have behaved like that with us. He does not have the right. We love Ali too much," his mother said. Realizing that her words could possibly make Aisha jealous, she added, "Your father and I love all our children very much. Allah has commanded us to do so."

"Mom, is Ali guilty if he loves that girl? Isn't there another option in that case?" Aisha asked, digging in her bag for her phone.

"Aisha, be quiet. What are you saying? We moved from Syria to Paris to create a safe and comfortable life for you, not to turn our back on Allah. To tell you the truth, your father had always been against this move. I convinced him that it would be better for our children. He said that it would be difficult to maintain our traditions in a big city full of temptations, but I said that Allah would help us get through all sorts of hardships. Now every time a problem occurs, he looks at me with accusation in his eyes. Of course, he says nothing. He doesn't actually make any accusations, but the looks he gives just kill me."

"Mommy, look at the photo a friend of mine posted on Facebook." Aisha held out her phone to her mother. She seemed not to have been listening to her speak at all.

Her mother picked up the phone and looked at it quickly. "Aisha, the girl that Ali sees… is she here?"

"Do you mean on Facebook? Of course she is. She's in Ali's list of friends."

"Will you show me? I want to see the girl whose beauty has enchanted my son."

Aisha looked for Liz's profile and then handed her phone to her mother. Her mother turned her attention to Liz's photo.

"She is pretty," her mother said with a gentle smile on her face. Then she immediately gathered herself and added, "But Ali is more handsome."

"She is not a bad girl," Aisha said. "But she probably has no idea that Ali is having problems with his family because of her."

"Aisha," her mother said, after thinking a moment, "What if you tell her about it?"

"Whom? Ali?"

"No, that girl. After all, Ali and his family are suffering because of her, but she does not know about it. Maybe if you explain it to her like a sister, she will understand. Aisha, it is unfair that she doesn't know about it. Ali keeps her in happy ignorance. That poor girl is going to suffer most of all."

"What can I say to her? 'Hello, Ali's family hates you.' Mom, you can't say things like that in this country."

"No, not like that. Just try to explain that Ali is a different kind of man and that their union is impossible. Just explain it to her in detail. After all, you are also a girl. Tell me, how fair would it be if you were dating a guy and you didn't know the truth about him?"

"Ok, Mom. I'll message Liz on Facebook."

Aisha went to her room, turned on the computer and opened Liz's Facebook page to write a message. She wrote: "Hello, Liz."

A few minutes later, Liz replied, "Hi! Do I know you?"

"I am Ali's sister."

"Really? Hello, Aisha, I'm happy to meet you. Do you know where Ali is? I haven't heard from him since yesterday!"

"Ali is at home. Liz, I think we need to talk."

"Ok, let's talk! Is everything ok?"

"Yes, in general, everything is ok. But Ali came home late yesterday, and our father is a little angry with him."

"Oh, I see. Ali went to visit my grandfather. If I knew that it would become such a big problem, I wouldn't have let him do it. But what do you mean he 'came home late?' Ali is a grown man and has a personal life. He is not a little kid."

"Well, I wanted to talk to you about this issue. Let's talk like two sisters. Please, try to understand me."

"Has something happened? I don't understand."

"Liz, Ali was born into a Muslim family, just like me. In a Muslim family, it is not customary to defy your parents' word or to be late for family gatherings or prayers. Maybe it sounds strange to you, but it is our culture. You come from another faith and nationality. I understand if what I'm saying, especially because it's in a Facebook message, may seem strange or not serious to you, but believe me, there is an insurmountable amount of cultural and religious differences between you and Ali."

"Wait a minute, what are you talking about? You said that we should talk like sisters. Ali and I love each other. Ali and I understand each other. What disconnect can there be? How can there be a disconnect between two people who love each other?"

"Liz, please! Listen to me."

"Doesn't Ali love me? Is there someone else in his life?"

"Ali loves you. Actually, he loves you very much. And it's because he loves you so much that he has created so many problems in his family."

"Problems in his family? What does his family have to do with us?"

"Liz, our father brought us from Syria to Paris to try to make our lives more secure."

"I don't understand. Do I pose some sort of threat to Ali?"

"Let me explain. Our father is against your union. He doesn't just feel that way for no reason. It's based on the requirements of our religion and culture."

"What does our 'union' mean? We are not married yet. Ali hasn't proposed, and even if he does, I'm not sure that I'm ready for marriage right now. As for your father's position, unfortunately, he does not have any influence in these matters. He made a choice once and he chose your mother. Only then did he have the right to have any position on being for or against marriage. Only then."

"Liz, that's not the way it works. This is why I said that there is a difference in mindset."

"And what is the difference? Is it the fact that you do not eat pork, but my parents do? You have become a prisoner of conventionalities."

"As a sister, I can tell you that the difference is not just about pork. I can't believe you have such a superficial understanding of our religion when the person you are going to spend your life with comes from that religion.

"You are assuming things again! I repeat: I'm not going to get married in the near future. According to my religion, marriage is too big of a responsibility and you shouldn't make such an important decision so hastily."

"Liz, Ali loves you. Judging from your reaction, you also love him. Why don't you try to understand me?"

"Do you understand how it sounds to me? You wrote me and said 'Hello, Liz, I'm Ali's sister. Ali's family is against you.'"

"The problem is not you."

"Well then what is the problem? My religion? My parents? My nationality?"

"Liz, even if Ali goes against his parents' wishes and continues to go out with you, you will still feel rejected. You will be the person who Ali went against his parents and religious beliefs for."

"Oh my god. You have insulted me in every possible way."

"This is the truth, Liz. If your relationship continues, Ali will also be rejected by his family."

After that, Liz did not respond for almost fifteen minutes. She had clearly seen the message, but there was no response. Aisha was about to shut off the computer when a message came from Liz.

"Aisha, my sister, I love Ali. He is a caring, sensitive man. Such men are rare these days. I feel like a princess when I am with him. I don't want to go into the details of our relationship, but I'm sure that what you said about your family's position is true. I am sure that because of me Ali has had a lot of trouble, which he hid from me. I do not want to hurt my beloved man. My presence in his life has made him suffer in secret. I have been a frivolous girl who didn't understand what was going on. Yesterday, he himself persuaded me that he wanted to visit my grandfather so that we could spend an extra half hour together. But it doesn't matter. We can't continue this. Today I will break all my ties with Ali. I will no longer see him, and I won't communicate with him by phone or Internet. Tomorrow, I'll go to my university and switch my group. I think this is the right decision. I can't become the reason for my beloved one's suffering. Stay well, Aisha, God bless you."

Aisha didn't know what to say, so she just turned off the computer and sat deep in thought. She knew how Liz must be feeling and could see the tears between the lines of her last message. Girls her age were usually obsessed with the torments and passions of love. At parties, they would talk about all the exciting things that happened with their boyfriends and sometimes even shared details of their sexual relationships. Aisha felt more comfortable playing the role of the audience, although some of the stories she heard would made her blush from embarrassment. She was only allowed to go on dates with her mother's permission and her father's knowledge, and only if the guy was going to start a family with her. Aisha sometimes felt envious of Liz and the way she remained brave and independent even in her sufferings. Liz at least had the power to make her own decisions about whether she should continue to see Ali or if she should break up with him, whereas Aisha was deprived the right to make decisions about her own destiny.

Aisha was deep in thought when the doorbell rang. She came out of her room and opened the front door. Patrick, Ali's classmate, was standing on the doorstep.

"Hello Aisha!" Patrick said and blushed slightly.

"Hello Patrick. Come in. I'll tell Ali that you're here," Aisha said.

"Ali! Your friend Patrick is here," Aisha said from the other side of the door.

Aisha motioned to Patrick to sit down on the couch. "Ali is coming out soon. Have a seat."

"Merci, mademoiselle," Patrick said with a smile and settled himself on the sofa.

Ali poked his head out of his bedroom door and saw Patrick. "Come to my room. We need to talk."

"Old chap, has something happened?" Patrick asked.

"Nothing special. Let's go to my room and I'll tell you."

The boys shut themselves in Ali's room to talk about their boyish topics. Aisha stood in the living room for a few moments with a smile on her face and then went to the kitchen.

Meanwhile, Ali and Patrick were having a very serious conversation. Ali told Patrick about the previous day's events and how his father had punished him by depriving him of all means of communication with Liz.

"Yes, old chap, you have problems. I don't even know what to tell you," Patrick said.

"Ok well while you're busy thinking about what advice to give me, give me your phone, I want to call Liz to explain everything, especially my absence in her life."

Patrick handed over his phone. Ali, unable to contain his excitement about calling Liz, dialed her number, which he remembered by heart.

"Hello Liz. It's not Patrick. It's me, Ali. Liz? Liz?"

"What?" Patrick asked, "What did she say?"

"The phone turned off. The connection probably was lost."

Ali repeatedly tried to call Liz, but there was no answer.

"Maybe it's not a convenient time. Maybe she's taking an exam or she's in class."

"I guess so," Ali said in despair. "Otherwise she has no reason to ignore my calls."

"Listen, will this punishment last long? What do you think?"

"I don't know, but my father is quite angry. I'm not sure, but it will probably last at least a week."

"And what are you going to do? How are you going to kill time?" Patrick asked, examining Ali's room.

"I have no idea. Maybe I'll just read to kill time until the punishment is over."

"Listen, you know what I am thinking?" Patrick said in a whisper.

"What?"

"If Liz doesn't call you back today, do you think you can sneak out tonight?

"Theoretically, yes. Anything is possible. But only after the rest of the family falls asleep. Where should I sneak out to?"

"Tonight we're all going to a nightclub to celebrate the successful end of the exam season. You're going to sneak out, come to the nightclub, do your hanky-panky with your beloved Liz all night, explain everything to her, and then come back to your room in the morning. By the way, you should bring Aisha with you." Patrick tried to utter these last words with indifference, but he obviously failed to. If Ali hadn't been so preoccupied with getting in touch with Liz, he would have noticed Patrick's face, which had turned beet red.

"Is the club far?" Ali asked.

"It's at the other end of the city, but it won't take you long to get there and come back home by taxi. Since you don't have a computer or phone, let me write down the name and address of the club on a piece of paper. I think you'll find it easily."

"Well, write down the address and I will try to come. I'm just wondering how I'll come back. Perhaps I'll take Aisha's keys."

Patrick wrote something on a piece of paper and put it on the table.

"Look old chap Ali Baba, I'm leaving the address here. When you get to the club, tell the guard that you are a participant of the student corporate event. Anyway, I will bring you a ticket and let them know we are waiting for someone. Should you have any difficulties, tell them to call Patrick. Ok, let me go finish all the things I have to do."

The two friends bid farewell to each other and Patrick came out of the room.

"Where are you going, Patrick? Let's have a cup of coffee at least," Ali's mother called from the kitchen.

"Thank you, Madame. Another time, though," Patrick said and left his friend's house quickly.

14. Crusader Knights' Letters to Pope Urban II (Clermont, AD 1096)

"What news do we have from the east?" Urban asked, settling himself on the palanquin. "How are the pilgrimages going?"

Odo placed a bundle of papers and parchments on the table and began to dig through them carefully.

"I will choose the most important ones now and report to you."

"Report all of them to me. I am not in a hurry," Urban said sharply, "Odo, in any case, remember that it's me who decides what is relevant and what is not. Report to me about every letter you have. I will decide the degree of their importance."

"It will take a few days to read out all the letters. They mostly contain good wishes and requests for papal blessings, which are accompanied by self-praise," Odo said, not even noticing Urban's obvious dissatisfaction. "I have selected the ones that more or less give detailed descriptions of military actions. These days, each commander is giving a large sum of money to his letter writer to present his feats with all sorts of grace, while sidelining others' activities. If we take those letters at face value, we will never know the truth. Each of the letters gives the impression that the commander is carrying out the entire campaign by himself and all the other commanders are pure cowards and parasites."

"Here they are," Odo continued, showing the bundle of papers to Urban. "Hugh, the younger brother of the King of France, wrote to you. He sends you greetings, reiterates his faithfulness, and requests papal blessings, not forgetting to mention that he is more devoted to the pope than his brother."

"Maybe that is so," Urban said.

"Maybe he has an eye on his brother's throne," Odo said with a grin.

"Listen, have you heard of the new commander? His name is Mark. He is said to be from Germany," Urban said. "It has been reported to me that he is known by the name Mark Ruthless. I heard that he is resourceful and strong-willed and that he fights like a lion."

"He is an unknown man of unknown descent who has become famous exclusively because of this campaign. We have no specific information about his past. It can therefore be assumed that he is an ordinary plebeian by origin. It is claimed that he served a knight as a groom and begun his own military career after the knight's death, though I can't guarantee the truthfulness of this information. Mark himself is carefully concealing his past. No one knows anything precise about him, though I can agree with you that he fights like a lion. His army suffers the least amount of losses in battle, and what is most interesting is that they always come out as the winners. He is said to be very strict with his soldiers, and there are a lot of interesting stories of his participation in battles. I'll rearrange the letters now in the necessary sequence and then I will refer to him by all means."

"And what do the other commanders write about him?" Urban asked.

"The other commanders are constantly complaining about him. They call him an illiterate man with no origins who has no mastery of martial arts, doesn't know anything about the differences between types of firearms, and even has to study battle strategies during the course of the campaign. His knowledge of Christianity is very scarce. He doesn't know theology at all. He is arrogant and rude with the knights and other commanders. I think we can confidently conclude from the various complaints made about Mark that he must be a very good commander. Otherwise, others wouldn't be filled with such envy and wouldn't be trying to smear his name."

"You are drawing quite an interesting conclusion, Odo. Do you think that if others are complaining about him then he must be a good man?"

"I didn't say that he is a good man. I don't know what kind of man he is and frankly that isn't so important. I just came to the conclusion that he is a good commander. After all, the driving force leading the other commanders to the east is the military glory, which I'm sure they are planning to turn into political power and influence in the future. The greater their glory in the battlefield, the greater their political influence will be in the future during times of peace. The commanders who are glorified in the battlefield the most will get the greatest number of benefits."

"It is quite logical," Urban said.

"It is also logical that there is now a fierce competition between the commanders. They are all spending huge sums of money to leave their mark on history. In that regard, their activity is first and foremost geared toward winning your favor. So essentially their fierce fighting is a performance being staged specifically for you. They are ready to take each other down in order to increase the value of their own exploits. Logically, the commander, who others see as the strongest rival, will be denigrated the most, and if everyone vilifies the same person independently of each other, that means that they will all consider him their archrival. Hence, it can be concluded that Mark is doing much more in the battlefield than all of them combined. By the way, we've received the least number of letters from Mark. Actually, we hadn't received any letters from him until recently, with the exception of a couple of good wishes and blessings. Mark started to write about his military actions only recently."

"And what did he write?" Urban asked.

"Nothing particularly interesting. As usual, he took an interest in your health and wrote a few words about the military situation. He mostly just described his own actions without mentioning the faults and shortcomings of others. If you are interested in the military situation, we had better read the letter from Raymond of Toulouse, in which everything is described thoroughly and properly. Of course, Raymond's letters need to be combined with Bishop Adhemar's letters so that then we can get a really accurate picture of what's happening."

"Very good. We will come back to Commander Mark later. Send him a letter with my blessings by all means. He earned it. And now, present Raymond of Toulouse's letter so that we can understand what's happening on the frontline of the Crusader's pilgrimage," Urban commanded, crossing himself.

Odo took out one of the letters and began to read. "To the Holy Priest, Beacon of God's Light, Urban II. Your Holiness, after walking for four months, the knights finally reached Constantinople. Emperor Alexander invited the chief commanders of the campaign to his palace that same day. The emperor received us with all due honors. At the evening feast, he demanded that all the lands and towns that will be liberated by the Crusaders pass under the domination of Byzantium, that is, to Emperor Alexander. He demanded from all the commanders participating in the campaign to take a solemn oath of adherence to his conditions. The emperor also said that his conditions stipulated that after the pilgrimage was over, the Crusaders would return to Europe and the protection of the liberated areas and their subjugation to the pope would be handled by him and his military forces. He said that we were all fighting for the same goal, and that goal was to destroy the non-believers and establish papal power."

"A quite interesting approach," the pope said. "It's a little hard to understand, but is still extremely interesting. First, Emperor Alexander asks the troops for favors, and then he sets requirements to those favors."

"Again, I will refer to logic," Odo said, interrupting the pope. "Alexander only asked for a small decrease in security from you, and we initiated a large-scale campaign. We may have named it a pilgrimage, but the essence of the campaign didn't change. The knights are not busy preaching in the east. They are liberating all the settlements, town by town. Thus, there arises the problem of subordinating those settlements, towns and castles. Do we have enough troops to keep the liberated castles under our control? Will our knights establish permanent residences in those towns? Alexander has raised very specific questions, and he did it with his usual trickery. Therefore, our knights began to beware of him."

"Well, keep reading," the pope commanded. "Let's see how this issue has been resolved."

Odo found the line where he had left off and continued. "At first, such conditions seemed unacceptable to us. Alexander was trying to convince us that it would be better for all of us, otherwise he threatened not to support the campaign in any way. By the time we reached Constantinople, the army's food supply was almost depleted. Without Alexander's help, we would be unable to move forward. Even the pope's representative, Bishop Adhemar, didn't know how to advise us. Finally, after consulting each other, the commanders accepted Alexander's conditions. We all took an oath to cede the liberated lands to Byzantium, but Bishop Adhemar set a condition that the oath must be approved by Pope Urban II, otherwise it would lose its power. Alexander fulfilled this condition and took the army to the Bosporus in the morning. We said goodbye to the European continent and made our way into the depths of the enemy's settlements. Emperor Alexander apparently didn't want us around much longer because our transportation across the

Bosporus was organized as quickly as possible. Five days later, there was no one left from our troops on the European coast."

"Look what a good response Adhemar gave," Urban said. "When they failed to make a decision themselves, they assigned the right to decide to me. Bravo! What a commendable solution!"

"A week later, the Crusaders surrounded the non-believers' town of Nicaea. Before the siege of Nicaea, a battle was fought, which was marked by a very interesting incident. We learned of the existence of a certain type of soldier in the Turkish army called a horse archer. They are very unique fighters if you think about how significant they can be. Horse archers surround their enemies during battle and begin to ride around them shooting arrows. They are not directly involved in the middle of the battle; thus it becomes very difficult to strike the horse archers with swords and nearly impossible for our archers to target them because their horses are moving too fast. The damage caused by these archers is incalculable since no armor can prevent you from getting hit by arrows at a short distance. After a short consultation, we decided we had to participate in the battle since God Almighty has our back and his curse is on the non-believers. Our cavalry moved to the battlefield and took up their positions. The non-believers released their horse archers. As it turned out, there was a large number of them. After the war trumpet sounded, the Crusader knights began the attack and, to everybody's surprise, the Crusaders' horses, which were exclusively military mares, went out of control and began to run toward the non-believers' horse archers. The non-believers' horses also didn't obey the commands they were given to retreat; they would run a short distance and then stop, thus allowing our knights to gain ground. As they approached the horse archers, the knights immediately killed them. It seemed that the horses on both sides had forgotten how to obey their masters and were just doing whatever they wanted. Our knights took advantage of this situation and quickly killed the non-believers' archers and won the battle without any difficulties."

"Do you see, Odo, what it means to have the blessings of the almighty God?" Urban smiled. "This is more proof that we are on the right track. Our cause is just! The non-believers do not have any chance of winning this fight, even though their troops are much more prepared than ours."

"I really can't find the right words, but I think that all this must have a logical explanation," Odo said skeptically and then continued to read. "After the battle was over, this interesting phenomenon continued; our knights' horses continued their unruly behavior and were running through the non-believers' field, chasing the horses left with no rider. Later, when the horses began to mate voraciously, everything became clear. As I noted earlier, our cavalry rode on the best mares, and as it turned out, the non-believers had bays. Our horses, seeing such an enticing group of females, couldn't resist and proceeded to sexually harass them on the battlefield. It seems the love between the animals won the battle, which had begun with unequal forces. Holy Priest, in your sermons and prayers you would always highlight the importance of love and the manifestations thereof in a Christian's life. Love is a tremendous power and it can create miracles, even if it is experienced by animals. We have seen it with our own eyes. With humility, we yearn for the blessings of Your Holiness. I must also add that we encircled Nicaea and the town surrendered after a two-month siege, but during this time a small event occurred that diminished the joy of victory in our eyes."

"Everything is in the hands of the Almighty," Urban noted. "Not a leaf falls without his knowledge. Continue reading, I wonder what happened during the liberation of Nicaea."

"I can already imagine that field after the battle, with hundreds of horses indulging themselves in amorous delights next to the dead bodies of the non-believers," Odo laughed.

"Odo, continue!" the pope yelled.

"Within two months of the siege of Nicaea, the troops in the castle became panic-stricken. According to our information, the food supplies were depleted and drinking water supplies were also coming to an end. The non-believers, with their small troops, had no chance of entering an open battle with us. Surrender of Nicaea was a matter of days. Two months later, the commandant of Nicaea delivered a speech in which he announced his intention to surrender the town, but to the Byzantine Emperor, not the Crusaders. It turned out that Alexander had sent a secret envoy to Nicaea who persuaded the commandant of the castle to surrender to the emperor, promising to protect the non-believers from our retribution. This fact was of course perceived negatively by the commanders of the campaign since we had already sworn to Alexander in Constantinople that we would hand over the liberated towns to Byzantium with your blessing. Alexander's step was a cunning conspiracy against the Crusaders, who left Nicaea empty-handed after a two-month siege. Of course, we were still going to stay true to our own oath and hand over Nicaea to Emperor Alexander, but through his actions Alexander did not receive the city from us, but rather took it out of our hands. Again, we expect your blessings, which your Vicar Bishop Adhemar conveys to us every day. Your prayers accompany us and make our army invincible. The non-believers are in a panic, and the Crusaders will reach Jerusalem in two or three weeks if they continue to advance with this energy. With humility, your unworthy servant, Duke Raymond of Toulouse."

Odo finished reading and glanced at Urban with a quizzical look.

"Alexander surely committed fraud," Urban said angrily. "He will definitely pay for it! Now send him a letter and congratulate him on the annexation of Nicaea with a sarcastic tone. Let the sarcasm be obvious and severe. I want him to understand that he has been deprived of my mercy."

"Is that all?" Odo asked in surprise. "Shall we confine ourselves only to sending him a sarcastic congratulatory letter?"

"It will be all for now. We won't undertake anything else yet," Urban answered nervously. "Our troops are almost entirely in the east. Much depends on Alexander now and he knows this, so he is pushing the limits of what is acceptable."

"But still, I don't see anything dangerous in Alexander's behavior," Odo announced after thinking about it. "Yes, his little act left an unpleasant aftertaste, but the end of the campaign is still far off, and our troops continue to depend on Alexander."

"What do you mean by saying that the end is still far off?" Urban asked. "Raymond wrote in his letter that they will be in Jerusalem in a couple of weeks."

Odo gave a quiet laugh.

"That letter was written four months ago. According to my information, the pilgrims are still in the Taurus Mountains. Taurus is impassable. It will be too difficult for them to overcome that part of the road, even without facing any battles. After the Taurus Mountains, there are several big cities in their way, like Edessa, Antioch, and Damascus. Only after overcoming all those trials will they approach Jerusalem. According to our data, Antioch is the toughest stronghold in their way. So, Raymond of Toulouse's letter should be viewed only as a military glorification."

"That's not good," Urban frowned. "What is your prognosis regarding this matter?"

Odo thought deeply about his calculations.

"I'm sure it will take more than a year," said Odo. "And that is only if no insurmountable obstacles arise."

Urban fell deep in thought. He did not like Odo's prognosis.

"Well, we'll talk about this further," Urban said. "And what were you going to say about Commander Mark? What has he become known for?"

"Nothing was known about Commander Mark until the massacre of the Jews in the German city of Worms," Odo explained.

"I seem to recall those events. You are speaking about the clashes before the actual campaign, aren't you?"

"Yes," Odo confirmed. "What's interesting is that Mark and his supporters already had problems with lack of nutrition and money long before reaching the city of Worms. He organized the massacres of the rich Jews living there as a way to fix his problems and justified it by saying that Christ was killed by the Jews, so they should be hated by Christians just as much as non-believers. His supporters destroyed everything in Worms, killing all the Jews and seizing their property and money. It was in that city that he gained the nickname "Ruthless." Mark's army humbly obeys him and is ready to execute even the craziest commands. He is said to be a born commander and his military talent is innate."

At that moment the door of the pope's study opened quietly, and a mace-bearing cardinal poked his head through the half-opened door and asked, "Holy Priest, may I come in?"

Urban's eyes rounded in anger. "Of course you may not! Can't you see that my advisor Odo and I are discussing issues related to the Crusade?"

The cardinal became flustered. "I am sorry, Your Holiness. I did not realize."

"And do you realize now? Leave and spare me the trouble of repeating the same thing over and over again. When I am with my adviser, try to never bother me for any reason."

The cardinal didn't say anything, he just bowed his head and walked out the door.

"I am tired of repeating the same thing over and over!" Urban said angrily. "Is it so hard to understand that they should not bother me when I am with you? I do not think that my cardinals are that dim; rather it might be because of your unfavorable attitude toward my courtiers. They don't like you, Odo, and they pointedly ignore your existence every time. Odo, please think about my words and try to do something about this unpleasant situation. Try to establish good relations, okay? Odo?"

But Odo was not in the room. The letters from Raymond of Toulouse and the other commanders were still lying on the table. There was no one else in the room except Urban.

15. Crusaders in Antioch (AD 1098)

The walls of Antioch were impregnable. They were made of stone as tall as ten people and were so thick that you could easily build something inside them.

Mark did not have a particularly large army. A considerable portion of his troops had abandoned their positions because of heavy rainfall around the Taurus. The rain had made the foot of the Taurus impassable, and it had turned into a graveyard for many soldiers. After the military incidents in Edessa, the number of soldiers had gone down. After every military battle, the army would grow more worn out and weary; only one third of the original army of Crusaders was now standing near the walls of Antioch and they were all strongly disheartened. Now, looking at Antioch's impenetrable walls, optimism among the Crusaders waned further.

None of the Crusaders, even those who had seen several wars and bloody battles, could imagine how they could take the castle of Antioch. Only a miracle from God could help the pilgrims conquer the castle. After all, they had walked thousands of miles to get there.

One of the commanders was trying to stand out by showing the rest of the army that he was the smartest commander and that his troops were the most blessed. Approaching the town gate, he suggested with a commanding voice that the residents of Antioch surrender themselves to the favor of the Lord's pilgrims, threatening to be relentless if they disobeyed. There was no response from Antioch. The town was silent, just like the stone walls surrounding it. There was nothing left for the Crusaders to try in their quest to seize Antioch.

A few months after the siege, at the call of Bishop Adhemar, all women were dismissed from their army camp. The bishop said that God had turned his back on the Crusaders because they had diverted from their sacred purpose and were indulging in fornication and other vulgar behavior that wasn't representative of holy soldiers. Even dismissing all the women from the Crusaders' camp didn't ensure any military progress in Antioch. The castle remained as inaccessible as ever.

In the evening, the military commanders, along with their advisors, convened in their tent to discuss the insurmountable problems that had arisen in capturing Antioch. It had already been two months since the pilgrims started standing under the walls of the castle and there was still no progress. Most of the commanders were encountering such a wall for the very first time. Of course, they were military leaders with great military experience, but generally European castles had walls made of wooden beams and were much smaller in size. The commanders hadn't experienced a month-long siege before, unless the irregular gatherings under Antioch's walls could be considered a siege.

"Our troops have tried all possible and impossible means to overcome the non-believers," Raymond of Toulouse announced. "I, as the head of the campaign, have organized this meeting so that we could jointly discuss our future actions. Initially, we had no idea that we would encounter such difficulties. It seemed to us that we would enter Antioch very quickly. The length of the wall was too big for our small army to completely encircle the castle and deprive its residents of their food supply. Only an army four times bigger than ours could have a chance to encircle a wall of such length. Emperor Alexander sent us weapons to attack the wall, but our soldiers didn't know how to handle them. Later he sent some people who came and showed us how they worked, but they turned out to be needless tools. It was impossible to destroy the wall with them. The tools were meant to throw at the wall, but they were so small that once they hit the gates they would break. Then one of the military leaders – if I'm not mistaken, it was you, Hugh – suggested that we use the tools to launch putrid animal heads and other body parts inside Antioch's walls to try and spread an epidemic inside. Hugh is the highest representative of the French court in the Middle East and was trying to show off his intellectual superiority over the others."

"Yes Raymond, you're right. That was my advice. But we need to wait a little for an epidemic to break out. It takes more than just a few days."

"And how long do we have to wait?" Gottfried of Lotharingia asked. "Please inform us, Hugh. How long do we still have to stand here being fried under the sun in hope that a plague will break out in Antioch?"

"Well, I do not know. Everything is in the hands of the Almighty," Hugh said.

"Everything is in the hands of the Almighty... usually people use this expression to conceal their own failures and misfortunes," Gottfried said. "Dear, this is not a royal romance, this is a war. Every day people are dying here. Half of my friends are already in another world. We need to understand everything. What if Antioch is our last destination and we have no chance of moving forward from here? What if we have reached the capacity of our troops? Anyone who comes after us will just be continuing our work. We conquered the capital of non-believers in Nicaea, we took Edessa, we passed through the floods of Mount Taurus, and this is our last harbor. Antioch will be conquered by people who will come after us, for whom we have already paved the way."

Gottfried was angry. He was tired of everyone's pointless actions. He was tired of this group of blindly enthusiastic young people who had no idea what war was and who didn't appreciate the life of a soldier. It would be another question if there was an open battle at Antioch; Gottfried only derived pleasure from life or death battles. But simply sleeping under a castle wall for months was not only boring, it was pointless. Gottfried could no longer make his troops understand why they were staying there. His troops, a military unit consisting of the most experienced fighters, laughed at the idea of throwing putrid horse heads. His army considered such a move as weak, which may be excusable for a young lover, but never for an army commander responsible for an entire army. Gottfried had been really looking forward to speaking out about all these things in front of everybody at the consultation. Hugh's only goal in life was to prove to his brother, the King of France, that he was also a descendant of the royal family, so he used every opportunity to stand out. His suggestions were full of youthful romanticism, which had nothing to do with military affairs.

Nevertheless, there were actually still soldiers on his side. Gottfried was surprised, especially since those types of naive strategies should have caused great losses among his troops, but oddly enough, Hugh's army had suffered the least.

"Gottfried, dear, what would you suggest?" Hugh asked with a smirk. "To surrender or retreat? Please, feel free to choose. Your soldiers make up such a small part of the total number of our troops that I really don't think your decision would affect the outcome."

"I can't understand why you think there is something funny about what I said," said Gottfried. "You, my dear, can't understand simple things. You're a nobleman whose whole life has been far removed from the battlefield. You are only here to oppose your brother. You don't really value a soldier's life at all, and winning this battle is just the same as winning a children's game. Hugh, you can't even imagine what a risky undertaking a war is."

"But my soldiers have suffered the least here. I know you're just going to say that most of your soldiers died at the foot of Mount Taurus in the downpours, but I do not think that is a justification. A skilled military leader should not just have strength, but also an above average intelligence and a particular set of military skills."

Hugh's last words made Gottfried smile broadly. Now it was his turn to mock him.

"I can't help but smile at the fact that I'm being told about intelligence and military skills from a child. I've participated in as many battles as years that you've been alive. I have led as many soldiers as you have hairs on your head. I began my service as a soldier, not a specialist of the lush life or of palace intrigues. Now I'm being lectured on morality by a man whose life goal is fighting his own brother and wandering across the Middle East in search of land to seize and proclaim his kingdom; a man who is looking for exploits and giving military lessons to those who are older and more experienced than him."

Raymond did not like the direction the conversation was going in. Two of the commanders were openly accusing and mocking each other.

"Excuse me if I am interrupting your logomachy, but don't you think that now is not the time for this? Today we have gathered not to criticize each other or praise ourselves, but to find a way out of this situation. I would like to ask you to speak only about this matter, without addressing anyone else. We have a situation that demands solutions, not criticism. Do we have intelligence data concerning the town of Antioch? I would like to ask the commanders to keep silent and only let the military experts speak."

One of the military experts came forward and began to speak. "The intelligence data is as follows: the walls of the town are the height of ten people, the width of five steps, and the length of forty kilometers. There are four hundred guard towers along the entire length of the wall. The food and water supplies in Antioch are more abundant than ours. It is impossible to completely encircle and take the town; the number of soldiers we have wouldn't even allow us to encircle half of the city. It is also impossible to destroy the walls. Even the siege engines that we waited two weeks for proved useless. Even approaching the castle is a problem because the guards are always awake and have their archers ready to strike any area under attack."

Another expert, who represented external intelligence directions, said, "I would just like to add that a large Turkish army is heading toward Antioch. Turkish princes have finally joined their forces against the Crusaders and their united army is moving toward us."

"And what would you advise in this situation?" Raymond asked.

The military expert looked confused. He knew how to present all the numbers and figures, but he had no idea how to offer any practical solutions.

"Please go ahead; we are listening to you," Raymond said.

"I have no suggestions," the military expert said with embarrassment. "It is the first time our troops have encountered such a problem. Our experience is useless here."

"What do you mean?" asked Raymond.

"I think we need to retreat and give way for the next pilgrims, who will probably know what to do," Gottfried said.

"Gottfried of Lotharingia, if you violate the consultation procedure once again you will not be asked to leave, you will be removed. There should be order at all times, especially during war."

Gottfried muttered something under his breath.

"Would you like to add anything, Hugh?" Raymond asked.

"First of all, as a nobleman, I would like to ask for your forgiveness for not restraining myself from being rude to Gottfried of Lotharingia. The impossibility of the situation is clear before us. The military experts are not able to suggest any solutions. We have tried everything in the battlefield, but to no avail. Maybe God doesn't want us to move forward for reasons known only to him; I do not know. Either way, it is clear we are desperate. If we do not find a solution during this consultation, I will consider Gottfried's suggestion and retreat to Edessa, which I had conquered. There, I will wait for the next generation of pilgrims who might know how to advance past the stone walls. I will join with them and come back to Antioch having made a final decision to capture it."

Raymond looked at the military leaders attentively. He could see despair on their faces. They had spent two years and four months walking to the Holy Land with the intention of liberating it, and now, when they were so close to their final goal, an impossible stone castle had halted them. It was not an easy decision to retreat. For one, it was almost as risky as going forward with the campaign. And if they returned home empty handed everyone would surely laugh at them. No one in all of Europe would ever take those men seriously if they tried to liberate the Holy Land and decided to change their minds right before they reached Jerusalem.

Raymond looked toward Commander Mark, who had been sitting quietly without interfering in the argument between Gottfried and Hugh or in the opinions of the military experts. He just sat there with his eyes glued to one point.

Raymond turned to him. "And you, Commander Mark? Maybe you could express your opinion so we can finish this consultation? As you heard, both the military experts and the commanders agree that we should go back. I also support this position, and after listening to your speech, I'm sure that we should choose the way back."

Mark listened to Raymond without interruption. There was silence in the tent. Everyone was convinced that Mark was going to share their opinion, at least to avoid staying alone in Antioch.

"Let's agree that Antioch will become the property of the commander whose soldiers manage to enter the castle walls first."

Mark's words seemed to be going in a completely different direction. The military leaders looked at each other trying to understand what he meant.

"I'm sorry, Commander Mark, but you might not have been listening to us carefully. We have been discussing the withdrawal of troops from Antioch. Even the military experts don't see any chance of victory."

"So much the better," Mark repeated clearly. "I think everyone should agree with me. After all, Antioch is under the domination of non-believers. I will welcome any commander who can conquer Antioch. I myself swear that I will consider him the ruler of Antioch."

"Mark, this is no time for jokes. Antioch is impregnable and you are suggesting sharing it. Before you can do that, you need to take it. Maybe you can clarify how you imagine doing that."

Gottfried tried to bring the conversation back to the matter at hand. The commanders had begun to whisper among themselves. One of them even snorted with laugh.

"Mark, we would like to understand your plan for taking Antioch. If you can, please explain it to us so that we can have the opportunity to assess the situation," Hugh said with a wide smile on his face and a secret wink to Gottfried.

"I'm glad you all stopped bickering immediately after I made my suggestion. From what I can see, Gottfried and Hugh have become allies, which works nicely for me. I suggest that we, the four commanders, headed by Raymond of course, swear to give Antioch to the one who can enter the city first. As far I can understand, I am the only one here who doesn't want to return to Europe without conquering Antioch."

"You're the only one with the stubbornness to stay," Raymond said. "And I, as the leader of the Crusaders' army, also think that staying here will be futile. You're very persistent, but you should understand that if you stay here alone your army will not be able to hold back the non-believers' army for even an hour. If you stay here, you will get caught in a trap."

Mark gave a smile. "But who said that I am going to stay if all of you leave, and thus make my small army an easy target for the non-believers? Do you think I'm crazy? Either we all swear on my terms, or we're all leaving together."

"Three against one," Raymond said, after thinking a while. "We, the three commanders, might have many differences, but we are unanimous about one thing: we are inclined to leave. So, Commander Mark, it seems the decision to return home will prevail. The agreement seems to have been reached; we only need to figure out how we should inform our soldiers about it. The news needs to be delivered very tactfully."

"Wait, Raymond," Mark interrupted. "Do not hurry. I have not finished my speech yet. If it is the final, combined decision of the three of you, then I have to agree with you. I am also accepting your suggestion and coming with you, but once we return, I will publicize both my suggestion and your decision about refusing it. I have the right to do that. It will be impossible to keep this conversation secret from people, especially Pope Urban II. After all, Bishop Adhemar, who is the pope's envoy during pilgrimages, is also here with us. By the way, let it be known that my suggested conditions for staying, namely just taking an oath to make Antioch the property of the commander who conquers it, were extremely fair. It wouldn't even be subject to recording. That's a very old military rule. Even so, it still remains incomprehensible to me why you are opposed to my suggestion. Aren't I right, Your Excellency?" Mark looked at Bishop Adhemar.

Adhemar nodded his head in agreement.

Raymond looked at Hugh and Gottfried. They were confused. They would be marked as traitors. It would be impossible to convince people that withdrawing the troops was the best option. The commanders realized that the decision to retreat had to be unanimous, otherwise somebody could be doing it just for their own reasons. Mark, upon returning to France, would announce that he was against turning back, and would become the only hero, whereas the others would be treated as cowards. Undoubtedly, Mark had thought up a good plan. The commanders, however, didn't really understand what he was doing; they felt his suggestions were too far-reaching.

"I think that Mark's suggestion is quite acceptable. And can you tell us, commander, how long we can remain at the gates of Antioch? A year? Two? Or maybe three?" Gottfried asked, demanding clarity.

"We can't wait long. You've heard that a Turkish army is moving toward us. Turkish princes from Damascus, Aleppo and Mosul have put aside their differences and are heading toward us with joint forces. If they find us in this condition, that will be our end. Our army is small and emaciated," Raymond explained.

Mark, who was listening to Raymond without interrupting, began to speak. "There is no need to wait long; it's useless and destructive. Give me a few days and I will tell you precisely when our group's oak will be. I'm not going to hand over Antioch to Emperor Alexander. Antioch will belong to those who take it."

"I agree," Hugh said.

"Me too," Gottfried uttered in a barely audible voice.

"I am also expressing my consent," Raymond announced officially. "Let this be considered the vow that the commanders of the Crusader pilgrims are making. Holy Father, would you like to say something?"

Bishop Adhemar cleared his throat and began to speak. "In any situation, my dear children, you are God's lambs, and it is very important to observe the principle of unity. God can only guide you if you act like a unified flock.

If you split up, God will leave you. One of the rules of war is that the liberated area belongs to the liberator. You all swore in Constantinople that you would surrender all liberated territories to the Byzantine Empire, but what happened instead? After a long siege, Nicaea's Turks surrendered the city to the Byzantine Emperor and not to the troops who had encircled the city for months. Pope Urban II has been informed about this unpleasant incident and, believe me, he does not approve of Alexander's behavior at all. Alexander's actions freed you from the obligation of keeping your oath. He was the first to break the agreement and thus the oath taken in Constantinople is now null and void. You are now left to your own discretion. You are free to act according to the rules of war, which say that an area belongs to the commander whose army has liberated it, and if several troops participate in the liberation then the liberated area belongs to the commander whose troops are the first to enter that area. But I am again calling on you to preserve the principles of unity. There may be disagreements between you, but you are here for the sake of God and his word. Your cause is common and sacred. You are God's soldiers, and you are brothers in this undertaking. Let the differences between you emerge after the pilgrimage is over. Long live Pope Urban and his uprightness! He will not let any hero commander be forgotten, and if there are any problems that you can't solve, leave them for the judgment of the pope's uprightness. It would be fairer."

Adhemar cleared his throat again to signal that his speech was over.

Mark jumped to his feet. "I suggest that we have a rest now. We still have a lot to do. I would like to ask you to keep your troops ready and alert. We will make it into Antioch if that is the will of God. I will not go into any details now so that we don't endanger our success. Tomorrow evening, I will lift the curtain of secrecy. Goodbye, gentlemen, and sleep well!" said Mark, and emerged from the commanders' tent.

The remaining commanders looked at each other with hesitation and bewilderment. They lingered in the tent for a short while before returning to their troops.

"I don't know. I don't trust him! If Mark lies to us, I will disgrace him for all of Europe to see," Gottfried threatened before leaving.

Hugh didn't say anything at all; he looked very concerned. If Mark went through with his decision, Hugh's suffering would be for nothing. After all, he had come here with the hope of taking Antioch, proclaiming it a kingdom and having the opportunity to show off his achievement and prove to his brother that he was worthier of the throne. His brother had never even tried to understand him. He had always turned up his nose at whatever Hugh had done. And now he had to deal with Mark, who had no origins or military service records but still intended to take Antioch from under their noses using tricks known only to himself. Raymond, being the leader of the campaign, was gradually giving way to Mark's pressure. Mark had a plan that even Raymond wasn't aware of. In Hugh's opinion, it was a shame. He obviously aspired to take over as chief commander of the campaign.

Mark lay in his gilded tent, trying to sleep. His thoughts had been so all over the place that they prevented him from falling into a deep sleep, even despite the fact that he already hadn't slept for days. The only thing he could do was drink a big glass of wine and doze off on the pillows in his tent. Mark realized that after that meeting, he was standing on the brink of greatness. He would either take Antioch and become a hero or everything would fail and, if he managed to remain alive, he would disgrace himself and become hostile toward all the commanders, whom he had put in an awkward position. Even the most beautiful and thunderous words needed to be accompanied by action, otherwise Mark would make a fool of himself. Bishop Adhemar's obvious support was unexpected, but extremely pleasing. Adhemar was a wise man and he understood that the strength of God's blessing was on Mark's side. Adhemar's main mission was to maintain the unity of the knights by keeping alive the atmosphere of togetherness and Christian love throughout the whole campaign. Otherwise, from the first battle onwards, the knights and commanders would quarrel and be at each other's throats without any help from the Turks. Adhemar's presence also held moral significance for the soldiers. Being away from their homes for the third year in a row, the pilgrims were often at their lowest level of morality. Adhemar had a deterring effect on them. The bishop did not allow the pilgrims to deviate from serving God. He was constantly reminding them that the pilgrimage should not be turned into an excuse for bad behavior. During the siege of Antioch, Adhemar had even delivered a sermon in which he angrily accused the pilgrims of turning away from God and indulging in sins. He would often try to link their behavior to their failures in battle. God had turned his back on the pilgrims and that's why they had failed. Instead of acting as instruments of God's justice, the pilgrims were indulging in fornication and sinfulness. After Adhemar's sermon, all women were dismissed from the Crusaders' camp in an attempt to distance the pilgrims from sin. A week had passed since that day, but God didn't seem in a hurry to take the Crusaders under his protection again. In addition, the alternating scorching sun and torrential downpour on Antioch was increasingly affecting the already deteriorating psychological conditions of the troops.

Adhemar, as the pope's representative, played a very important role during the military consultations. It can be said that the bishop's words held the most weight, even against the opinions of all the commanders combined.

"Commander!" Mark heard the voice of his assistant call out to him from afar, but it seemed as if it came from a dream. He opened his eyes and gave a questioning look at his assistant, who was standing in front of him.

"He is here. Would you like to see him?" the assistant whispered.

"Bring him in!" Mark commanded.

The assistant bowed before Mark and left the tent. A few minutes later, he returned with another man. Mark gave the newcomer a close look. He was a slim man wearing a Muslim soldier's uniform. He behaved very calmly, despite wearing the enemy's uniform. The look in his eyes showed signs of neglect.

"Your name?" Mark asked.

"I am Firuz."

Mark picked up the purse lying next to him and held it out to Firuz.

"There are fifty pieces of gold inside."

"Commander, I did not come here for gold. I do not need gold."

"Firuz, do you really want to help us? Explain why you are here" Mark said.

Firuz glanced at Mark's assistant. He was hesitant to speak in the presence of a third person.

"You can speak freely," Mark said, reading his mind. "If you're in my tent, nothing will threaten you. Now answer me: why do you want to help us?"

"The commander of the eastern guard towers has his eye on my wife. He has a high rank and I can't call him to order. In these troubled times of war, every little misstep is punishable by death. I just have no other choice. It is my decision and that concerns only me."

"How strange and unfair your management is that commanders can antagonize the soldiers like that. You have made the right decision," Mark said. "Do you know who I am? Are you aware to whom you are speaking?"

"Everybody knows you. You are Commander Mark Ruthless, the most famous commander of the Franks. You are known for your ruthlessness and cruelty toward the Orthodox Muslims."

Mark could not hide his grin of satisfaction. Of course, he had always been flooded with praise by his adherents, but it was a whole other pleasure to hear it from the enemy.

Mark was deeply convinced that his soldiers were the only ones among the Crusaders to actually be fighting; the other commanders were either bandits, busy plundering peaceful civilians, or charlatans, writing indecent letters to the pope and giving heroic descriptions of their own military activities, when in reality they run away at the sight of the troops of Saracens. Or they were hot headed losers who suffered defeat after defeat, leaving numerous dead bodies and prisoners on the battlefield. Mark would severely punish anyone who dared praise another commander or allude to the military successes of others in his presence.

Mark's influence reached a point where the soldiers around him would not only remark on his clear superiority out of fear of brutal punishment, but would also downplay the reputations of proven military leaders like Alexander the Great.

"Commander, if the Macedonian King had a teacher like you, he would have conquered the whole world."

"Commander, Caesar would have lost this battle."

"Commander, even Hannibal would have retreated by now, but you fought to the end with such courage."

Mark had surrounded himself with musicians who only wrote songs of praise about his deeds. He kept a whole platoon of scribes who would compete with each other to see who could write a more heroic description of Commander Mark's military path. But even all that couldn't compare with receiving praise from an ordinary soldier of the enemy's army. The peak of military glory is when you are recognized and praised by the enemy.

"On which guard tower do you carry out service?" Mark asked.

"On the fourth tower to the right of the eastern gate. It is my permanent post."

"Very good," Mark said, drawing out the words. "Give the details to my assistant. The plan is as follows: a small group of forty soldiers will approach your tower tomorrow at midnight. You will throw down a rope. My soldiers will use the rope to climb the tower and from there move to the eastern gates and open them, and then our army will enter Antioch, putting an end to your suffering. Did I present the plan correctly?"

"Yes, commander! Everything is correct. I will be waiting for your soldiers at my guard tower tomorrow at midnight."

In the morning, Commander Mark's troops partook in a demonstration march. Soldiers passed through a small ravine wearing shiny helmets. Mark watched from above as the troops marched like water flowing from a river. As they emerged from the ravine, their lines widened out. In front of them were the riders, who made up a third of the troops. After the horsemen, the infantry came out, followed by the archers. Discipline and order were Mark's favorite things. No matter what had happened or how troubling times were, Mark would first and foremost punish the soldiers who had disturbed the order. Once, during a battle near Nicaea Castle, Mark ordered the soldiers to retreat and attentively watched for the order to be carried out strictly. His servitors were well aware of the commander's sensitivity when it came to observing order.

Everybody was afraid of Mark. His whole army was terrified of getting in the commander's way. He was ruthless and brutal. He did not particularly stand out for his righteousness of Solomon. Should there be any disagreement among the soldiers, he would punish all sides severely, even without knowing who was guilty. Mark had another peculiarity as well. Each morning when he woke up, he liked the troops to greet him in a line. It was a whole ceremony. The commander came out of his tent to wash himself, and in the meantime the trumpets played. Once he cleaned himself up, he would approach the troops so that they could greet their commander one by one as he looked on sternly. The soldiers would shout in unison, "Hello, Commander!" Mark would then nod slightly and approach the next regiment. Thus, every morning the soldiers had the opportunity to wish a good morning to their commander, battalion by battalion.

Mark rode along the line of soldiers in the parade, looking at their faces carefully trying to get a sense of their morale and fighting spirit. Every commander knows by heart how many soldiers, weapons, defensive measures, and horses he has. A military parade serves one major function: to showcase the full readiness of the soldiers before the commander and before themselves. The soldiers get a chance to see what a formidable force they are together. The military parades reinforce the soldiers' belief that they are part of an invincible army, and that belief is the key to victory on the battlefield.

At midnight, according to Mark's plan, a group of forty soldiers secretly and silently headed toward the eastern gates of Antioch. The voices of the guards could be heard from the wall. They were talking to each other very loudly, almost shouting, and the language they were communicating in was unknown to the soldiers. The guards frequently interrupted their conversation with loud and unruly laughter. Mark's soldiers made their way to the fourth citadel from the right of the gates and squatted low. Compared to other towers, this one had an eerie silence. No whisper could be heard. The soldiers sat on the ground close to the castle walls so as not to be visible from above and waited with tense anticipation. An ominous silence surrounded them. The soldiers sat frozen, not moving. Even the wind seemed to have halted and was waiting for something to happen. Suddenly, a barely audible whistle could be heard from the top of the tower, and several ropes came down from the window. The soldiers began to climb up the ropes silently and cautiously. They entered through the tower window one by one. A quarter of an hour later, not a single soldier was left under the wall.

Firuz was giving instructions to the soldiers inside the tower. He explained how the soldiers should reach the gates of the city, how many military groups they would meet along the way, and how to open the city gates once they reached them. Firuz urged them to wait a bit longer until the final night shift was over and fewer soldiers were hanging around the gates. Besides, it would soon be dawn, and the best time to attack was twilight, or owl light. It would be much easier then to catch the enemy unaware.

A group of soldiers who had taken up positions inside Antioch came down from the tower and started running toward the gates. The people they met along the way looked at the soldiers in their unfamiliar uniforms with surprise, but didn't really pay much attention to them and assumed they were Turkish soldiers carrying out a regular training. During the last few months, the residents of Antioch had witnessed so many strange things that everything had become normal for them, even Crusaders running around the streets of Antioch. The troops maneuvered through the streets with few obstacles. The only thing the Crusaders encountered were three Turkish soldiers, who were stabbed to death before they could even understand what was going on. Finally, the group reached the eastern gates of the city suffering no losses. The muezzin's quivering voice could be heard coming from one of the city's minarets. It wasn't clear what the muezzin was saying, but it was certainly a delayed signal of alarm. The gates opened with a squeak and the Crusaders charged through, yelling. The light of dawn revealed a terrible scene: blood flowing through the streets of the city. The number of dead bodies was so great that some parts of Antioch had become impassable. The massacre of non-believers continued until noon the next day, as Crusaders continued to find them and drag them into the streets to be killed. The screams and cries had gradually decreased, but they could still be heard in some parts of the city. In some places, deep ponds of blood had formed that reached up to the knees. It was only in the evening that the commanders finally signaled their troops to gather in the central square to partake in the ceremony of seizing Antioch.

After a whole day of military operations and mass killings, the exhausted troops began to arrive from different parts of Antioch and gather in the central square, where thousands of lit torches were creating a solemn atmosphere. The Crusader leadership and papal representative Bishop Adhemar stood in the center. Among them, Commander Mark stood tall and proud. He already had the look of being the ruler of Antioch. He seemed to be telling everyone that he was a man of his word and that he succeeded in taking Antioch. Adhemar stood beside Mark, blessing everyone with his hand and making the sign of the cross over them. The crowd began to shout.

"Dieu le veut!" Gradually, the shouts became louder and came in unison.

"Dieu le veut!" resounded across the square. The troops were unspeakably happy. After so many months, they finally managed to conquer the seemingly invincible city with almost no losses. Surely divine powers were behind such a success.

Halting his blessings, Bishop Adhemar addressed the troops that had gathered. "Dear pilgrims, we have been walking to the Holy Land, the final destination of our pilgrimage, for days, weeks, and months. Overcoming various difficulties, we did not lose hope for the liberation of the Holy Sepulcher. The Lord Almighty put those difficulties on our shoulders as severe trials. The Lord wanted to test our faith in the light of Christ, our will, and our commitment to the divine cause. It is these difficulties which separate a pilgrimage from a pleasant walk. The more severe and insurmountable the trials seem, the sweeter and more blessed the reward will be. You are not ordinary people. The almighty Lord is carrying out his divine will through you. Through you, he is establishing justice on earth, about which Pope Urban II spoke during the Mass in Clermont. God's light has guided us all to places thousands of miles away from our homes. It has helped us defeat a much larger enemy in his own house. It has helped us conquer Antioch, which stands out because of its exceptional inaccessibility. When we first approached the gates of Antioch, despair weakened our faith for just a moment. We had been trying to overcome Antioch's impregnability for months. These attempts called for experimentation of new scientific and military methods, all of which ultimately failed, and which may have affected the faith of many of you. Antioch succumbed only when God wanted it to. This was another trial that we have overcome with our joint efforts. The trial of faith is the most serious trial that a Christian can ever be subjected to. That trial can now be considered over, and after this military miracle, I can't imagine someone could cast doubt on the divine nature of our cause, even in the deepest corner of his mind. It is impossible to defeat us because our cause is blessed. You all are instruments in God's hands through which heavenly justice is maintained. That is God's wish. Dieu le veut!"

"Dieu le veut!" the soldiers shouted.

The crowd shook with fanatical outcries. People were in a trance. They were convinced that they had become instruments in the hands of God. Antioch's occupation, indeed, was from a series of military miracles, and because very few people were aware of the meeting that had taken place with Commander Mark in the combat tent, the opening of Antioch's gates was tantamount to a miracle for many. Isn't it a miracle to wallow aimlessly for months under the walls of Antioch, losing all hope of entering the town, and then suddenly witness the city open its gates hospitably?

As soon as the shouts and exclamations stopped, Bishop Adhemar continued his speech. "As we know, one of the military rules is that if a battle is fought by more than one commander, then the liberated city falls under the domination of the one whose troops were first to set foot inside. In this case, there can be no exceptions, and I, as the representative of High Priest Urban II throughout this sacred pilgrimage, am proclaiming Commander

Mark the ruler of Antioch, conveying the high priest's blessings to him in his difficult but just cause of ruling Antioch."

Upon saying this, Adhemar pointed to Commander Mark, who stood next to him, and placed his right hand on Mark's head as a sign of blessing.

"Now rule by God's will!"

Mark stood beside Adhemar with a stern look; not a single muscle on his face seemed to be moving. It was impossible to determine whether he was happy or not. Mark looked around at the soldiers silently and proudly. He looked to the left and right, singling out his soldiers among the crowd.

"Antioch also has great spiritual significance for our pilgrimage," Bishop Adhemar continued. "Saint Peter the Apostle served as a bishop in this city. Christianity as a religion originated here. This city is also the foundation of the Catholic Church, and here you can find the temple from which the word of Christ spread. Antioch's liberation is crucial: it's a sign from the Lord Almighty that we are on the right path and that our pilgrimage is acceptable to him. By liberating Antioch, we recaptured one of the most powerful Christian landmarks from the clutches of the non-believers. So, thrice blessed are all those who participated or who fell victim in this sacred battle. The Kingdom of Heaven will welcome us when our time comes. We will continue the good cause of our fallen friends, deserving their constant blessing from heaven. After all, they joined God's army in heaven and will give us strength, patience and strong will so that we can reach the Holy Land and liberate God's Sepulcher from the non-believers."

"Dieu le veut!" the crowd exclaimed in approval, waving their torches. Their fanaticism, which had already reached its peak, was being inflamed further by Bishop Adhemar's words. The army had finished the widespread massacre of Muslims in Antioch just a few minutes prior, and now they were standing in clothes crimson with blood, waving their bloody hands and asking for strength from the Lord Almighty to continue what they had begun. No one among the troops had any doubt that their cause and struggle were sacred. People felt that they were, as Adhemar had said, God's instruments. They were convinced that all killings committed with their hands were favorable to God.

A group of soldiers tried to light a large fire in the center of the square to further inflame the emotions of the night. Pieces of wood were being carried to the square from various places.

The commanders, standing on the platform, were having an active discussion with Adhemar. After Adhemar's speech, all the commanders approached Mark and congratulated him on his brilliant victory. Mark did not show his joy. He was lost in his thoughts.

He was standing in complete isolation when one of the bodyguards approached him and whispered something in his ear. Mark went pale, then leapt slightly forward and shouted out to the troops. "Close the gates of the city! Close them immediately! Put out the fire! Each of you, take up your combat positions!"

Everyone looked at each other with bewilderment. Adhemar approached Mark, trying to understand what was happening.

"The army, the Turkish army, is reaching Antioch," Mark said gasping for air. "The united army of Turks from Aleppo, Mosul and Damascus is reaching us. May God help us, bishop!"

Adhemar crossed himself and stepped down from the platform.

As it turned out, there was a reason for their panic, and it was a very serious one. The Turkish army approached Antioch within a few hours and surrounded most of the city like a large river. The besieging army was large in number. The Turks were like a human ocean whose waves had come and crashed into the castle gates. They had all types of troops; the Crusaders had never seen such a large cavalry. Their riders circled the castle as close to the walls as possible to show off their power and allow the enemy to examine them better. Aside from horsemen armed with hooked swords, there were also archers among the Turkish troops, which was a new phenomenon for the Crusaders. Of course, the defensive gear of the Turkish army could not equal the strength of the Crusaders' breastplates, but the Turkish infantry's advantage was that there were so many of them. The Turkish army was also well fed, unlike the Crusaders who were malnourished from walking and fighting for years, and this made them even more threatening.

This was the first large scale meeting of the Turkish army and the Crusader pilgrims, and it was taking place when the resources of the Crusaders' army were on the verge of depletion. The Turkish army, on the other hand, was just starting their military operations.

Confusion spread through the Crusaders' army. They weren't necessarily panicking, because they believed they had the protection of God, but the situation was just too ambiguous. Those who had been trying to seize

Antioch for months were now being besieged. Apart from being confusing, the situation also caused certain difficulties. Resources were already scarce; there was still some water, but after the occupation it was necessary to check all the wells in order to avoid poisoning. Food was also running out. Since there was little food to sell, the nearby urban markets had closed down. A bread shortage led to the swelling of its price. People would pay up to five pieces of gold for a small loaf of bread. Domestic animals quickly died, becoming dinner only for the richer Crusaders.

The moderate use of food was having an impact on the troops. The soldiers had lost their liveliness, and the number of fainting cases had increased. In addition, a plague epidemic suddenly broke out in the city. Apparently, diseases excreted from the putrid bodies that covered the city were spreading. At the beginning of the siege, the Crusaders had thrown the corpses of animals and people inside the castle walls in hopes of causing a plague epidemic within Antioch. In the end, they succeeded, but unfortunately it happened when they were already inside the city. The wave of sickness spread to such an extent that even Bishop Adhemar fell ill and lay in bed with a high fever. He could hardly walk or speak. For safety reasons, Adhemar wasn't asked to join meetings of the military leaders. He stayed in Saint Peter the Apostle's cave, where the founder of the Catholic Church had preached about Christianity thousands of years before. Adhemar prayed in the cave for days, asking for a victory for the Christians. His health deteriorated day by day because of lack of proper medical care. His high fever would sometimes cause him to go crazy. Regaining consciousness, he would tell everyone about the visions he had seen. The other commanders tried not to visit Adhemar so they wouldn't be infected.

The cautious atmosphere from the army camp was slowly manifesting itself in the atmosphere of the city. The streets had become empty. The movement of people could only be seen during the guard change. Each commander had shut himself in his shelter, isolating himself from others, and didn't leave except out of extreme necessity. Communication was mainly conducted through envoys. In the meantime, the Turkish troops continued their siege of Antioch, each day getting closer to causing despair for those inside.

Even Commander Mark, who was known for his ruthlessness, did not leave his shelter for days. Sometimes, he would come out to tour the guard towers with a concerned face, but he only did that in areas protected by his army. The soldiers would look at Mark's face and try to assess the hopelessness of the situation. If the Crusaders had the option before of leaving without capturing Antioch, they certainly didn't have that option now. With each day, the Crusaders felt the cold chill of imminent death get closer and closer. They realized that they would either die from a Turkish sword or starve to death, unless of course the plague epidemic killed them before that.

"Only a miracle can save the Crusaders. There is no way to fight against the Turkish army," a centurion said to Mark during one of his tours.

"We are blessed. Do not forget that we are instruments in the hands of God. This is a trial – a trial of faith," Commander Mark said and walked away.

The third week of the siege was marked by Bishop Adhemar's death. As the representative of Pope Urban, Adhemar was buried in Saint Peter's cave, according to a special Catholic right. The leaders of the campaign came together for the first time since the capture of Antioch during Adhemar's funeral ceremony. It was the only time that everyone forgot about the risk of being infected. When the funeral ceremony was over, Mark asked the other commanders not to leave.

"We need to talk. I want to consult with you all about something," he said.

All the commanders of the campaign were gathered inside Saint Peter's cave near Adhemar's grave. The last time they had met, they had tried to make a decision about leaving Antioch. Raymond of Toulouse had ceded his commander position to Mark and hadn't organized a meeting since then. Other things had happened so that there was no need to hold a special meeting of commanders again. Hugh had taken offense and all of his plans had failed after seizing Antioch. He was more concerned with restoring his name and reputation rather than the next steps of the campaign. Gottfried was also depressed. Almost no one was left from his troops. By some providence, the majority of deaths in battle had fallen on his troops, and then the plague epidemic inflicted the most damage on his remaining soldiers. The Crusaders started a rumor that God had turned his back on Gottfried, and it was becoming increasingly difficult for him to lead his surviving soldiers. If it wasn't for the agreement between commanders that you couldn't accept each other's soldiers, Gottfried's troops would have passed to the supervision of Mark in one day. The commanders had been weighed down by their thoughts, but soon the consultation began.

"Before his death, Bishop Adhemar had a vision," Mark said. "With his last breath, he told me what it was."

The aromatic smell of incense had spread across the entire cave, sanctifying Adhemar's tomb and creating a mystic atmosphere at the meeting. Numerous hardships had weakened the commanders' will, and they subconsciously hoped for a miracle.

"Saint Peter the Apostle had come to Adhemar like a vision and, pointing to the temple tabernacle, said that the Holy Lance, the spear that killed Jesus as he hung from the cross, is buried under the altar. Saint Peter said that the army that possesses the lance is undefeatable."

Mark said this and looked into the eyes of the commanders. He was waiting to see looks of skepticism, but to his surprise the commanders were listening carefully and respectfully. Mark did notice, however, that the commanders' eyes looked a bit strange. Was it despair and hopelessness that he saw? Faith was probably the only feeling that had survived inside them. The commanders were attentively listening to Mark and looking forward to the continuation of his story. Mark continued his speech.

"Adhemar said that if we find the Holy Lance in the temple, then all our brothers that we have lost during the pilgrimage will come down from the Kingdom of Heaven and fight with us against the enemy. I repeat: the army owning the Holy Lance is invincible. We'll be able to attack the enemy troops and defeat them no matter how huge and strong they are. Our victory will be guaranteed. Once we find the Holy Lance, it will be pointless for us to shut ourselves in the castle and wait for death. We will counterattack and destroy the non-believers."

Complete silence fell on the cave. It was not clear what the commanders were thinking. Mark looked at their eyes, trying to figure out if they agreed with him or if his words fell empty. Noticing that no one was going to break the silence, Mark continued speaking. "But that's not all. The secret is that we, the four of us together, must believe in the power of the Holy Lance and look for it together, and then it will become the property of all four of us. He who tries to claim the lance will be cursed, along with his whole family, and the lance will lose its power for everyone else."

"Well, why are we wasting time? Let's find the spear," Hugh said excitedly.

"Yes, why are we standing here perplexed? Are we waiting to see when we'll die of the plague?" Gottfried joined in.

Raymond was still thinking.

"If we do not follow Adhemar's words, we will die. We have no choice. After all, we aren't here to have fun. We are soldiers of God and we have relied, and continue to rely, on him. There is no mightier power. If God is for us, who can ever be against us? Let's begin the search without delay. God has been with us throughout the pilgrimage, and he hasn't left us now, but we have turned away from him," Commander Mark concluded.

The four commanders picked up the spades and began digging. For anyone watching, it must have looked very strange. Men who were known for their ruthlessness, their courageous deeds on the battlefield, and some for their royal ancestry that set them apart from ordinary mortals, were working together with spades in their hands, dripping with sweat.

Even Mark, who had previously lived an ordinary life, was holding a spade. He was the only commander who was digging with displeasure. Physical work reminded him of his past, when he would have to massage the leg of his aristocratic master's horse and perform various humiliating tasks. Other commanders didn't have this problem, so they didn't treat the situation very seriously; they were even enjoying the work since they had never done it before. They were used to a life where physical work was performed by others. The only physical activity that was appropriate for a man was fighting with a sword on the battlefield; the rest was for the lower class. And now, after their religious fanaticism had destroyed their senses, they were digging up the floor of Saint Peter's cave in search of the Holy Lance with no worries.

It was after five or six hours of digging, when they were close to despair, that Gottfried's voice could suddenly be heard. "I found it! I found the lance!"

16. Habibi: Sayid's First Discovery in Alamut (Persia, AD 1117)

One night, as he entered his shelter, Sayid noticed that his bed sheets were ruffled. As he fixed them, he noticed a piece of paper under his pillow. Whoever had put it there clearly did not want anybody else to see it. He tucked the paper into his breast pocket and left the room under the pretense of washing himself. In the washroom, he took out the paper and read the following: "Do you want to see me? Do not drink anything, just pretend to be drunk."

At first Sayid didn't understand the meaning of the letter, nor could he guess who it was from, but he kept a small glimmer of hope in his heart that it had some connection with Habibi. Of course, he didn't know what the connection could be, but the hope did not abandon him.

Sayid washed himself and returned to his shelter to sleep. There was a pitcher full of water by each of the four beds, from which the Assassins could drink water at night. Before going to sleep, the Assassins had to drink half of the jar. That night, Sayid decided to skip that ritual. He put the jar to his lips, lifted it, and pretended to drink. Sayid had become so tired that day that he fell asleep as soon as he lay down. Someone's voice woke him up.

"They are sleeping, come on, let's go!" whispered the voice.

"Don't shake him, you'll wake him up," another voice cautioned.

"Quiet! He has been put into such a deep sleep that he would not wake up no matter what."

Two men lifted Sayid out of his bed and were carefully carrying him somewhere else. He pretended to be fast asleep and not to feel anything. He even started to snore lightly to seem more believable. Those acting classes he had gone to hadn't been in vain.

Sayid could feel that he was being taken downstairs. He was then carried through a long corridor. Even though his eyes were closed, he could sense how many steps were being taken and in what direction he was being carried. From the corridor, they made a sharp turn to the left, then they went up a few stairs and were outside in open air. After walking for almost fifteen minutes, the men who had been carrying Sayid carefully put him on the ground and left. Someone else came up to them and asked, "Was Sayid on today's list?"

"Yes, he was on our list."

"How strange. There is a totally different person on mine. Well, anyway, go. He will regain consciousness in about two hours and you can come pick him up in ten hours."

Sayid realized that he had to pretend to be asleep for two more hours.

"Houris! I am speaking to you. Where are you?" the voice called out.

"Here we are," said a woman's voice.

"Are you ready? He will soon regain consciousness," the voice said. "Tell me what you have prepared."

"Well, first I will approach him and caress him a little. Then the next houri will approach him and begin to lick his body. Then I will copulate with the boy in the 'doggy style' position and give him juice to drink, after which he will lose consciousness again. Then I will call you."

"Ok, but in the meantime, you need to repeat this constantly: 'Oh, brave soldier, warrior of Allah, we will be waiting for you anxiously.' Do not suddenly forget that! Without these words, all of this turns into trivial prostitution. He must feel like he is in paradise, not some seaport brothel. His time here must be unforgettable. Do you understand what unforgettable means?"

Sayid understood that they were talking about him, and that those unforgettable moments were apparently awaiting him. "Let's see," Sayid thought. "We shall see how unforgettable these moments will be."

"Yes, you have made yourself clear," said one of the houris in an offended tone. "It is not the first time we are doing this, you can go easy."

The man gave a few more instructions and muttered, "All the empty-headed prostitutes have gathered here and they want me to work with them properly. It is impossible; they can't even tell a simple lie about sending a soldier to death."

There was complete silence for a moment. A bird could be heard in the night. There were at least five hours before the start of dawn. Sayid lay motionless for one more hour, after which he started to move around with his half-open sleepy eyes. A ringing laughter could be heard from the other side of the garden. Sayid approached the houri and hugged her from behind. Everything from the previous night's dream was repeating, only this time Habibi whispered something else in Sayid's ear.

"I have missed you to death, Sayid. I managed to change the order without anyone noticing and wrote your name on the list. I wanted to see you again. Sayid, I have been thinking about you since I met you in the desert. Fate has brought you here so that we could meet again."

Sayid wanted to respond, but Habibi covered his mouth with the palm of her small hand.

"Hush! Do not say anything; they might notice us. Listen to what I am saying; should you want to contact me, leave a note in the bin near the blacksmith's workshop. The next day, you will find my response in the same place. Sayid, be careful. This is not a joke. If you don't write to me in the next three days, I will assume that you have forgotten about me and I won't hold it against you. Again, this is extremely dangerous. Sayid, you do not know the truth about this place."

Upon saying this, Habibi hugged Sayid, her youthful naked breasts heating Sayid's rough, hairy chest. She began to feverishly move around and groan in Sayid's arms. It sounded sweet to Sayid's ears. He had never heard a sweeter voice; even the most beautiful music sounded like a pig grunting compared to Habibi's gentle moan. Sayid realized that Habibi's moans of pleasure were because of him. The scene repeated just like the previous time they met. After a few hours, Sayid pretended to have drunk the elixir that should have put him to sleep, when really he secretly poured it out on the ground. He lay under one of the trees and pretended to fall asleep.

The houris approached Sayid and made sure that he was really asleep. Habibi kissed his face as if she was just checking, but really she was saying goodbye.

"He's sleeping," Habibi said quietly.

"Listen, sister, you're a very interesting girl. You were moaning so naturally; I was listening to you from the other side of the garden," the other houri said with a laugh. "At one point I even thought that maybe you really love this guy."

"Do not say stupid things," Habibi said quickly. "Falling in love with him is the last thing I need. I might not come to the garden for a few days, so we need to find someone to replace me. We should think about it."

"Wait a minute, sister," the houri said angrily. "What do you mean you might not come? The new girls will be here in a month and my monthlies are about to start, so that means I can't come to the garden either. Maybe you better wait a little."

"Well," Habibi said thoughtfully, "I think you should ask Mr.; he will know what to do. Come on! Let's call the porters to take Sayid back."

"Sayid? Wow, you even know his name. Sister, you seem to have really fallen in love," the houri laughed.

"He himself said his name to me when I was caressing him. Otherwise, I don't need to know it!"

The girls, chatting lively, left Sayid, and after an hour the very same men who had brought him to the garden took him back to his shelter. One of the Assassins was awake at the time and saw the men carrying Sayid in their arms. "What has happened? Why is he unconscious?"

"Quiet! Everything is ok," said the porter. "He didn't feel good during the night and he lost consciousness and white foam was coming out of his mouth. We took him to the medical post. Such things happen sometimes when a person becomes very tired. He will wake up in a few hours."

The porters left quickly.

Sayid rolled around in his bed for half an hour and then "woke up." He was immediately surrounded by his brother Assassins, who began to question him.

"Brother, how are you feeling?"

Almualim was worried the most.

"Sayid, what happened? I was sleeping and didn't even notice that you weren't well. How are you feeling now?"

"Very good, Almualim. I feel wonderful now," Sayid said with a wide smile on his face.

And indeed, he was not lying. Sayid had never felt so good. A huge weight seemed to have been taken off his chest and his soul seemed to have become lighter. Sayid felt very relieved.

17. Almualim's Head: Sayid's Second Discovery in Alamut (Persia, 1117 AD)

A month had passed since that strange night in the garden. Twice a week, Sayid would write a letter to Habibi and leave it at the previously agreed upon place in the bin near the blacksmith's workshop. The letters never mentioned their names; the lovers knew who wrote them. They also didn't contain any specific information about events or actions. Instead, they were full of beautiful words of love and a mutual promise that a day would come when they could be together forever. Neither Sayid or Habibi had a clear idea of the future of their relationship, though it wasn't much of a relationship yet. They had had three dates, two of which had been secret, and the third was in the desert oasis next to a well and only lasted a few seconds. Their love was centered around the bin near the blacksmith's workshop, where they continued to carry out their secret correspondence. Not a single night passed in which Sayid didn't see Habibi in his dreams, and not a single minute went by where Sayid stopped thinking about Habibi. In those days, Almualim had gone off to carry out an assignment. Sayid never saw him at the shelter anymore. He hadn't heard any news about Almualim yet and it wasn't acceptable in Alamut to make inquiries about the whereabouts of another Assassin, even if he was a close friend.

The day before he disappeared, Almualim, with a glint in his eyes and a mysterious expression on his face, quietly told Sayid that he had been given an extremely important assignment. Sayid didn't pay much attention to his words, writing it off as friendly boasting. Later, Sayid thought back on this conversation, trying to remember what task Almualim had been entrusted with. Almualim hadn't really stood out for his high achievement scores, or for his success in training. In fact, the trainers were always dissatisfied with his results. If it wasn't for the trainers frequently turning a blind eye to his failures, he may not have had the possibility to pursue a full course of study.

Sayid had already begun to worry about Almualim's long absence, but he decided to wait one more day before asking the trainers where he was. He began to wonder if Almualim had been kicked out of Alamut. That day, the ceremonial soldier on special assignments visited the Assassins' shelter and informed them that all Assassins, without exception, must visit the Hall of Truth in festive attire right after dinner. The Old Man of the Mountain was going to be speaking.

Upon hearing the news, everybody made a fuss taking out their festive clothes and laying them out neatly. The Assassins' festive garments were long white hooded robes, embroidered in gold thread. "Allah's soldier" was written in Arabic on the back of the robes and the secret emblem of the Assassins, the woven triangle, was embroidered on the hood. That very same emblem was on the letter that granted Ahmed entrance into the castle. Sayid remembered that that triangular seal had made a special impression on the Assassins receiving it at Alamut's gates.

Sayid took out his festive garments as well. At the appointed time, immediately after dinner, the Assassins entered the Hall of Truth and lined up along the wall by rank. The lighting in the hall was very poor and the atmosphere was very solemn. There was a round table in the center of the hall. On the table, something lay covered in a silk cloth.

As soon as the Assassins lined up, the Old Man of the Mountain, Hassan-i Sabbāh, entered the hall and the atmosphere grew even more solemn. Hassan greeted the Assassins with a slight nod of his head and began to speak. "Soldiers of Allah! Celestial sentinels of the Lord's glory and humble servants of the Lord! I, as the only connecting link between heaven and earth, the only mediator between Allah's heavenly kingdom and the sin-soaked world, want to thank you for your dedication and your faith, which has only increased with each day. There are soldiers among you who have completed their cherished studies and I appeal to them now. You will see the strength of your arms multiply with each day. Rest assured that it is Allah who is blessing you and giving strength and power to you. You are not ordinary people. Your minds differ from the minds of ordinary men. Your strength and power have a divine nature."

The Old Man of the Mountain walked to the other side of the hall. "I am appealing to the soldiers who have been serving Allah for several years already, whose dagger's blow has destroyed numerous Shaitans. Your cause is just. You will always be compensated for your efforts and for your contributions. Be sure that there will come a day when you will also deserve death and will be awarded with eternal bliss."

The Old Man of the Mountain moved toward the table in the center of the hall. "One of our brothers was entrusted with a very important task. He killed one of the Shaitan's chickens with honor, but the enemies caught him and beheaded him."

With these words, the Old Man of the Mountain pulled the silk cloth off the table and revealed a round brass tray on which sat a bloody head. Sayid's heart stopped. He could barely restrain himself from screaming out loud, although he failed to hold back his tears. It was good that the lighting was so poor so that no one could see him crying. His heart filled with emotions that he had never felt before. It was a mixture of regret and powerlessness.

"As you can see, our soldiers reclaimed our hero's head from the enemy, and he is here now. The hero is now at the feet of Allah. He enjoys the presence of Allah, he walks through the gardens of Eden, and he will be in eternal bliss. The same fate is awaiting each of you who become Allah's dedicated soldier and will die for the glory of the Lord."

The scene was not particularly convincing. The prospect of being a bloody head on the table would hardly encourage anyone. In fact, it might have even deterred a few soldiers.

"Soldiers of Allah, are you ready to continue Almualim's feat, who in turn was continuing Bu Tahir Arrani's good cause?"

"Yes," everyone in the hall said.

The Old Man of the Mountain looked dissatisfied. It was clear that there was little enthusiasm in their response, and he didn't like it.

"I do not hear faith in your answer. The breath of suspicion and skepticism blows from among your ranks. There are people among you who do not want to be Allah's soldier with all their heart and soul. Maybe their fears have awakened in them. I do not know."

The Assassins avoided Hassan's examining gaze. The Old Man of the Mountain shook his head in reproach and went up to Almualim's head. He took a bottle of powder out of his pocket, opened the bottle and emptied the powder on his head, saying words of prayer in a low voice.

"Uallahayimbahanatra, we want to talk to him. Allah's soldiers want to see the Lord's miracle. Open your eyes, Allah's soldier," the Old Man of the Mountain shouted.

All of a sudden, Almualim opened his eyes.

Even all their discipline trainings couldn't help the soldiers suppress their surprise. Sayid could not believe his eyes. Almualim, or rather his head, had opened his eyes and was looking at the Assassins in surprise, as if trying to understand why they had all gathered.

The Old Man of the Mountain stepped aside and turned to Almualim's head. "Dedicated servant of Allah, I asked Allah to let us speak to you for a while. We want to exchange a few words and make sure that everything is alright with you. Tell us, where you are now?"

Almualim looked at the Old Man of the Mountain and began to speak. "Old Man of the Mountain, I am grateful to you for giving me the opportunity to once again see my friends. I hope I will meet them again in the near future. I wholeheartedly hope that that meeting takes place as soon as possible. I am now in the Garden of Eden, where everything is just the way it is described in wisdom books and as our teachers taught. There is no pain, there is no fear, there is no discomfort; there is only bliss here."

"Almualim," the Old Man of the Mountain said, "Would you like to answer your friends' questions? They suffer from the desire to join you. It's possible that anxiety born from uncertainty has nestled in some of their hearts. I am sure that it would be better if you served as a guide for them on some of these issues."

"I would love to, Old Man of the Mountain. I am indebted only to you for my present happiness. You opened my eyes, and thanks to you, I approached the light of the truth. Thanks to you, I am now in the Garden of Eden."

The Old Man of the Mountain turned to the Assassins. "Anyone may ask their brother Almualim a question."

"Do you feel pain?" the bravest Assassin asked.

"I have actually forgotten what pain is. There is only one feeling here – bliss," Almualim replied.

"What do you do there?" another Assassin asked.

"Houris do not leave me much free time, but there are different perceptions of time here. I do not know how much time has passed in your world, but I feel like I have always been here."

"How is the weather in the Garden of Eden?" someone else asked.

"It's neither cold nor hot here. And I never feel too hot or too cold. The weather is what you want it to be."

"Do you remember your friends?" Sayid shouted from his seat.

Almualim's looked directly at Sayid. He saw who had asked the question and gave Sayid a knowing wink, unnoticed by the others, and then replied with a smile on his face. "Of course I remember, and I am looking forward to seeing my friends here. I am waiting for all my friends."

The Old Man of the Mountain approached Almualim's head, slowly closed his eyes shut with his hand and said, "This will end your earthly suffering, my son. Enjoy the bliss you deserve."

Almualim became breathless once more. Sayid noticed something strange on the left side of his head. It was a black stain that looked like it couldn't have come from getting his head severed. As he looked closer, he realized what it was. The black stain was in place of where Almualim's neck was. It was covered in black dye, which was meant to hide that part of his neck so that it didn't show.

Sayid realized everything all at once. The poor lighting, the talking head, Almualim's smile and wink of the eye, the important task that he had been entrusted with...

They had just taken part in a staged performance aimed at proving the existence of the heavenly world, the Garden of Eden, and the bliss of the afterlife. Of course, Hassan-i Sabbāh's divinity was also proven that day. After all, he was able to resurrect a "dead" man, or rather his severed head, at least temporarily. What a sham! And all of these lies and falsehoods were conducted in the Hall of Truth. It was hard to imagine anything more disgusting yet simultaneously ironic. Sayid suddenly smiled; something had just occurred to him. If everything had been staged, then Almualim was still alive. Praise be to Allah, there was at least one good thing in all this mess. Sayid didn't care about why they did the fake show or who was responsible for it; he was comforted by the thought that his friend Almualim was alive. This meant that they must have cut a hole the size of his head in the tray on the table. He was safe and sound; his body had just been hidden under the table. Sayid promised himself that he would find Almualim.

At night, as he lay in bed, Sayid kept smiling about how he actually believed for a moment that a severed head could speak. He thought of how much he would berate Almualim for causing him such suffering. Eventually, Sayid fell asleep and had a strange dream. He was in the Hall of Truth, where a bunch of severed Assassins' heads were floating around. The heads were smiling happily.

"Sayid, brother, present your head to the Old Man of the Mountain. Keep the rest of your body for yourself," the severed heads urged him. "The Old Man of the Mountain will show you the door to happiness and bliss. He loves you. Do not be ungrateful; he only wants your head in return."

Sayid walked through the heads to the center of the hall where the Old Man of the Mountain was standing with his back to him. When Sayid approached Hassan, he turned around. In the old man's hands was an apple.

"Sayid, take this apple. You already know everything."

Sayid stretched out his hand and took the apple. The apple transformed into a hooked dagger that emitted a glaring light, illuminating the dark hall and wowing him. Sayid then woke up from the dagger's glaring light.

It was already morning, which meant it was time for classes.

Every dawn, the Assassins would get up, wash and clean themselves, and have sword training until breakfast. They worked on the techniques they had learned, inflicting blows to the scarecrows in the center of the sports circle. Sometimes they would duel to imitate real fights. Even though the swords designed for trainings had blunt blades, the duelers would often get serious injuries. Their swords would clash together, causing sparks of light to fly around.

Sayid was concerned that he was not able to train vigorously. He thought that maybe it was because of Almualim's performance or the previous night's dream. Allah sometimes speaks to people through their dreams. In that case, what could the apple that the Old Man of the Mountain gave to him mean? Why did the apple turn into a dagger? These thoughts followed Sayid throughout the day. Anxiety and uncertainty had nestled themselves in his heart. For a moment, he wondered whether Allah even needed to do all that. Maybe the Heavenly Father thought that he had sinned.

Before breakfast, Sayid went to visit the blacksmith. He browsed the beautiful, newly forged swords and daggers. The blacksmith was convinced that Sayid's frequent visits had to do with his weakness toward weapons. Every time Sayid came by, the blacksmith would excitedly showcase the new weapons, explaining their significance, different forms, and aesthetics. Sayid would listen to the blacksmith silently, pretending to be very interested in what he was saying. Then he would wait for a suitable moment to burrow through the blacksmith's bin in hopes of there being news from Habibi.

"This dagger is made of a mixture of four different metals. Each type of metal gives the dagger its properties. Steel gives it its durability and flexibility, cast iron gives it its hardness, copper and brass give it permanent acuity," the blacksmith explained.

Sayid listened, picking up the dagger and fumbling with it.

"And how much does this dagger cost?" Sayid asked.

"This one is not for sale. Only the Assassin who earns the greatest trust from the Old Man of the Mountain gets this dagger. He personally hands it to the Assassin in the Hall of Truth. Along with this dagger, its owner gets the wisdom of the experts who created it."

Sayid put the dagger back on its velvet pedestal and began to think deeply.

"Sayid," the blacksmith said in a low, hushed voice, "I see that you like this sword very much. You are my constant customer." The blacksmith looked around to make sure no one was watching them. "Take this dagger. I'll let you keep it for one day but keep it to yourself! Let it give you strength. But don't forget to return it tomorrow. I am sure that one day you will be receiving this kind of dagger from Hassan."

Sayid took the dagger and hid it in his bosom. He thanked the blacksmith and quickly left the workshop. The blacksmith hadn't even noticed that he searched through the rubbish bin and took a letter out.

Sayid frantically ran to the refectory so he wouldn't be late for breakfast. He was hiding two things in his bosom: the dagger and the letter.

Breakfast had just started when Sayid entered the refectory. A high-ranking Assassin reprimanded him for being late and ordered him to stay after breakfast to wash the dishes as punishment. In his head, Sayid rejoiced at the opportunity. After all, if he didn't stay and wash dishes, he wouldn't find any privacy to read his letter until evening. Hiding behind a pyramid of dirty dishes, Sayid took out the letter and began reading: "Tomorrow I will no longer be here, and you'll never see me again. At midnight, I'll be waiting for you near the house where you got this letter from. It's now or never! It's up to you."

Sayid was shocked by the drastic change of events. He knew that he had until midnight to decide. Habibi was leaving Alamut. But why? Perhaps she was suspected of something. Maybe she was no longer fit for service. Sayid couldn't understand, nor could he decide what to do.

"There is still plenty of time until midnight," he thought, and began washing dishes. By the time he finished his work, the trumpet sounded, signaling the start of spear training. Sayid ran out of the kitchen and headed toward the training ground.

The Assassins walked from all different directions to the central square of Alamut. The trumpet sounded once more to signal that it was an important meeting and that the Assassins should hurry. As they made their way, they tried to guess what the urgent meeting was about. Entering the square, Sayid saw two beams, about the height of a typical man, which were placed at the very center of the square. There was something attached to their ends and covered with a cloth. Next to the beam, two burly soldiers were standing with their arms crossed.

The bellman shouted, "Devoted sons of Allah, we are saying goodbye to our brother. We hope to meet him soon. By the Heavenly God's will and, of course, by order of the Old Man of the Mountain, we will strive to achieve what our brother has."

Upon hearing this, one of the burly soldiers lazily approached the beam, pulled the rope attached to the cloth, and revealed what was on the top of the beam. It was Almualim's severed head again. This time, there was no presentation, no dark room, no painted head, no table under which the body was hidden, and no tray with a special hole. Almualim had really been beheaded. Sayid realized that this was only possible if Almualim had been beheaded after the performance held the day before. He had been deceived in the worst way; he had been convinced that he was carrying out a special task by partaking in the performance, and then he was beheaded so that they could show off his head and there would be no doubt that it had been real.

Almualim, however, knew only about the first act of the performance. Now the Assassins were approaching his head one by one and bowing down.

"Sayid, don't you want to say goodbye to your hero friend?" an Assassin asked him.

Sayid didn't answer.

At midnight, Sayid quietly left his shelter. He listened carefully and made sure that everyone in the room was asleep and that no one was following him. Skillfully avoiding the night guards and assessing the situation from the street corners from time to time, Sayid reached the blacksmith's workshop, which was closed at that time. The blacksmith and his family lived upstairs on the second floor of the building. The light was off in the window of the blacksmith's house; craftsmen usually went to bed very early.

Sayid hid in a dark corner of the sidewalk and waited. He was completely invisible from the street. Sayid himself didn't really understand what was supposed to happen next. He thought about running away from Alamut with Habibi, but he had no idea how he would manage to do it, nor could he imagine what would await them when they escaped.

Life had been changing so fast recently that Sayid was constantly failing to keep up with events. He barely managed to find solutions to one problem, and then destiny would throw him another surprise.

Who would have thought that the Old Man of the Mountain, who was idolized and worshipped throughout Alamut, was a despicable liar? Any ordinary market in an eastern city is full of people like him.

From the other end of the street, Sayid could see somebody walking toward the blacksmith's house with a hood pulled over his head. Sayid tried to look closer. The person's face was not visible, but he was sure that it was Habibi. Despite the fact that they were wearing masculine clothing, their careful, steady gait hinted to Sayid that it was a woman. A few minutes later, she reached the front of the house and began to move around anxiously. Sayid emerged and approached her.

"Habibi?" Sayid called in a low voice.

The stranger did not answer. It seemed like maybe she hadn't heard him.

"Habibi!" Sayid called again, this time a little louder.

The woman in a hoodie turned around to see who was calling. It was not Habibi. It was the other houri who had been with Habibi that day. Sayid was surprised. The woman looked confused and frightened.

"Do not move! We will tear you to pieces," a husky voice said from behind.

Sayid turned around. Three burly soldiers stood behind him armed with swords.

"Go ahead! We've got an order to accompany you," one of the soldiers said.

"Where?"

"You'll find out when we get there," the other soldier said and punched Sayid in the stomach. Sayid felt the wind blown out of him and the soldiers waited quietly while he caught his breath. The blow was not actually intended to inflict injury on Sayid; it simply served as a warning that they were serious and not joking around.

Sayid started to walk in silence. One of the soldiers was leading him while the other two followed. They walked for a while in silence until reaching the home of the Old Man of the Mountain. Two of the soldiers remained at the entrance and the third entered the house with Sayid.

A lamp was burning on Hassan's table where he sat reading a piece of paper. Sayid and the soldier entered in silence. Hassan seemed to be so absorbed in reading that he didn't even notice them enter the room.

"Poetry helps me escape reality," Hassan said calmly.

Sayid didn't answer.

"It teaches us beautiful things; it polishes and refines the human soul, making it more beautiful and favorable to Allah."

Sayid again remained silent.

"Physical love is nothing compared to spiritual love. A man bound by physical love is not fit for acts favorable to God. Such a person ties someone else's body to his leg." Hassan turned abruptly to Sayid and asked angrily, "Sayid, why did you tie that girl's body to your leg?"

"I love her, Old Man of the Mountain," Sayid said.

"Shut up!" Hassan shouted suddenly. "You love her, do you? And do you love Allah? Do you love your spiritual brothers? Do you value their devotion? You are in love with yourself; you are just hiding it behind that girl. Do you understand that you have condemned her to death with your actions?"

Hassan continued, pointing out the window. "I have sent an order for her to be brought here and beheaded in your presence. Her death will weigh on your conscience, that is if you have a conscience. A traitor's death is inevitable. Didn't you know that?"

Sayid shrieked in pain like a wounded beast. They had already beheaded Almualim and now they were going to behead Habibi. Sayid suddenly felt like nothing else in the world mattered; his life was worth nothing to him. He wasn't even interested in any of the rewards promised to him in the afterlife. Sayid seemed to have fallen into a vacuum of emptiness, as if he was in a bad dream. He looked at Hassan with a meaningless expression, as if waiting for him to take out an apple and give it to him just like in his dream. Now, that dream seemed closer to reality than everything that had just happened, even the rows of severed heads that had greeted him.

Emotionless, Sayid took out the dagger that the blacksmith had given to him and thrust it into the guard's throat. It all happened so quickly and unexpectedly that neither Hassan nor the soldier understood what had happened. It was only when the soldier crumpled to the floor, creating a crimson pool around him, that Hassan looked at Sayid in bewilderment.

Nobody in Alamut was allowed to carry a weapon without his permission, especially a dagger like that. Sayid didn't even give Hassan a chance to think twice. He put the dagger against Hassan's throat and said through clenched teeth, "You're a liar, but you're making yourself out to be a prophet. You have created hell on earth. You're going to die, but what you created will live on. The monster you have created lives on blood, and a lot of blood will be shed after you."

Hassan smiled scornfully. "You are so stupid! I could give you heavenly joy. What is the difference between getting that joy here or elsewhere? Have you already forgotten about the poor vagrant you used to be? Were you happy then, being poor, hungry and persecuted, wandering from town to town?"

"Yes, it was probably the only happy time of my life, and do you know why? Because even being persecuted or hungry, I was free. I was my own master."

"Didn't you want to kill me? Then go ahead and kill me! Why are you delaying it?"

"No!" Sayid gave a devilish smile. "An onlooker would think that Sayid had gone completely mad. I won't kill you, Hassan-i Sabbāh. You're going to help Habibi and I leave Alamut. Together we will go to the first settlement, and then you will be totally free; we'll all go our own way. If you don't lose your temper and help us leave, I won't kill you. But if I notice you doing anything else, I will cut your throat without hesitation. You have achieved your goal, Hassan; I have nothing left to lose. I am not afraid of death. Life has no value for me."

Hassan obeyed Sayid's wishes. He ordered for Habibi to be brought in, and the three of them walked out toward Alamut's gates together. Hassan lowered his headscarf to avoid being recognized. The night was already coming to an end. The mountain peaks loomed in the east. Hassan accelerated his steps; he wanted to leave Alamut by dawn to avoid infamy. He would have chosen death if he could, but in this case, death would have been dishonorable and shameful. He had created legends about his own invincibility and divine origin, and now a greenhorn young man had taken him hostage with a stolen dagger. Most likely he had never even performed a murder assignment before, and perhaps the soldier whose throat he cut was his first and last victim. It was a murder committed in the name of love.

Love as a feeling was odd and incomprehensible to Hassan. There was only one kind of love for him: love of the heavenly Lord. Looking at this love between a vagabond and a common slave proved to him that all the preaching he had been doing for years had been for nothing. Hassan really could not understand where he had gone wrong or what more he could have done.

Sayid wasn't thinking about anything. There were no thoughts or ideas in his head. He moved after Hassan mechanically and it didn't even occur to anyone who saw them that the captive was Hassan. Sayid tried to keep up with Hassan as if he was simply accompanying him on a walk. Even in that situation Hassan was trying to make himself look like the master. Together, they reached the gates of Alamut. These were the gates through which the Assassins were leaving to commit another murder.

"Stop! It is prohibited!" the guard called.

"We're leaving Alamut," Sayid said.

Hassan stood with his head lowered so that the guard could not see him.

"Hassan-i Sabbāh has given an order not to let anyone out," the guard said, placing his hand on the hooked sword hanging from his belt.

Hassan lifted his headscarf and said, "Open the gates! It's me!"

Confused, the guard gave a low bow. The gates opened and the dawning light could be seen. Hassan stepped outside the gates. Before following him, Sayid turned to the guard and asked, "And when wouldn't you execute Hassan-i Sabbāh's command?"

"When Hassan-i Sabbāh himself orders us not to fulfill his command," the guard replied without hesitation.

This answer, for some reason, amused Sayid. He laughed loudly and left Alamut. It wasn't until long after, when Hassan, Sayid and Habibi were long gone in the winding mountains, that Sayid's laughter stopped haunting the guard.

Two days later, Hassan returned to Alamut. He continued to rule Alamut just like he always had until the end of his life. Afterward, Hassan's son ruled in his place.

Nothing was ever heard of Sayid and Habibi again. Sayid was said to be involved in the arms trade and to have become quite successful. He lived a rich life and his business flourished. It turned out that the Crusades would never leave Sayid jobless; weapons became the most sought after commodity.

Human life was several times less valuable than the weapons with which those lives were taken. There was also another peculiarity – all the caravans laden with Sayid's arms were said to never have been subjected to attacks by Alamut's Assassins – a surprising and inexplicable exception in those times.

18. Pope Urban II's Secret (Clermont, AD 1099)

It had already been twenty days since Pope Urban II hadn't left his room. There were whispers among the courtiers that Urban had health problems, which was correct to some extent. Urban had suddenly started experiencing uncontrollable coughing fits that would last at least an hour. He would gasp for air and his eyes would become bloodshot and watery. Doing work was out of the question. After his coughing fits, Urban would feel so weak that he needed to sleep for at least one or two hours, so he ended up just spending his days coughing and sleeping.

Being a man of deep religious convictions, Urban did not particularly like doctors. He had great faith that everything was in God's hands, including health. Urban refused medical care until one day Odo himself had the same symptoms. Urban concluded that they were both infected with some disease. As soon as Odo's coughing fit finished, Urban's would begin, so that even basic communication between them was becoming impossible. Eventually, the pope began to worry and sent an order to bring in Doctor Fukeh.

Meanwhile, the military and political conflict in the east was close to resolution; the Crusaders had almost reached Jerusalem. Every day Urban waited for news about the liberation of Jerusalem, although his terrible disease had made the waiting unbearable.

Both joyous and sad news came from the east. Because of his condition, Urban was unable to properly communicate the news with Odo. Therefore, a lot of letters had piled up on Urban's desk, almost completely covering it. Inside the letters was written that the Crusaders had eventually conquered Antioch and sent the Turkish army fleeing with the help of the Sacred Lance.

After the death of Bishop Adhemar, the post of the pope's vicar remained vacant. Urban hadn't thought to appoint anyone to be the spiritual leader of the pilgrims and it had had a very bad impact on the campaign. The only person more or less constraining the brutal and aggressive army was Bishop Adhemar, and now, after his death, the army had somewhat deviated from their spiritual path. Every little thing would evolve into a large brawl at the camp, which sometimes ended with multiple killings. Theft among the troops had reached enormous proportions. Immoral women felt themselves masters among the soldiers and commanders.

One disgusting incident near the village of Maarat signified the peak of their demoralization. As they reached Maarat, the Crusaders killed and ate all of the village residents. According to one letter, the Crusaders roasted young men and boiled elderly people. This cannibalistic feast drained away any remaining morals the Crusaders possessed, and that's how they continued.

But Pope Urban hadn't kept abreast of this news. Odo's illness had put any official work on the back burner. The decision to call a doctor was of national importance. Over the last ten years, Doctor Fukeh had personally dealt with Urban's health problems. He would visit the palace every Tuesday and carry out a detailed medical examination during which he would also reveal the results of the previous week's examination. The courtiers were already accustomed to his regular visits.

Apart from examining Urban, the doctor would also visit the papal kitchen to oversee the regulation of the pope's meal plan. Fukeh would open his carriage bag full of multiple vials and begin taking food samples. Besides the Pope, Fukeh also served one other person: Odo. Doctor Fukeh would examine and treat Odo in the same way that he did for Urban. Every time Fukeh left, Urban would start asking Odo whether he had given him the same advice or whether he had followed that advice.

Fukeh was in Germany at the time that he was urgently called to the pope's palace. The doctor spent the entire trip back to France worrying and shaking his head along with the wobble of the chariot. He had a feeling that something bad would happen. Arriving at the palace, he ran into the pope's room and almost forgot to even greet him. He took out his carriage bag full of vials and drugs and put them all on the table in a special sequence. Their wide-ranging significance and application were known only to him.

"Doctor," Urban called from his bed, "I called you in today not for me but for Odo."

"What happened, Your Excellency? I examined him two days ago and I did not see any reason for worrying," Fukeh said, not even looking in Odo's direction. The pope was the main reason for his concern.

"I don't know. Last night he had a coughing fit and was choking. Fukeh, I'm afraid for him. Be very careful with him. Odo absolutely does not care about his own health. All of his attention is focused on the Crusader pilgrimages. He did not sleep all night because he was waiting for the herald to bring news. The Crusaders have already reached Jerusalem. They have destroyed the non-believing Saracens and are spreading the word of God. The non-believers must feel the power of the Lord Almighty and they must..." Urban began coughing and couldn't continue until it subsided. "Fukeh, promise me that you will be as careful with him as you are with me."

"I promise, Your Excellency. It's always been like that. I have never treated you and Odo differently, you can be absolutely sure of it," Fukeh said.

He took one of the vials, examined it under the light and, pouring a few drops into a medical spoon, brought it to Urban. "Drink this, Your Excellency! It is a sedative with your favorite mint extract."

Urban drank the concoction, then laid down and instantly fell asleep under its influence.

Fukeh proceeded to work. He mixed together different liquids and powder, made a schedule and wrote down instructions for taking the prescribed medications, some on an empty stomach and others after a meal. Aside from preparing the medications, Fukeh also scrawled something on a piece of paper, leaving it near the vial of medicine. After about two hours of meticulous work, Fukeh emerged from the pope's room as quietly as possible. The pope's two cardinals were waiting for him in the hallway. Seeing Fukeh's anxious face, they began interrogating him.

"Doctor, how is the high priest? Will he recover?"

"Everything is in God's hands," Fukeh said.

One of the cardinals gave a half-suppressed laugh. "Fukeh, don't you find it strange?"

"What?"

"The fact that you, a man of science, are comforting us, mace-bearing cardinals, with the hope of God."

"As a doctor, my opinion is that the pope doesn't have long to live," Fukeh replied.

"And what about Odo? How is he?" asked one of the cardinals with a smile on his face.

Fukeh clenched his teeth.

"I do not think that now is the time for jokes. Goodbye."

The cardinals looked at each other meaningfully, smiled and walked away silently. They retired from discussing issues related to the inheritance of the papal throne.

Fukeh was right. On the morning of July 29, in the year 1099, Pope Urban II died. Urban II was the name that the high priest had been given during his anointing, but his secular name was Odo of Châtillon, or Otho de Lagery.

Epilogue (Paris, AD 2015)

It was already ten o'clock at night. Ali put his ear to the wall to make sure that everyone was asleep, then he quietly put on his clothes and walked into his brother's room. He opened the window as gently as possible and climbed out, clinging to the windowsill with both hands. A police car passed by blaring its siren.

Ali looked back at the window in fright. No, everything was fine; he had closed the window after himself. His brother definitely wouldn't wake up from the sound. Ali maneuvered to the window rail of the bottom floor with agility and jumped down to the street. It troubled Ali that he could still hear the police car. There were screams and shouts from the next street. Women's voices were heard crying loudly from the windows of the front building. Ali walked to the edge of the street in hope of finding a taxi. He waited for half an hour, but for some reason all the cars seemed to be speeding by like madmen.

Ali had a strange feeling inside that unrest had gripped the city, but he couldn't understand where the feeling had come from. There was a strange, inexplicable commotion in the streets. Everyone seemed to be rushing to get somewhere. Ali thought about finding a car.

The club where Liz had gone was located in the suburbs on the opposite side of Paris. It wasn't realistic to think he could get there on foot. Ali decided to cross the street and walk for a bit and try to catch a taxi on a busier street. He barely walked a few steps when a police car, hurtling by at high speed, stopped suddenly next to him. Two policemen got out of the car and approached Ali.

"Who are you?" one of the officers shouted.

"My name is Ali, I'm a student," Ali replied, trying not to seem frightened.

"What are you doing outside at this hour?"

"It's Friday night so I decided to go out to a club to have fun with my friends," Ali said. "Isn't that allowed?"

"Don't give us lip! Provide proof of identity!"

Luckily, Ali had brought his student ID, assuming that he wouldn't be allowed into the club without it. He took his student ID out of his breast pocket and held it out to the police officers, trying to keep an expressionless face. Ali noticed that as he was taking out his ID, the officers were watching his movements with rapt attention. One of the officers grabbed the ID from Ali, shined his flashlight on it, read it, then shined the flashlight on Ali's face. He repeated this twice.

"Kristo, everything seems to be ok," the police officer said to his friend, turning off the flashlight.

"You can't be sure; everything needs to be checked thoroughly," said the other officer, casting a skeptical look at Ali. "Hey, student, which campus do you live on?"

"I live at home with my parents."

"Where is your house? What block?"

"Our home is on the next street, just two-three hundred meters away," Ali said. He immediately realized it might not have been a good idea to tell the police officers where he lived.

"Are there many Arabs in your neighborhood?" the officer continued.

"Almost half of our building is populated by Arabs, but I don't really know about the whole block."

Ali couldn't understand why they were asking such strange questions. He thought maybe the police officers suspected him of being involved in the hashish trade. Some of the young Arabs, mostly Moroccans, would often sell hashish in passageways near railway stations in Paris. They would transport the hashish in the form of black, olive-shaped balls. That's why hashish was often referred to as "olives" in the streets of Paris. The buyer would approach any passerby who was either black or looked Arab and ask where he could purchase "olives." The dealer would give a meaningful smile and sell them a highly addictive "olive" for one hundred euros.

"You seem to be a clever guy," one of the police officers said with a grin. "Let's go! You're going to show us your house."

"'Excuse me," Ali said, "But why do you want me to show you my house?"

"We would like to pay it a visit," one of the officers said, mocking him. "Hurry up, our time and patience are not inexhaustible."

"Sir, I'm not a drug dealer. I want you to know that in case you suspect me of it," Ali said sincerely. "I snuck out of the house and if my parents find out that I'm not home at this hour, I'll be in big trouble."

"Come on and show us your house. We don't have time for foolish stories," the officer threatened.

Ali hung his head and walked toward his house.

"Mustafa, someone is knocking at the door," Mustafa's wife said, waking him up.

"Who could it be at this hour? What a city this is! What a country this is! Whose idea was it to visit us at this hour?" Mustafa put on his dressing gown, muttering under his breath.

"I'm coming," he shouted toward the door. "May the Devil take them all; I haven't gotten a wink of sleep all night."

Coming out of the bedroom, Mustafa saw that the whole family had gathered in the living room. Perplexed and alarmed, they stared at the door with sleepy, half-closed eyes.

This made Mustafa even angrier. He wondered who had dared to disturb his family's sleep. He was so angry that he didn't even notice that his youngest son was not there.

"Who is it?" Mustafa said approaching the door.

"It's the police. Open the door," a man said from behind the door.

"The police? What has happened?" Mustafa asked anxiously.

"Open up, we need to talk," the officer replied.

"I don't understand, we are law-abiding citizens," Mustafa said and opened the door.

Ali stood at the doorstep with his head bowed. Next to him were two police officers.

Someone gave a bitter sob behind Mustafa's back. It was his wife, who assumed the police had arrested their son. She started weeping.

"What has happened?" Mustafa asked, surprised. "What has my son done?"

"Monsieur, your son has not committed any crime. We escorted him home for his own safety," one of the officers explained.

"We wanted to make sure that he really lives in this house," said the other officer.

"Yes, he lives in this house. He is my son. Now please explain to me why he is coming home in the dark at this crazy hour? And escorted by the police, no less!" Mustafa was extremely angry and didn't seem to care that there were men of the law standing in front of him.

"Let us come in and we'll explain everything," the first officer said. "Especially since this is a matter of consequence for you."

Mustafa turned to the living room, shouted something in Arabic so that the police officers couldn't understand, and waved them inside. Mustafa's behavior could hardly be considered hospitable. He was not happy to see the night visitors and it showed in his manners.

The officers walked into the living room studying every object they came across with skepticism. They took off their hats, and then one of the officers announced, "Monsieur, an unprecedented terror attack happened in Paris just two hours ago. The suspects are young people of Arab appearance; the possible motive is religious terrorism. We wanted to make sure that this boy is indeed your son and that he lives in this house."

"Neither I nor my son have any information about any terrorist attack. You came to our house and disturbed my family's rest. I am the Muslim Mufti of this district, and I demand respect for my religion and my family. Tomorrow I will make a complaint to the municipal gendarmerie and ask them to take arbitrary actions."

"Monsieur, please calm down. It's certainly your right to make a complaint to the gendarmerie, but please listen to us until the end," the officer said, trying to defuse the tense situation. His partner obviously did not agree with him and was panting anxiously. He would have preferred his colleague take a much stricter approach.

"Monsieur Mustafa, as we said, there has been a large-scale terror attack in Paris a few hours ago. As of this moment, the number of victims has exceeded one hundred. All of Paris is awake. Several cases of xenophobic attacks have been registered already. People are angry and they are blaming all Muslims, Arabs or blacks – basically anyone who looks different from them. You see, there are a large number of victims, and the number of people wounded is also very large. A few Arab shops have already been destroyed, for example the hookah shop in your neighborhood."

"Monsieur," the other police officer interrupted, "We brought your son back home for his own safety. Walking in Paris as a young Arab man is not very safe right now. People are very angry. Also, on behalf of the Paris Police Force, we will have to order you and your family to stay indoors for a few days."

"What do you mean?" Mustafa asked angrily. "What does 'stay indoors' mean? This is a gross violation of our freedoms."

"Monsieur, this order is given for your own safety. Please do not leave your house for twenty-four hours. Again, this is done only for your safety."

Mustafa did not answer. The police officers, realizing that they had nothing else to add, left the apartment, closing the door quietly behind themselves. The whole family was still awake and gathered in the living room. A heavy silence fell upon them, the kind that is usually followed by an explosion.

"My son, you trampled on my word. Well done, son!" Mustafa said sarcastically.

Ali stood in the middle of the living room with his head hung low.

"What will people think about our family? What will they think of me?"

Ali was silent.

"Speak, Ali! You have spat upon your parents. You refuse to recognize us as your family, don't you? What will be next? Will you disown Allah for the love of that faithless girl?"

"Dad..."

"What?" Mustafa said louder. "Ali, that girl has enchanted you. I used to be your age, and I myself encountered temptations, but at the last moment when I was so close to the wicked path of sin, I sobered up. I got married to your mother. I knew all her ancestors, even those who had lived five hundred years ago. Your mother is a believer and a woman devoted to her family. Imagine what would happen if I got married to some faithless woman of unknown descent. Who would have been your mother? Wouldn't you be ashamed and want to curse my momentary weakness?"

"One cannot be ashamed of his mother," Ali said courageously. "I would have loved my mother no matter who she was. I would have loved her the same way."

Mustafa thought deeply. His son had grown so much! He could already present reasonable arguments that were hard not to consider.

"Ali, you're on the wrong path. Your mother and I want to prevent you from making irrevocable decisions."

"Wrong way?" Ali suddenly exploded, interrupting his father for the first time in his life. Mustafa's eyes rounded with surprise. "And which is the right path, Dad? To love but suffer? To have a profession that you hate, but still do it just because your parents like it? To suffer, suffer, suffer and ascribe it to Allah? Dad, Allah is love; Allah is not torment and suffering. Allah loves us like his children, and a father can't cause pain and suffering to his child. Allah can't punish us. If we are supposedly causing each other pain in the name of religion, how do we differ from them?" Ali pointed to the TV, which was showing photographs of the terror attack suspects.

Ali gave a bitter sob and ran into his bedroom. Mustafa was left standing motionless in the middle of the living room, shoulders hunched over, in complete bewilderment. He looked like a decrepit old man.

Ali spent the whole night trying to reach Liz by phone or Internet, but it was in vain; Liz's phone was turned off. Ali's other friends either weren't responding or they too had turned off their phones. He couldn't reach anyone the entire night.

In the morning, Ali's mother called her son to breakfast. She hadn't been able to sleep either. She couldn't understand her son's suffering, yet she herself was suffering and trying to find a way out. When he arrived in the kitchen, she was pouring tea into cups and watching television out of the corner of her eye. She held out one of the cups to Ali and kept the other one for herself.

"My son, don't spare yourself. I understand that love is so colorful and bright when you are young. Everything around you seems so beautiful, and perhaps you think that the only people who wish you bad things are your parents. Your father did not close his eyes the whole night; he sat in anxiety. Your father loves you very much."

Ali was listening to his mother's words with his eyes glued to the television. He had decided to keep silent and not respond to his mother's words. Suddenly he went pale and seemed to have lost the ability to breathe evenly. He started gasping for air.

"Ali, look at me," his mother screamed. "What happened?"

Ali did not say anything; he just continued gasping for air. He raised his hand and pointed a trembling finger at the TV. The TV journalist was speaking quickly, reporting the details of the previous night's terror attack from the scene. He stood in the street in front of the place where the attack had happened. The footage clearly showed that the name of the place was Bataclan Club.

Ali jumped to his feet, knocking over the cup of hot tea, and ran into the corridor. He opened the door and rushed into the street like a madman.

It was cold outside, but Ali could no longer feel anything. He started to run down the street. He didn't know how long he had been running, but soon he noticed a taxi, jumped into it and shouted to the driver to take him to Bataclan Club. The driver looked doubtful, muttered something under his breath and started driving in that direction.

They hadn't even reached Bataclan Club yet when they hit a traffic jam. The driver turned around to Ali and said, "It is impossible to go further; there is a bad traffic jam."

Without answering, Ali paid the driver, got out of the car and ran toward Bataclan Club. When he reached it, he saw that it had been cordoned off with police caution tape. People had gathered from all sides. Some people were just curious, while others were either plain clothes police officers or relatives of victims who were frantically trying to find out information about what had happened. Policemen were trying to keep the crowd away from the scene.

"Please step away! There is nothing to see here. There is no one here; all the victims have been taken to the hospital."

"Can you tell us where each of them was taken?" a woman asked the police officer from within the crowd.

"No, Madame, we do not possess that information. Everything will be announced on TV."

"Can you tell us anything about the number of victims?" asked a young journalist.

"There is no information at this moment. Please step away and let the police work."

After walking around the outside of the club aimlessly for several hours, Ali realized he had no reason to be there. He decided to go see Liz's grandfather to try to get information from him.

He walked around a little thinking about his plan, and finally went to Liz's only relative in Paris – her grandfather Matteo.

The doors of the nursing home were already closed; it was late at night, and visitors were not allowed then. Ali rang the doorbell and left his finger on the button until a very displeased nurse appeared and gave Ali a questioning look.

"What happened? Who do you want?" the nurse asked, clearly annoyed. "Visiting hours are over. Come tomorrow."

"Madame, please, let me see Matteo! He lives in ward 216. It's very important."

"All of you think you are so important," muttered the nurse. "I said it isn't allowed. The gendarmerie has warned us not to let anyone in or out after the scheduled time. Leave and come back tomorrow."

"Madame, I'm begging you! I need to see Matteo at all costs. It's a matter of life or death."

The nurse looked at Ali from head to toe. He must have looked really pathetic, because she was suddenly filled with compassion and opened the door. "Just be quiet. You only have a few minutes."

"Thank you, kind woman! May Allah bless you and your family."

Ali ran up the stairs to the second floor. He found the familiar corridor, opened the familiar door and entered Matteo's room. One of the two beds in the room was empty and Matteo was lying on the other one, fast asleep. Ali approached him with hesitation. He felt bad about waking Matteo up, but the situation was extreme. Defying some of the rules of etiquette was excusable in such cases. Ali approached Matteo's bed and gently shook him.

"Grandpa. Grandpa Matteo, please wake up."

"It's useless," a voice said from behind Ali. "The doctors have injected him with high doses of sleeping medication. He'll be asleep until morning."

Ali turned around and saw Professor Moshe standing in the middle of the doorway watching Ali. "Professor, what happened? Why did they inject him with medication?" Ali asked anxiously.

"Don't you know?" the professor asked. "The police visited him today and asked him to come verify a body."

The professor hung his head.

"I guess you don't know what happened. Liz died in the club. The police came to inform Matteo about it. I'm so sorry. Find strength, my son."

Ali couldn't hear anything he was saying; his ears had stopped working and his eyes had gone blind. Ali fell to the floor and began making strange hand movements.

"Sheitan! Satan! Where is Liz?" Ali was muttering words that had nothing to do with each other. He wasn't crying, but he was gasping for breath.

Suddenly Ali jumped to his feet, shook himself and quietly exited the hospital. A cold, windy blast of air hit his face. Ali wandered the streets of Paris aimlessly. There were few people out in the streets except for police officers, firefighters and emergency physicians, all of whom looked frightened and confused. He passed by them, but they didn't seem to notice anything around them.

A car slowly made its way down the street. From the car, an African man started shouting from a loudspeaker. "This is the end! Judgement day is coming! Repent, true Christians!"

No one looked toward the man. A red-haired girl in her early twenties was sitting on the ground on the corner of the street. She was crying and howling with pain. Ali tried to find some resemblance between Liz and the girl. No, Liz had very delicate features. Incomparably delicate.

Ali thought about Akhenaten. His Jewish professor's story had been imprinted in his mind. Akhenaten, being blind, established the worship of the sun. He was the first person on the planet to understand that God is one, and that God is love. But everyone knows how that turned out. The clergymen did not allow that love to last long; they took matters into their own hands.

Police vehicles continued to speed through the streets of Paris with their sirens blaring. It seemed to Ali that everything in the world had lost its meaning; even the sirens made no sense to him. They were simply sounds accompanying terrorism, murder and violence. After all, terror attacks are always accompanied by the sounds of cars rushing past with terrifying sirens, right? They only seemed to double people's fears and uncertainties.

Interestingly, the sirens of Paris's police cars were completely different from those of police cars elsewhere in the world. The French police had introduced the use of acoustic melodies for their sirens. Police cars would rush to the scene with melodious sirens even in cases of robbery, theft, and murder, adding a touch of elegance to everything in a way that only the French could understand. Take the Eiffel Tower, for instance. If one were to judge by the highest standards, what exactly is the Eiffel Tower if not a pile of iron? Towers like that are usually built far from city centers so that they don't ruin the architectural landscape of the city. The French, on the other hand, show the whole world what a bulky iron tower could look like according to their interpretation. People come to Paris from all over the world to see what a tower should look like according to the French.

A few Africans were standing outside the entrance smoking hashish in secret. Of course, they only thought they were doing it in secret. The obvious smell of hashish had actually wafted up to the end of the street, and to anyone who looked closer, their red eyes said everything. Ali didn't know why, but he started to run. He passed two streets, then stopped and caught his breath. An old woman passing Ali gave him a condemning look. Ali could read what her eyes were saying: "That's what happens when Muslims are given so much freedom. I used to say that we shouldn't let those bearded people into our country, but no one listened to me. Who would have thought that an Arab teenager would be running through the streets of Paris like a hooligan? Who knows, maybe he's also a terrorist hiding a bomb under his shirt."

Actually, the woman recognized no religion. She came up to Ali and asked, "Is everything ok, my son?" She tried to sound as stern as possible.

Ali did not answer and ran away. He wanted to escape from everything and everyone. He didn't need the woman's questioning or his university studies or his parents' goals for his future.

Ali's steps slowed. It was getting dark already. The few pedestrians that had been walking in the streets of Paris had already shut themselves in their homes. Later on in the night, Ali noticed that more and more people had actually started coming out of their homes and were all walking in the street in the same direction. Ali decided to join the spontaneous march. The crowd continued to grow until it resembled a human river. Like a leaf fallen from a tree into the water, he surrendered himself to the flow of the river.

Two streets away, the sight of the Notre Dame Cathedral opened up before Ali. The crowd was going to Mass. Ali automatically turned his steps toward the courtyard in front of Notre Dame and his eyes unexpectedly rested on Point Zero, the stone near which he and Liz had first kissed. Ali stood paralyzed for a few minutes. All of his memories of Liz flashed before his eyes and he felt weak in the knees. At that moment his body seemed to realize that he hadn't had a wink of sleep for two nights. He also couldn't remember the last time he ate something; he had been wandering the streets of Paris all day. He felt so powerless that he started to sob.

Ali knelt down on the stone in front of the cathedral and cried loudly. That stone was the only thing left of his great lost love. He screamed and lifted his eyes to heaven and asked Allah for help. If he had done that on any other day, he would have attracted the attention of passersby who would surely approach him and wonder what misfortune had happened to him. But that day, Paris had no time to focus on one person's misfortune. That day, Paris itself knelt down on its knees, moaning and mourning.

A large crowd of Christians had gathered in the courtyard in front of Notre Dame. People had been coming to the church to find comfort to answers to the questions they had been concerned about for centuries.

Inside the cathedral, the bishop was delivering a liturgy dedicated to the memory of the victims of the terrorist attack. The bishop, wearing a garment sewn with golden thread, was walking near the chancel and saying a prayer in Latin.

"Dieu le veut!" the believers murmured in response to the bishop's prayers. "Dieu le veut!"

Ravens before Noah

by Susanna Harutyunyan

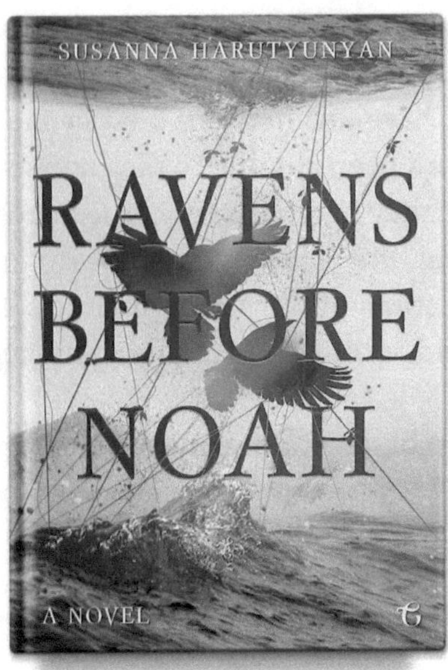

This novel is set in the Armenian mountains sometime in 1915-1960. An old man and a new born baby boy escape from the Hamidian massacres in Turkey in 1894 and hide themselves in the ruins of a demolished and abandoned village. The village soon becomes a shelter for many others, who flee from problems with the law, their families, or their past lives. The villagers survive in this secret shelter, cut off from the rest of the world, by selling or bartering their agricultural products in the villages beneath the mountain.

Years pass by, and the child saved by the old man grows into a young man, Harout. He falls for a beautiful girl who arrived in the village after being tortured by Turkish soldiers. She is pregnant and the old women of the village want to kill the twin baby girls as soon as they are born, to wash away the shame…

Buy it > www.glagoslav.com

Jesus' Cat

by Grig

Jesus' Cat is the first book by this young prose writer. The stories involved in this collection reveal, on the one hand, a unique writing style, and on the other, an original perspective on the world and people. This combination allows characters to develop in Grig's creative space that helps readers discover another invisible side of life.

This book was published with the support of the Ministry of Culture of the Republic of Armenia under the "Armenian Literature in Translation" Program.

Buy it > www.glagoslav.com

Goodbye, Bird

by Aram Pachyan

For a twenty-eight-year-old young man who returned from the army several years ago but has yet to reacclimatize to ordinary life, every step, gesture, word, and vision is a revelation, which takes him back to the beginning, to a time when reality had lost its shape, and turned into a new and imperceptible world. In his imagination, he embodies a number of different characters, he feels the presence of his girlfriend again, and remembers friends from his childhood and from the army, who are now gone. This is a book of questions, and the answers to these questions are to be found by the reader. The novel is like a puzzle which needs to be pieced together, and the picture is not complete until the last piece is in place, until the last word of the book has been read.

This book was published with the support of the Ministry of Culture of the Republic of Armenia under the "Armenian Literature in Translation" Program.

Buy it > www.glagoslav.com

The Door was Open

by Karine Khodikyan

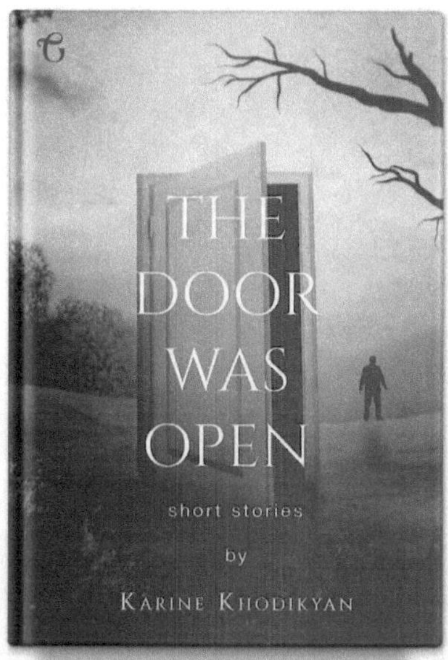

The short fiction of Karine Khodikyan can be described as intellectual fiction for women. These short stories with a "mystical touch" tell stories about women – young and old, happy and sad; even when the protagonist is not a woman, the story will immerse you into the life of a woman, revealing her role in anything and everything.

This book was published with the support of the Ministry of Culture of the Republic of Armenia under the "Armenian Literature in Translation" Program.

Buy it > www.glagoslav.com

- *A History of Belarus* by Lubov Bazan
- *Children's Fashion of the Russian Empire* by Alexander Vasiliev
- *Empire of Corruption - The Russian National Pastime* by Vladimir Soloviev
- *Heroes of the 90s: People and Money. The Modern History of Russian Capitalism*
- *Fifty Highlights from the Russian Literature (Dutch Edition)* by Maarten Tengbergen
- *Bajesvolk (Dutch Edition)* by Mikhail Khodorkovsky
- *Tsarina Alexandra's Diary (Dutch Edition)*
- *Myths about Russia* by Vladimir Medinskiy
- *Boris Yeltsin: The Decade that Shook the World* by Boris Minaev
- *A Man Of Change: A study of the political life of Boris Yeltsin*
- *Sberbank: The Rebirth of Russia's Financial Giant* by Evgeny Karasyuk
- *To Get Ukraine* by Oleksandr Shyshko
- *Asystole* by Oleg Pavlov
- *Gnedich* by Maria Rybakova
- *Marina Tsvetaeva: The Essential Poetry*
- *Multiple Personalities* by Tatyana Shcherbina
- *The Investigator* by Margarita Khemlin
- *The Exile* by Zinaida Tulub
- *Leo Tolstoy: Flight from paradise* by Pavel Basinsky
- *Moscow in the 1930* by Natalia Gromova
- *Laurus (Dutch edition)* by Evgenij Vodolazkin
- *Prisoner* by Anna Nemzer
- *The Crime of Chernobyl: The Nuclear Goulag* by Wladimir Tchertkoff
- *Alpine Ballad* by Vasil Bykau
- *The Complete Correspondence of Hryhory Skovoroda*
- *The Tale of Aypi* by Ak Welsapar
- *Selected Poems* by Lydia Grigorieva
- *The Fantastic Worlds of Yuri Vynnychuk*
- *The Garden of Divine Songs and Collected Poetry of Hryhory Skovoroda*
- *Adventures in the Slavic Kitchen: A Book of Essays with Recipes*
- *Seven Signs of the Lion* by Michael M. Naydan

- *Forefathers' Eve* by Adam Mickiewicz
- *One-Two* by Igor Eliseev
- *Girls, be Good* by Bojan Babić
- *Time of the Octopus* by Anatoly Kucherena
- *The Grand Harmony* by Bohdan Ihor Antonych
- *The Selected Lyric Poetry Of Maksym Rylsky*
- *The Shining Light* by Galymkair Mutanov
- *The Frontier: 28 Contemporary Ukrainian Poets - An Anthology*
- *Acropolis: The Wawel Plays* by Stanisław Wyspiański
- *Contours of the City* by Attyla Mohylny
- *Conversations Before Silence: The Selected Poetry of Oles Ilchenko*
- *The Secret History of my Sojourn in Russia* by Jaroslav Hašek
- *Mirror Sand: An Anthology of Russian Short Poems in English Translation* (A Bilingual Edition)
- *Maybe We're Leaving* by Jan Balaban
- *Death of the Snake Catcher* by Ak Welsapar
- *A Brown Man in Russia: Perambulations Through A Siberian Winter* by Vijay Menon
- *Hard Times* by Ostap Vyshnia
- *The Flying Dutchman* by Anatoly Kudryavitsky
- *Nikolai Gumilev's Africa* by Nikolai Gumilev
- *Combustions* by Srđan Srdić
- *The Sonnets* by Adam Mickiewicz
- *Dramatic Works* by Zygmunt Krasiński
- *Four Plays* by Juliusz Słowacki
- *Little Zinnobers* by Elena Chizhova
- *We Are Building Capitalism! Moscow in Transition 1992-1997*
- *The Nuremberg Trials* by Alexander Zvyagintsev
- *The Hemingway Game* by Evgeni Grishkovets
- *A Flame Out at Sea* by Dmitry Novikov
- *Jesus' Cat* by Grig
- *Want a Baby and Other Plays* by Sergei Tretyakov
- *I Mikhail Bulgakov: The Life and Times* by Marietta Chudakova
- *Leonardo's Handwriting* by Dina Rubina
- *A Burglar of the Better Sort* by Tytus Czyżewski
- *The Mouseiad and other Mock Epics* by Ignacy Krasicki
- *Ravens before Noah* by Susanna Harutyunyan
- *Duel* by Borys Antonenko-Davydovych
- *Absolute Zero* by Artem Chekh
- *An English Queen and Stalingrad* by Natalia Kulishenko

More coming soon...